EARLY PRAISE FOR DISPOSSESSED

A beautiful elegiac masterpiece which begins with the fictional life of a young Mexican American boy, Manuel, as he navigates a new life in Los Angeles' Chavez Ravine without his biological parents and sister. Author Désirée Zamorano reveals her great love and respect for her community as Manuel perseveres against racist laws and attitudes through key moments of his adult life in Southern California. Readers will be firmly in Manuel's corner, rooting for his personal happiness and also transformation of American politics. *Dispossessed* is such a necessary work; I laud Zamorano's dedication to realize this story that deserves a large readership.

— NAOMI HIRAHARA, AUTHOR OF MARY HIGGINS CLARK AWARD-WINNING *CLARK AND DIVISION* AND *EVERGREEN*

Few novels have captured the scope of Latino L.A. the way *Dispossessed* does. Sweeping, lyrical, gut-wrenching — yet hopeful.

— GUSTAVO ARELLANO, LOS ANGELES TIMES COLUMNIST

What an epic, immersive tale Désirée Zamorano has woven, a beautiful, moving story of family, of longing and belonging, of injustice, of friendship, of love, of the deep power of place. Just as Manuel could see his story reflected in *Fiddler on the Roof*, I could see my own family reflected in *Dispossessed*. By the time I finished reading, Manuel and his loved ones had become my own kin; they and this novel will forever hold a place in my heart.

— GAYLE BRANDEIS, PEN/BELLWETHER
PRIZE-WINNING AUTHOR

Dispossessed is a compelling novel set against the hidden history of the terrible treatment of Mexican-Americans in 20th-century California beginning with the forced expatriation of Mexicans, including naturalized citizens, during the Depression, the destruction of the vibrant neighborhoods by real estate speculators and the ghastly medical procedures practice on unsuspecting Latinas. Yet through it all, as this novel eloquently shows, the community survived and thrived. An important addition to Latinx literature.

— MICHAEL NAVA, AUTHOR OF *THE
CITY OF PALACES*

Dispossessed by Désirée Zamorano is a beautiful and necessary story, tenderly told, that spans the vicissitudes of Mexican American history in twentieth-century California. Richly detailed yet quickly paced, *Dispossessed* offers the moving tale of one man, one family, and the extraordinary endurance of love. "We are all each other's families," as one character says, and Zamorano's enchanting storytelling makes it feel true. Admirers of Gregory Nava's 'My Family/Mi Familia' will love this heartbreaking, heartwarming novel.

— JOY CASTRO, AUTHOR OF *ONE BRILLIANT FLAME*

Dispossessed is a heartfelt, moving work about an episode of Los Angeles history long erased from our collective memory. Désirée Zamorano brings to light the human toll of the mass deportations of the 1930s, and the fortitude of those who endured them.

— HÉCTOR TOBAR, AUTHOR OF *OUR MIGRANT SOULS*

Epic in its scope yet intimate in its storytelling, *Dispossessed* is a deeply powerful novel about injustice and resilience, racism and wholeness, separation and longing, and the ways that sometimes, knowing who we are and staying soft in this hard world is the journey that shapes a lifetime.

— NATALIA SYLVESTER, AUTHOR OF *EVERYONE KNOWS YOU GO HOME*

As the whitewashing of American history takes a terrifying turn, *Dispossessed* is essential reading. Focusing on one man, Manuel, Désirée Zamorano embarks on a heartbreakingly honest journey through the history of 20th-century Mexican Americans in California. She bravely breaks silences, knocks down stereotypes, and demands that crucial stories be listened to with compassion. At the same time she explores the intimate beauty of a maligned culture and illuminates the dignity that every human being deserves.

— KIM FAY, NATIONAL BESTSELLING
AUTHOR OF LOVE & SAFFRON

DISPOSSESSED

DÉSIRÉE ZAMORANO

RUNNING WILD

To the separated

The first official repatriation train left Los Angeles for Mexico with more than 400 on board. Within about six months, another 50,000 had been caught nationwide and put on trains and ships.

By 1940 more than 1 million people across the country, mostly Mexican Americans, had been deported.

— Antonio Olivo, "Ghosts of a 1931 Raid," *Los Angeles Times*

CHAPTER ONE

1939

Manuel shrieked against the waves as he and his big sister went further into the water. Lulu clutched his hand. He braced himself against the next wave and felt the cold water collide against his body. The sand sucked at his toes as the water retreated. They danced on the receding foam, Manuel following wherever Lulu led. Another wave crashed against them, then pulled him farther into the ocean.

Lulu squealed and laughed. Manuel laughed until a wave of water pounded against him. He lost Lulu's hand, fell into the sea, and panicked, airless, until his father hoisted him up, patted his back, and swung him around.

"You're an airplane," his father said.

The beach, the sun, the waves were a blur, and he was flying!

His father set him down again, dizzy, unsteady, as a wave headed toward Manuel. This time he looked away from the sun, buried his head in his father's trunks, and clutched his father's leg, which stood steady and firm.

1

"It's okay, I'm here, Manolito, I'm here with you," his father said.

"Lulu!" Manuel shouted. She wasn't here anymore. Where did she go? He spotted her in her red and white polka dot swimsuit, digging on the beach. He ran to help her dig a hole. Sand crabs appeared, then burrowed into the slick sand, leaving bubbles behind. Manuel dug and dug, catching them to watch them burrow into the sand again.

His sister grew bored and ran to their parents. "Wait!" he said. "Lulu!" She kept running and laughing as he chased her.

"Manolito," his mother laughed, "you are a fish, let me catch you!" She held out a towel and wrapped him in it.

* * *

Two men stood in their home. There was crying. Who was crying? Was that him? Was that Lulu? She hugged him tight, whispered to him, held his hand, tugged him alongside her, and told him they were police officers. Why were there police officers? Where were their parents? The men spoke to each other while Manuel wrapped himself around Lulu. She wore a gray dress with a black bow and a sweater their mother had knitted for her. He touched his own sweater, remembered that their mother had made this for him too. Lulu smoothed down his hair. Her black hair was brushed out and fell straight against her shoulders. She dressed him, looked for their night clothes, and placed them in a cloth bag. Everything looked wrong, blurry, out of place.

Lulu understood what the men, the police, said, but he did not. Their words sounded harsh and ugly, like their faces. He and Lulu slid across the slick backseat of a car. The police officers' car. The seat was cold against the backs of his legs, exposed in his short pants. The car smelled of cigarette smoke and sour milk. In the car he and Lulu held hands, her nails jabbing into his palm, her teeth colliding, chattering. Where were they going? Where were his parents? Were they going to be with them?

The same disquieting odor of the car followed them into the house where they were led while a small dog yapped angrily at them. Manuel's ears were assaulted. Like the car, the house smelled wrong, unfamiliar, and unwelcoming.

In this house of strangers, they gave him clothes which scratched at him and smelled of someone else. Lulu came over and laughed and bounced on the bed, making the springs sing, and he laughed too. Lulu's large brown eyes brimmed luminous. She wore her own nightgown, flannel, soft, and faded.

If she laughed, he laughed, if she cried, he cried, if she was going to brave, he could be too.

Lulu put her arms around him and prayed and told him to repeat what she said. Normally their mother prayed with them at bedtime, but she was not there. Manuel listened to Lulu and repeated what she said that night as best as he could.

The two of them moved from home to home together. "I want to go home," he told Lulu. "When do we go home?"

When she said, "I don't know," he felt as if he was underwater. For a moment he was unable to see or breathe, airless in darkness. Only when Lulu was with him, her hand in his, her arm around his shoulders, was there any light or warmth in the world.

He caught his breath with a sob. "Where are we?" he asked her. "Where are Mami? Papi?" Why did they leave?

She bit her bottom lip and said, "I don't know."

They met strangers. They slept in strangers' homes, sometimes in the same room as their children. Other kids who looked at them with big eyes. Manuel didn't understand what the kids said, but Lulu answered them. Then a new home. The strangers always seemed to like Lulu because she understood them. Manuel stood behind her.

One day Lulu hugged him tight, crushing him against her. Little tears fell down her face as she said, "Portate bien, seas un buen niño, seas mi hermanito, valiente y bueno."

He promised her he would be good. He promised her he would be brave.

She kissed him and hugged him and then she was gone.

His sister's warmth, her sunshine, vanished. The ocean water was everywhere now, filling every room and corridor, every crease and seam, his eyes, his body. When he could make out shapes and images, he found himself by a murky swamp, filled with mud and quicksand. His feet dragged through mud; his body waded through deep water. He slept on the bottom of the sea. He awoke to baying wolves and strangers. He called for Lulu. He cried for his parents.

* * *

He didn't recognize the faces or hands that pushed his arms into shirt sleeves, his legs into rough dungarees, then held his hand tightly, until it hurt, and walked with him.

He was led into a room filled with lupine children being heckled by a witch.

To avoid the hungry look of the wolfish children and the scalding eye of the evil-looking woman, he stared out the window. A crow caught his eye and winked. Manuel winked back. Lulu had told him about magical animals who could talk, about people who would sleep for a hundred years, about marvelous places. She used to tell him stories to make him laugh, to scare him. He had cried when she told him about La Llorona who searched for her babies.

Manuel blinked and looked up. That's who that woman was, La Llorona, shrieking for her children.

How would he get out of here? How could he be safe? Lulu would know.

Lulu had shown him how to wink, how to cross his eyes. How to be valiente y bueno.

Would it be this way forever? Today and always? he asked the crow.

The crow flapped her wings, uninterested in his questions.

He put his head down. Maybe La Llorona wouldn't see him this way.

She rapped on his desk with her knuckles so forcefully he startled. The crow scattered; the children sprayed mocking laughter. Bueno y valiente, he told himself and looked up at the shrieking woman. Her eyes were fierce with anger and her mouth a round O out of which came accusations he didn't understand; he wanted to cover his ears, but how would that be brave? Brave would be to continue to look at her, the angry green eyes, the strangely colorless face, the lips moving and moving around the sounds she emitted, until she turned and went back to her place in front of the class.

The children laughed again. Their laughter lasted his lifetime.

At night he slept at the bottom of the sea; in the mornings he awoke to strangers; during the days he tread through mud and marshy overgrowth; he returned to the classroom with its mocking children.

"We're Mr. and Mrs. Powell," one of the faces had said. Manuel wasn't sure what that meant. Mrandmrspowell was a long name. They were both called that? Mrandmrspowell looked very much like each other, washed out faces, wire-framed glasses over watery eyes, invisible eyelashes, downturned mouths. Manuel had to look at their clothing to tell them apart. One wore an apron, the other black pants. When he woke up from the bottom of the sea, they made him wash his face with cold water. They dressed him. He sat at a small wooden table with Mrandmrspowell and tried to eat the biscuits. They were sawdust. They gave him a pail with a thermos and a sandwich and cookies, and later he would smell them, inspect them, tentatively lick the cookie—more sawdust.

A hundred days, a hundred years passed. The angry woman was now replaced by a towering vulture. A long time ago Manuel's father had pointed out the vultures pecking at a carcass. That day had been bright and cool, but the birds happily feeding on a dead animal made Manuel nervous, nauseous. This vulture came to school every day in a gray suit, a white shirt, and a black tie. His hair was slicked back, looking thin and slithery, his face pale, the color of contempt. He stood and glowered at the front of the room for what seemed to be days, or months. Manuel did not speak, did not say anything, and this seemed to appease the gray bird, for which Manuel was grateful, since he for a long time didn't understand a word that was said. Gradually, by listening to the children chatter at each other, he understood the rhythms and the words of this language.

The vulture held a deep gray staff with knots, black grooves, and twists as if it had been hacked from a dead tree then polished with the worry and sweat and tears of thousands of stricken children. The staff and its grooves fascinated Manuel, who now studied it, instead of the birds that appeared and disappeared at the window.

The stories Lulu had told him had never been half as frightening as the towering vulture before him.

He saw that gray staff swung against the underpants of boys and girls, for hours, days it seemed. The girls appeared more humiliated than wounded, their faces dirty with crying and tears before the staff even touched them. The boys were all bluster and swagger and bit hard their bottom lips until the gray vulture swung so hard that he beat tears out of them.

Manuel didn't speak, didn't move, so the vulture left him in peace. At recess he wandered alone, at lunch he sat alone. Sometimes the vulture offered him a bit of food, a piece of rock candy, some coffee from his thermos, an extra biscuit from his lunch pail.

Manuel looked at the deadness behind the vulture's eyes and shook his head. He did not want to become a vulture, and he was certain taking that man's food would turn him into one.

* * *

Every night he slept on the bottom of the ocean. It was cold there, and he summoned memories to keep him warm. His mother patiently brushed and braided Lulu's hair while music from the radio played. He colored on scraps of paper. There was a braided rug on the floor, there was music on the radio. Lulu came home from school, a young woman made them dinner while they waited for their parents. Lulu read to him from a comic book. They waited a long time. Then the police officers came.

What had he done, what had he done, what had he done? Without the words but with all the sensibility, he examined his short life to see what he had done to chase them all away, forever and for eternity, for as deep as the sea and as far as the marsh.

He awoke to the faces of strangers who pushed his body into a cotton shirt and stiff dungaree overalls. He leaned down to tie his shoes; Lulu had taught him, patiently, over and over, and Lulu was not here to show him how to do it right again. He was waiting for her to come back. He broke one of his shoelaces in his frustration to tie them, and the mouth of one of the strangers' faces went hard and grim.

He set off with his book bag and lunch pail to cross the marsh. A hundred days, a hundred years passed. Lulu had told him to be brave. He would be brave. He went to school, he stared at various teachers, and he learned to eat sawdust.

One morning when he was ready to go to school, a trio of strangers arrived at Mrandmrspowell's home, two men and a woman. The trio said words to him, but Manuel didn't understand. A brown man with gold-rimmed glasses spoke in a way Manuel recognized and said, "You're coming with us. We're taking you to a new home. Now, gather your things and thank your hosts." Manuel understood but said nothing. As he left with this new set of strangers, Mrandmrspowell shook his hand and said goodbye.

Manuel sat in the strangers' car and stared out the window. A huge building raised itself in the distance—as they approached it grew larger and larger. The driver pointed to the building, but Manuel couldn't make out what he said. Were they taking him to his parents at last? Was Lulu going to be there?

They drove on a bumpy dirt road in a hilly neighborhood where the homes scattered around like pebbles. Over the car engine birds chittered and a rooster crowed. He sat up to find them. Instead, a man with a deep brown face and a broad straw hat loped alongside a horse. He nodded at the car as they passed.

As they came nearer to the homes, a goat bleated, tethered to a pole. Chickens strutted in yards, and the car slowed down as a few hens wandered into the road. The car honked; the hens clucked and scattered.

Lines of sheets, serapes, pants, and undergarments hung in the yards. A group of girls and boys waved at the car as it passed. Before Manuel could decide whether or not to wave back, the group was far behind them.

The car parked, and he walked with them up wooden steps to a porch where a bird cage hung, and inside a small yellow bird sang. Manuel stopped to stare. The bird cocked his head and sang again. To him.

The door opened. A short, brown woman with a wide smile squatted down to his height. "I see you've met Mimi. I told her to expect you! She only sings for people she approves of." When the woman spoke, he could understand, effortlessly. "Welcome, Manolito. My name is Amparo. You can call me Tía if you like. And if not, that's okay, too." She stood and welcomed the trio in, making sure they all wiped their feet before coming inside.

Inside there was a kitchen table close to the counter and cupboards, and a sofa and on the end table a Santa Biblia. He knew because that's what his mother had called it. Was she, could she possibly be here? He looked around. There was a pipe wood furnace, cool to the touch. The floors were bare, scratched wood, the walls pale gray.

There was a dark wood cabinet with a collection of items inside. On top of the cabinet was a framed photograph of a young man in uniform smiling at the photographer. Manuel inspected this photograph. His teeth were so strong and bright, his smile so wide. He looked happy. Manuel wondered who this man was.

Stored on the cabinet shelves behind closed glass doors were oddly shaped, strange items. Manuel opened the cabinet door and pulled out a small rectangle of glass. He picked it up and turned it around—light refracted out of it in different colors.

Amparo crouched down next to him. "This is my special cabinet. Some of these things my son sent me from all around the world," she said, pointing to his picture. She pulled out a trio of tiny ceramic bowls. "These come from the Philippines," she said, handing them to Manuel. They were tiny clay plates, like a small doll would eat off. Amparo said, "Toño, my son," she pointed to the framed photograph, "told me the people there speak Spanish, too. He fights for our country, Manuel. He's brave, and I'm proud of him. God bless him. When he comes home, Palo Verde will have a big parade. Even La Loma and Bishop will be there. Everyone in Chavez Ravine. Let's put this back now."

Manuel nodded, put the rectangle of glass back where he had gotten it while a thought tickled at the back of his mind. His mother had had a cabinet, too, he was sure. He and Lulu would stare at the tiny clay animals inside, and silver... A silver cup? A silver buckle? A photograph of him? Amparo firmly closed the cabinet door.

She introduced him to the chickens in their coop and the tangle of vegetables that grew in her plot. She told him about zucchinis, that you could eat the flower and the fruit.

With Amparo came the familiar scent of freshly made flour tortillas, cinnamon in coffee, and a new one: detergent. Amparo was always laundering clothing, it seemed to Manuel, and now the clothes he wore were impeccably clean and softened by countless washings.

His family was not here, but he no longer slept on the bottom of the ocean. He no longer crossed marshes or deserts, trailed by packs of predatory animals, but a sidewalk that sloped up the hill. Now he slept on a mattress in a small room next to Amparo's sewing machine, and he awoke to her face, brown and spackled with age spots. She would stroke his cheek, lift him out of his bedding, and point him in the direction of her bathroom. On the nights he dreamed he was a dog, a whimpering dog, running, running, running, the next morning he'd find himself in Amparo's bed, she already awake and moving in the kitchen.

When he emerged, there would be a plate full of beans, a scrambled egg, and an almost toasty, slightly charred flour tortilla. He ate.

Amparo was either cleaning or cooking or ironing or sewing. She was round and brown and soft, and she explained to him everything she did, from trimming the needles off the nopales to how to thread the bobbin in her sewing machine. She often pulled him toward herself and gently said, "Ay, when will you speak to me, little one?"

When would he speak to her? He wanted to ask her so much. Where was he? What had he done? Where was Lulu? Where were his parents? It was nice here, nicer than any place he'd been since Lulu left him alone. But when could he go home to all of them? Inside his chest a softening began, filling his lungs, and choking the words in his throat before they could escape.

She stroked his face with her warm dry hand. He put his arms around her.

Maybe Lulu would join him here. Maybe his parents would know to look for him here.

CHAPTER TWO

1943

After a week at Amparo's, his new home, Manuel whimpered in his sleep. He knew he was dreaming, he knew he was not a dog, lost and hungry. He knew this, really. Then he was lifted up and placed somewhere warm and comforting. He inhaled and smelled corn masa and chicken broth. He was in Amparo's bed, her hand stroking his face.

"It's all right, mijo, it's just a bad dream. You're fine, you're here with me."

He awoke, the heavy misery of his nightmare clung to him, cloaked him in dampness, and infected what he saw, this stranger, the old lady, far away from what he had once known.

He began to cry.

"Oh my," she said, startled. "Oh my. There, there, there. Now, now, now." She held him and hugged him as his tears turned into coughs, then hiccups, then tears again.

He wanted Lulu. Where had she gone? He was distracted by his sister's voice, "Portate bien, seas un buen niño, seas mi hermanito, valiente y bueno." Her eyes had been shining, her lashes had been wet. Her hair had been brushed straight and pulled back into barrettes. Had their mother brushed her hair? Had their mother come and not even said goodbye to them? Had their mother taken Lulu and not him? He continued to cry. He cried until his stomach muscles ached and his throat was dry.

"That's it, son, that's it, let it all come out, like an illness, like a sickness. Let's get that pain and sorrow out. You're allowed." She heated him a mug of milk and handed it to him.

He wiped his eyes. He breathed between tears, then breathed without tears. He thought of the laundry on the line. He had watched Amparo trample, beat, and push laundry through the machine, then, damp, hang it on the clothesline. He felt like those clothes. He took a drink from the cup. He looked at her.

"Better now?"

He said nothing.

She smoothed the sheets and blankets and made space in her narrow bed for him and herself. "Finish your milk. It will make you feel better. That's it. Good. Lie down. I won't crowd you." He lay down and put his arm out to her. She drew him in and rested his head on her chest. He listened to the steady beating of her heart until he fell asleep.

* * *

The morning of the first day of school in this new place there was mist on the windows as he readied himself. There was icy dew on the few clumps of grass they passed. Amparo, Tía Amparo, she called herself, walked with him up the dirt road while pointing out the houses they passed, saying hello to the children that goggled at him. She introduced Manuel, and they stared, then scattered.

"They're excited to see you," she explained.

13

He held her hand a little tighter. Some of the homes they passed were leaning into each other, almost falling apart. Others had their own yard, surrounded by flowering hedges, looking fresh and newly painted. Birds clustered in the bushes, others darted overhead. The dirt road they walked on climbed higher. Birds and flowers were everywhere. As they climbed, he could see a winding road in the distance below them, and beyond that a tall gleaming building that was so high it almost scared him. He was shivering, but not from the cold. He was nervous. Another clump of kids heading to school paused to gawk at them, then said, "Good morning, Doña Amparo," and passed them by. Amparo gave his hand a squeeze. He decided he was excited too.

They approached the squat buildings. "This is your school," Amparo said. She led him through a door and pointed at a wooden bench for him to sit on. He sat. Amparo spoke with a woman behind the counter, in the school's language. She followed the woman into an office, closing the door. Manuel stayed still.

When Amparo reappeared, she crouched down next to him on the bench and spoke to him in their home language. "This nice lady will take you to your classroom. Last year with the other family you went to kindergarten. Now you are in the first grade. You are a smart boy, but because you don't speak, they are going to give you extra help. I need you to do two things. Listen to your teacher and be good. Do you understand?"

Amparo's face was serious, so he made his serious as well and nodded.

Amparo glanced at the woman standing nearby, as if to say, "See?"

Manuel followed the new woman who walked briskly, clacking her heels against the flooring. They left one building,

14

entered another, passed through the hallway, then outside again. They walked to a room apart from the other buildings. The woman opened the door and swept Manuel inside.

A boy lay on a rug on the floor, rhythmically pounding two blocks together; two children at a small oval-shaped table copied words onto their slates, boys and girls sat at their tables or desks, two girls were seated in wheelchairs. He had never seen a wheelchair before, and Manuel stared at the machinery while the woman spoke to the teachers in the room.

"These are your new teachers, Mr. Reed and Miss Woods," she said.

Mr. Reed seemed impossibly high above Manuel, a giant, who leaned down to rub Manuel's head, messing the hair that Amparo had so carefully tended to. He smelled of cigarettes and something sickly sweet. Miss Woods said, "Hello!" and "Welcome!" and took his hand and walked him around the classroom, showing him the slates, where he could place his book bag, where the toilets were. Then she sat him at a desk by himself with a few broken crayons and pieces of paper. She smelled of flowers.

Miss Woods was not La Llorona and Mr. Reed was not a vulture. The classroom of hyenas sitting behind desks had disappeared. Now he recognized the squat building and all it encompassed as a school. The classroom was a classroom, the teachers simply teachers, the students merely children.

Still, there was something different about his new classroom.

The girls in the wheelchairs were Jessica and Ileana. Jessica had sharp features, strong arms, and tiny legs under the peach-colored crocheted blanket. Jessica propelled her wheelchair back and forth, in a kind of rocking motion, until Miss Woods, clearly irritated, locked the brakes and Jessica in place. Jessica scattered her crayons and work angrily. She made sounds, not words. Her arms and hands moved jerkily. Sometimes she held a pencil and dropped it, sometimes the teachers would retrieve the yellow pencil, sometimes they were distracted, and it lay there as she blinked furiously at it, then made squeaking sounds. Manuel scooped it up and placed it in her hand.

Ileana was a despondent girl who lay her head on the desk and blinked at all who passed by. Slender, dark, listless, her head lay on the arm rest most of the day, her eyes wandering back and forth, occasionally resting on Manuel. "Hello," she said. Manuel nodded and waved.

At lunch time everyone in class other than Jessica, Ileana, and Manuel disappeared.

"Aren't you going home for lunch?" Miss Woods asked, her very narrow brows brought together in concern. It was then that Manuel remembered, and he went to his cubby, rummaged through his satchel, and pulled out the bean burritos Amparo had packed for him. Miss Woods wrinkled her nose. "Go eat those outside," she said.

At the end of the school day Mr. Reed took Ileana's wheelchair in hand while Miss Woods unblocked Jessica's and the troop walked toward the school entrance. Manuel was disoriented. How was he to get home? A flush of fear, of self-consciousness, that he would be here forever and ever until he saw Amparo, her wavy gray hair at her shoulders, a gray dress with a pattern of tiny green flowers, walking toward him.

She held out her arms, and he fell into them.

"How was your day at school, my boy? Did you enjoy yourself?"

He peered up at her and shook his head. She laughed. They walked back down the hill holding hands. "Tomorrow you will walk home by yourself, so pay attention." She pointed out a row of ramshackle houses at the bottom of the hill. "That is where the old white bachelors live. They used to work on the railroad. They keep to themselves, so don't go bothering them. When they're on the left of you, you turn right here." She pointed out the tall building in the distance. "That's City Hall," she said. "It should be on your right when you walk to school, and your left when you come home." She moved his hands around so he would understand right and left. "It's so tall they put a light on top so the airplanes don't bump into it. Really!"

As they walked Amparo pointed to a two-story home with a white porch. "Good day, Doña Romero!" she said. "This is my boy, Manuel!" She squeezed his hand and the two women talked. As they walked away, she said, "Good sons. Even better daughters." She crossed the unpaved road to the other side and said under her breath, about the home whose walls were slats of wood and the roof, like Amparo's, was tin, "Over there, the Arechigas. Stay away from them and they'll leave you alone. The boys are wild."

Waving, she said, "Hello Doña Garcia! This is my boy, Manuel!"

To Manuel, "She makes beautiful dresses, for the girls' weddings."

They passed a home with a goat tied up on the side. "The Lujans live there, God bless them, and their daughter, Ileana."

They passed houses surrounded by shrubbery, others standing alone, aloof. Amparo spoke to everyone. Birds darted back and forth between the palo verde trees, the path, and the homes.

A group of children surrounded them, stared at Manuel, then scattered.

Back at her home, the yellow bird puffed her tiny chest and trilled at them. "Mimi likes you!" she told him again, then she had him wash up.

The next day as he set off for school, a boy shorter than himself appeared at his side. "I'm Beto," he said. "I heard about you. You're new to the neighborhood, my neighborhood, and I like to know what's going on." Beto eyed him critically. "You're the kid who can't talk. Manuel, right?"

Manuel examined Beto. He had thick eyebrows and big black eyes that appeared as if he'd seen the entire world and thought it was a pretty funny place. Beto walked with his hands in the pockets of his chinos and bent forward against the steepness of the hill.

"We go to the same school, heck all the kids in Chavez Ravine go to the same school, whether you live, like us, in Palo Verde, La Loma, or Bishop. Palo Verde's the best, the birds here are the loudest. Cisco, he plays his guitar on Friday nights from the water tower. Now when you hear him playing, you'll know who it is. I can't stand Bishop, the priest blasts music early Saturday morning to get everyone out of bed. He ruins good music that way!"

Beto kicked a clog of dirt, which skidded Manuel's way, and he kicked it back at him. "You go to the chueco kids' room. To tell you the truth, most of those kids give me the creeps. Not you. You're like me, but you keep your mouth shut. What's the big deal about that?" Beto shrugged. "More people kept their mouths shut, there'd be a lot less trouble in the world. What grade're you in? First?"

Manuel nodded and Beto didn't remark or appear surprised in any way that Manuel understood him just fine. "I'm in second. Yeah, I know, everyone's shocked. I'm short, okay? But my brother's tall, my dad's tall, so there still might be some time. In fact, I'm counting on it!"

Beto pulled a hand out of one of his pockets and offered Manuel a tiny ball. Manuel picked it off Beto's palm.

"Chew it, ya goof," Beto said, popping one into his mouth. "It's gum!"

Manuel's chewed tentatively and then, as the sugar filled his mouth, more easily. He smiled and nodded thanks at Beto.

The two of them chewed and walked up the dirt path. A car drove by, scattering dust in their direction. "See that." Beto jerked his head in the direction of the disappearing car. "I'm gonna own two of those one day. Maybe even an entire parking lot. They can't mess with you when you got a lot of money. That's what I'm gonna do." He kissed his fingers and waved his hand in front of him.

"See that?" Beto pointed to the tall building in the distance. Manuel felt moved by how tall it was, and already used its position to find his way back home. "That's City Hall. Important people work there. The mayor, you know?" Beto looked back at Manuel.

"You know, this is kind of fun. Kind of interesting. I talk to you, but you don't say anything." Beto moved faster than Manuel, even though he was shorter, so he was always outpacing him and doubling back. He settled on moving sideways, to keep pace with Manuel. "You're a priest! You listen but can't tell things, simón!" Beto smiled, and Manuel wondered, was this a good thing?

Beto now walked taller, believing Manuel was a confidant like a priest, but if there was something revealing Beto wanted to share, some secret fit only for Manuel's silence, none was forthcoming. Beto kicked at a random piece of wood on their trail to school.

"All the kids from the neighborhood come to this school. Another reason I like our neighborhood best is cuz it's closest to the river. A bunch of us go there on the weekend, and all through the summer. Me, Chavela, Kiko, and Kiki, they're twins, Isaac, and Peludo. You'll see. You'll come with us. Peludo's in your class, he's the bald kid who always wears a cap.

Can't grow hair. So we call him Peludo." Beto grinned, and so did Manuel.

It was easy getting to school with Beto. As they walked, Manuel watched the sporadic stream of kids, especially the girls. Most of the kids were barefoot, making him self-conscious of the shoes Amparo insisted he wear. Maybe Lulu was there, or nearby. Maybe she even went to the same school?

Each school day when Manuel finished his breakfast and stepped outside, Beto stood at the latched chicken-wire gate waiting for him. If Amparo stood behind Manuel, Beto would tap his head as if tipping a cap and greet her. Then the two of them trudged the dusty trail up the street to Green Oaks Elementary School.

Manuel watched the colorful birds flitting in the bushes, flying in the trees, or hanging in cages on the porches of the neighboring homes. Amparo talked with her neighbors, Sarita and Pedro Vasco on one side, Hermelinda and Tiburcio Casares on the other, in the evenings as she watered the vegetable garden or the pots of succulents or gathered her animals into the shed. Mimi trilled and chirruped as the sun set and the adults talked. Manuel listened.

On Sundays Amparo got up even earlier, before the sun came out. She ironed his Sunday clothes, the dark blue pants that she had recently re-hemmed, letting out an inch or so. First, she showed Manuel how to polish the stiff black leather shoes she had bought him, then made sure he did so on Saturday nights. These shoes he wore only to church, the shoes he could barely move his toes in. Amparo made a face when she saw how hard it was for him to squeeze his feet into each shoe but said nothing.

Sunday mornings the house smelled of something wonderfully savory, budin azteca, a casserole of layered corn tortillas dipped in a red sauce sprinkled with the bits of meat or chicken

Amparo had reserved for this occasion. The casserole dish was heavy and still warm, smothered with dish towels. By the way she fussed and worried Manuel knew Amparo was proud of the food she prepared and shared for the potluck after the service. She set the casserole of food on the bottom of her collapsible shopping cart, which he dragged behind them as they walked to Sunday service.

Manuel concentrated on pulling the cart away from divots in the dirt road, from puddles and uneven parts.

Amparo said, "Many people here go to the Catholic church." She sniffed. "They drink. We do not. I used to believe as they do, in priests and incense, and statues, and lucky charms, but then the Lord opened my eyes."

Did his family believe in incense and statues and lucky charms? He couldn't remember. He thought of his father picking him up out of the waves and making him fly like a bird. He remembered his mother singing a song about a ranch that went on and made him and Lulu laugh. He remembered being on his father's shoulders watching Lulu run ahead of them.

This morning their walk to her church, their church, Iglesia de Dios Pentecostal, was quiet and uneventful. He unstuck the cart from the mud the rain had made the night before. The shopping cart trailed behind him, the heavy casserole pot making a muffled thunking sound as Manuel hauled it onto the curb. A rush of congregants surrounded the two of them, with cries of "Hermana Amparo!"

"Hermano Sebastián," she answered. "Hermana Filomena, Hermana Luisa! This is my boy, Manuel."

The two women smiled at him eagerly as if holding themselves back. Hermano Sebastián leaned down to Manuel, gold-rimmed glasses on his full brown face, a timid mustache above his mouth, and took Manuel's hand and covered it between his own. "It is an honor, young man. You are blessing to us all."

The two ladies behind him in the bright floral dresses happily echoed him. Manuel glanced over at Amparo, who appeared to glow. Hermano Sebastián released Manuel's hand, then took Amparo's shopping cart, lifted it, and took it downstairs to the community room.

Amparo took Manuel to the children's room.

There, a young woman led them in a lesson about brothers. Manuel wondered if there was a lesson about sisters. He sat like the others in a half circle around the teacher, but his eyes and mind wandered. The classroom was filled with sunlight, different from the class where he spent his weekdays. There were paintings of Jesus, with blindingly bright eyes, his head and hair nearly shining.

A mother stepped into the room, interrupting the young teacher to drop off her daughter, a girl dressed in lavender ruffles. An ache started in the center of his chest and began to spread. The bright sunshine he had blinked his eyes against grew dark. Manuel was clammy, the mist returned, and the sea threatened to envelope him. The kids disappeared. He blinked hard, focusing on the young woman, who talked about one of the brothers doing something bad. The classroom disappeared.

He was at the bottom of the ocean. He didn't know what it was, but he had done something so bad his family was gone.

He opened his eyes. The young teacher offered him a paper cone of water. He sat up and drank. She tugged on his hand. "Let's go find your family," she said. Manuel's heart leaped, but then realized she meant Amparo. He shook his head and stood. Everyone else had already left.

Manuel went up the stairs into the main congregation and spotted Amparo. Her face erupted into pleasure and delight as Hermano Sebastián leaned down and spoke to her conspiratorially. He rushed over. She didn't even notice him approach until he clutched at her hand. She gave him a dismissive pat.

He wandered downstairs to the common room where the others were gathering. He moved folding chairs into their places with the other children. The Sunday school teacher and other ladies set out covered casseroles and pots.

Despite the cold mist that was close by, Sunday was a good day. There were people and colors and music and children and Amparo and food. Lots and lots of food. Pots of beans, soupy, refried, different rice dishes, Amparo's casserole, enchiladas, tamales, albondigas, simmering meat stews, warm and spicy, chiles, and mounds of tortillas.

As they walked home, Manuel's belly was full, and Amparo held his hand while she dragged the shopping cart and the casserole pot, now filled with a combination of other people's food. She said to him gently but firmly, "Little one, I am happy you have a good appetite. But can you eat just a little less? People will think I don't feed you right!" She squeezed his hand, and Manuel squeezed back.

In his little bed that was warm and snug, Amparo covered him with a clean sheet and an old quilt. She placed a pillow and another quilt next to him, just in case, she said.

"You may not believe me, you don't have to. It's all right. You are small and lost, with this crazy lady. How strange and terrible it must all seem to you. It won't always be this way. You won't always be this way. You'll get your voice. I know you will. You will grow strong and healthy, certainly if our hens have anything to do with it!" He could hear the smile in her voice, he smelled her scent of masa and chicken broth, and his mind started wandering. His lids were heavy, as she continued to speak.

"Oh, my little one, every night I pray for you. And every night I thank God that he has given you to me to care for." Amparo had him fold his hands reverently and above him prayed to God.

As she prayed aloud, he silently prayed to Lulu.

Lulu, wherever you are, I am here in Chavez Ravine. I made friends with Beto who's funny, he makes me laugh. I'm living with this lady named Amparo. She's very nice. Where are you, Lulu? Will you come and find me? Why am I alone here, will you come and find me? Please talk back to me, wherever you are, whatever you're doing. I'm being as good and brave as I can be. Please. Tell me where our family is, please? I want to see you again. I want us to all be together again.

As Amparo ended her prayer, he, too, mentally added, *In Jesus's name, Amen.*

CHAPTER THREE

O n school days Beto waited outside the latched gate Amparo had to keep her pecking hens safe, his hands in his pockets, entertaining himself by kicking at the stones and pebbles in the pathway. Manuel waved him in for breakfast, a warm tortilla filled with buttered beans or eggs and a dollop of cream, but Beto would shake his head and frown as if to say he'd eaten plenty.

Beto had a younger brother, Trini, who everyone called Peanut, and a younger sister, Alicia, everyone called Chavela. Chavela was still too young for school, and sometimes Peanut would walk with them, but he liked to pick up sticks on the road and annoy Beto, who would then chase him away. That always made him think of Lulu—she would never chase him away, would she?

On their walk to school Beto told him for the hundredth time about his plans. Manuel always listened, attentive. The language Amparo spoke at home was the same language she spoke at church, and the language that Beto spoke when he, at last, would come into her home. But on their walks together,

Beto talked to him mostly in the language that was spoken at school, English, Miss Woods said. Everyone was to speak English at school. Manuel understood English now, but he hadn't when he lived with Mrandmrspowell. Not at first. He had just listened. There was no Spanish there.

If Manuel awoke in the morning and could not hear Amparo in the kitchen or sense her presence in the house, he hopped out of bed and went looking for her. Sometimes he'd find her in the backyard, feeding the chickens, talking to Bessie and Ana, or visiting on Sarita's doorstep, or with Hermelinda. He hovered underneath the Vascos's window and heard her voice. "He is as good as gold, and more precious to me." Hermelinda murmured something, and Amparo's voice came back, clear. "He will talk. I am sure of it. God told me so."

One morning he searched for her, and she was simply gone, a plate of food for him was kept warm by the pilot light in the oven.

Come back, come back, come back.

The sea rose around him, cold and gray. A wave rose, it would swallow him, drag him to the bottom, again.

She's not coming back, she will never come back, she won't ever come back.

He sat at the table, rigid, unable to reach into the oven for his food. *I promise to be brave, I promise to be a good boy, she will come back. I promise not to eat too much, she will come back. I promise to call her Tía, she will come back. If I promise to—*

Amparo walked through the door. Manuel was seated at the kitchen table, miserable, his food in the oven, dried out, his lip trembling as he watched her walk through the threatening waves.

She hugged him, he burst into tears.

"Ay my little one, I was not far!"

I was by myself, his eyes accused her. *You abandoned me, Tia.*

She kissed the top of his head.

"Eat your food," she scolded. "You should hurry, Beto is waiting for you."

At school, Manuel examined Miss Woods, the slight woman who worked with him in the room with all the children. She had light freckles on her face, thin lips, even teeth. He stared at the tiny crosses that tugged at her earlobes.

She said, "Copy this, Manuel. February 17th, 1943. Then copy this. This is how your name is spelled."

She wrote the words on his slate, and he copied what she had written, slowly and carefully, feeling the chalk firm between his fingers. He knew how to spell his name already, but he worked slowly. She smelled pretty. He watched her as she moved to work with Peludo, with the distinctive brown cap. Peludo seemed to melt sideways, he couldn't sit very long. He worked on his slate then sprawled out on the floor. That afternoon the school had a fire drill. Manuel helped Jessica with her chair. She reached behind her and patted his hand.

Friday night Manuel awoke in his small room in the dark. He wasn't afraid: he had awakened to distant music. A voice singing. That must be Cisco, like Beto had told him. The guitar was sweet, soft, and very sad. He heard the words: "los animalitos / se mueren de hambre / porque son huerfanitos / de madre y padre." The song made him feel tremendously sad for those animals dying of hunger. He knew he, too, was an animalito, huerfanito.

In Lulu's stories the animals talked and were smarter than the people. There was a mole that led to buried treasure, a donkey that found the village all the water they would ever need, a bird that brought lost children home. He wished he could find that bird.

He fell back asleep.

On Saturdays Beto came in for breakfast. Before he ate, Amparo, now Tía, as he had promised, made him change into Manuel's spare clothing, so she could mend his shirt and pair of pants where the threads were fraying and give them a quick press to neaten him up. "If you two are going to deliver my clothes, you have to look sharp," she said.

Beto ate until Tía laughed, pulling charred flour tortillas off her griddle, finishing the beans that she had fried in a pan of sizzling chorizo.

Tía's broad face broke into dimples and white teeth as the boy thanked her and complemented her cooking. "Who knew I could eat so much?" he said, covering his mouth to hide a burp.

Manuel finished and watched with admiration as his friend kept eating, and talking, and smiling.

The two of them took Tía's shopping cart, filled with washed laundry, tied and tagged with the names of whom to deliver it to.

On occasional stops Manuel and Beto got pennies as tips. The first time that happened Beto was confused. "Do you want us to give this to Doña Amparo?" he asked Mrs. Garfas.

"It's for you, tonto, but if you don't want it," she threatened to take it back.

"No, no, no, it's good." Then, "And thank you!"

Mrs. Garfas closed the door, and Manuel and Beto delivered the rest of the laundry, dragging the shopping cart back with them, dividing the pennies evenly when they got back to his home.

A month of penny tips later, Beto appeared thoughtful. His thick eyebrows drew together. "What are you gonna do with all your money?" Beto asked.

Manuel shrugged. He had a vague idea he would give it to Lulu when he found her.

"Do you trust me? Give me your money. It's like an investment. I have an idea how we can make it grow."

Manuel went into his room, the small room that he shared with the sewing machine. Under his mattress he pulled out the small brown tarnished coins. Six. He had six cents.

In the back of his mind shook a memory. *Coins jingled, his father gave him coins. They were buying something.* He tried to grasp the memory, but there was nothing more.

He ran through the kitchen, onto the porch, past Mimi, down the steps, and handed the coins to Beto.

"Between us we got twelve cents. Remember that. You gotta keep track of things when you invest. Unnerstand?"

Manuel nodded.

"Great," Beto said. "Good. See you Monday, mano!"

Monday morning Tía was not in the home, but this morning Manuel was filled with expectation, despite her absence. What would Beto bring?

He pulled his plate out of the oven, scrambled eggs, a slice of bacon, and two flour tortillas now crisp and dried from the pilot light. He ate, enjoying the crispness of the bacon and the creaminess of the eggs.

He washed his face, brushed his teeth, and waited on the porch for Beto. When he saw him walking up the street he waved. Now Beto dragged his feet and lowered his head.

Manuel ran to the gate, latched it, and moved his arms, as if to say, "Hey, what's wrong?"

Beto walked toward him slowly and reluctantly raised his sorrowful face to Manuel. Then he broke into a smile. "I'm just kidding you!" he said. "Look. We're in business!" Out of Beto's book satchel he pulled a crinkly paper bag. He held it out to Manuel for inspection.

Jawbreakers and gumballs! It looked like a dozen or more. Manuel reached to take one when Beto pulled the bag away.

"No, ya goof, you can't eat the investment. I'm gonna sell, see, at school during recess. You're what is known as the 'silent partner.'"

Beto laughed and Manuel's body shook with silent laughter as the two boys headed to school.

After school ended Manuel approached Beto, who had yet to see him. Beto looked, not upset, but thoughtful.

He turned and spotted Manuel.

"No sale," Beto said. "I'm not sure what's going on. I told Carla, you know, the girl with the ringlets?

"Anyway, that's not important." He scratched his chin as they walked home. "I give it a week." He patted Manuel on the shoulder. "If it doesn't work out, I guess we're eating the profits. Not such a bad thing."

Tía brought him to Bible study on Wednesday nights. Hermano Sebastián led a group of twelve or so with a handful of appended children. Manuel scanned the faces: no Lulu. The children played together in a room nearby, then the entire group gathered for a closing hymn and prayer.

Often, during the final prayer, people changed. The first time Manuel watched, it was a quiet woman, prim and deep brown, like Tía, who tilted her head back and began speaking something incomprehensible to Manuel. She babbled, gesticulated, spittle running down the side of her mouth, her body swaying, her arms spread upward with a complete sense of abandonment. Soon a man older than Hermano Sebastián raised his arms to the ceiling, and he, too, began speaking words that made no sense to Manuel. It was not the language of his classroom or of his home. Tonight an older man lifted and lowered his arms and moved unsteadily as he spoke. Others followed, an outpouring of unrecognizable words. Manuel watched Tía and Hermano Sebastián: their eyes were closed tight in silent prayer.

Hermano Sebastián walked the two of them home. Manuel was between them, half-listening to their discussion of church members. At the base of the steps to their home Sebastián said a final, brief prayer, then shook Manuel's hand.

Tía said, "Good night, and God bless."

* * *

That week Manuel watched as Miss Woods pointed her finger to each word and read it aloud to him. She asked him, "Where are the children going?"

As she had just read, the yellow-haired children were clearly going down the path to pick berries. And it was right there in the picture. He looked up at her with eyes that should have demonstrated he knew how obvious it all was.

She wasn't looking at him. "What is her name?" she asked, pointing to Jane.

This was a stupid question. He reached for the book, to close it to point to the girl's name that was on the cover. Miss Woods flinched and snapped the book shut. She glared at him hard. "Seriously. Why do I even bother? With all of you, with any of you?"

The tone in her voice made her meaning clear. Manuel spent the rest of the day ignoring Peludo's movements, other interruptions, and stared out the window, where a starling sailed, then later a flock of geese.

Beto frowned when they spotted each other after school. "Carla tells the teacher, the teacher sends me to the principal, so the principal can confiscate the candy. That means so he can take it away." Beto examined Manuel to be assured he was understood. Manuel's mouth was wide in dismay.

"Yeah. Exactly," Beto said. "You know, I had a feeling about Carla. She's sneaky, like me, you know? I didn't bring any candy today. And see those kids over there?" Beto pointed at a group that headed down the hill. "They gave me twenty-five cents for my entire supply, and tomorrow morning we'll meet them before school. Anybody finds any candy after that—well, it won't be on me."

Manuel nodded encouragingly.

"Now don't get too excited with your new-found wealth," Beto said. "We've got to reinvest the profits. Don't worry, partner. Trust me."

Soon Manuel had an assortment of pennies and nickels which totaled a small fortune: fifty cents. All tips they earned went into candy. After they invested their funds into inventory, he and Beto split the profits, although it was a little fuzzy to Manuel why he got any money at all since it was all Beto's idea, all Beto's negotiating skills, all Beto's understanding of what the other kids would like.

Genaro, the liquor store owner everybody called Jerry, got to know both of them pretty well, and soon he started shaking his head over the sweet tooth the two of them had, and if their families knew how they were wasting their money.

"Investing," Beto told Manuel with a poke in the ribs.

There were some times when they actually ate their merchandise. Manuel was fond of the brown barrel-shaped candies that had a hint of burned sugar in them, while Beto disdained his and the kids' choices. "I don't like 'em," he said. "They just melt away. Give me gum. That's something you can chew on all day."

At home Tía made coffee while Manuel stared at Hermano Sebastián. He was dressed in a light gray suit over a pristine white shirt. His brown silk tie was fastened with a small black pin. He had a round shiny face with a neatly trimmed mustache. Now he recognized him. He was one of the men who brought him here, to Tía Amparo. He seemed to have a lot of hair covering his head. Tía smiled and laughed. Manuel stared at the white tablecloth with distended flower petals she had set out just this morning. She placed a coffee cup in front of Sebastián and herself and poured coffee from a speckled blue kettle. She asked him if he wanted anything. Hermano Sebastián set his Bible gently on the table, first brushing it for crumbs. Manuel was immediately offended on his Tía's behalf, who rid her home of crumbs and motes of dust in a nearly unceasing battle. Manuel hadn't heard what she was laughing at, he had been too involved studying Hermano Sebastián. He said, "How's your week been, young man?"

Manuel shook his head. It was better when he had Tía all to himself. He wandered over to his small room, then, restless and bored, stepped outside.

He stepped behind the home and looked at the three hens. Bessie and Ana always lay eggs tinted greenish blue, while Daisy's were dirty brown. He could hear the Vascos' goat baying.

The light of the sky changed. The sun had dipped behind the hill now, and the air would soon be cold. City Hall stood, reflecting dying sunlight, turning green, turning gray as the sun sank. The hills smelled of wet dirt, of animals, and faintly of diesel wafting up from the roadway below. Heading back to his home he saw the light in Tía's home. Through the window, he could see they were still talking.

He poked around the chicken coop. The hens sat on their pegs and ignored him.

He looked at the light that shone through the windows. Despite his mood her home was warm and inviting. Tía's home. He closed his eyes against it. He thought of being swung around by his father and laughing. His mother had read to him, he was certain, from the Santa Biblia. Not even Lulu was there, just the two of them. He thought of Lulu and wondered where she was. He remembered walking with her, his hand in hers. Something was checkered. Her dress? His shirt? One day he would go find her. He would find them all. When he was older, when he would know how.

Manuel stepped onto the porch and walked into Tía's home. His home now.

Hermano Sebastián said, "I wanted to be sure to have a moment of prayer, the three of us."

The three held hands across the table. Manuel bowed his head. Hermano Sebastián cleared his throat and said, "Lord God of the Universe and all Creation, thank you for this moment. We know that whenever two or more are gathered in your name, you are present."

Manuel heard Tía's interjection of "Thanks be to God."

Sebastián continued, "Forgive me, God, it is not my habit to pray in the manner of the Pharisees, out loud, somewhat boastful, but I want to thank you, God, for bringing Manuel into Doña Amparo's life. We thank you, Lord Almighty, for the love between the two that is unfolding, for the mercy she is showing him, and for you bringing Manuel into all our lives. May he honor your blessings with his awareness of your hand in his life. May you help him to recover his words and his language. Thy will be done. In Jesus's name, Amen."

Manuel blinked against the light. Tía dipped down and kissed the top of his head, while Sebastián ruffled his hair. Manuel looked at Tía. She had tears in her eyes and smiling so wide. He smiled back at her. The room filled with light.

* * *

On the weekend he and Beto delivered laundry, collecting random tips. From one woman, Beto's blinking brown eyes attracted a tug on the cheek in lieu of a penny, and Beto spent the rest of the walk to the next house muttering about the nerve some people had, helping themselves to pinch his cheek! His face was his business and they could all—

This way, Manuel met a few of Beto's friends, Chavela, the twins, Kiko and Kiki. Peludo sometimes walked with them, smiling and joking, but Beto would tell him to beat it before deliveries. "As my mom would say, 'algo tiene,'" Beto explained. "But so do you, huh?"

Manuel nodded and wanted to laugh, but it stuck in his throat. It was more something he *didn't* have. Always, on their deliveries, he kept his eyes open for a girl he might recognize, a girl who looked, maybe, a little like him. But no. No Lulu.

Some houses they never visited, like Ileana's home. Occasionally they went down the gulley to inspect the row of "bachelor" flats, scruffy shacks that even made Jessica's home look good.

"My Dad told me those gabachos used to work on the railroad." They sat on the hill and watched, Beto chewing gum, Manuel staring at the ramshackle homes. Tall and scruffy men with white hair and dirty beards wandered about. Sometimes the men waved, often they just ignored them.

Beto stared at the tips in the palm of his hand. "You still good with this, Silent Partner?" Beto said with a wink. Manuel nodded, and Beto pocketed the change. "One day I'm gonna have two cars. That's right! And each day I'll have to decide which one I want to drive, which one feels best for the day. I'll have a house so big it'll have two bathrooms, *two! Both* of them inside." He nodded to himself. "I'll have men working for me. For me! And they'll take off their hats and say, 'Good morning, Mr. Lopez,' or 'Good afternoon, Mr. Lopez,' or 'Good evening, Mr. Lopez. How is your wife? How are the kids? Beto Jr.'s a real smart one, isn't he, Mr. Lopez? You must be so proud.' Simón!"

Manuel recognized the keen and distant look on Beto's face. There was no point in interrupting him, pointing out Peludo playing in the field, or El Cementerio Andando pulling his donkey ahead. Beto was alone in a world he had created, where he was the most important one of all. Manuel wondered if he was in this world with Beto.

When Beto came out of his trance, Manuel clapped him on the back. Beto could dream about the future. Manuel could not see anything of his future—all of it was blank to him. His daydreams were about right now: finding his parents at Tía's church, discovering his sister while walking to school.

Even reinvesting in the candy business, Manuel and Beto had coins to themselves. When Tía was in the backyard feeding the chickens, Manuel pulled the change out from under his mattress and inspected the coins: the dirty, tarnished pennies with a man's profile and a building, the nickels with another man's profile and an animal. He liked the weight and the thickness of the nickels. He made stacks of the pennies. He had forty-seven cents. What was he supposed to do with it all? Could he use it to find his family?

He heard Tía call him; he swept his coins back to where they belonged, flattened out underneath his slim mattress, and ran out to her. Together they patched a hole in the chicken-wire fence. Tía explained patiently how to do it. Manuel concentrated and followed directions, then showed her that he could twist the wire himself, more neatly and efficiently than she had shown him.

Hermano Sebastián led their Wednesday night group while Manuel and the other children played. The two groups joined for the final words and blessings. Manuel waited for what was called the Holy Spirit to descend upon the congregation and watched with a growing throbbing at the base of his throat.

He stared at the previously calm and sedate men and women who started moving sideways. Some started moaning.

"Let us raise our hands and lift our voices to the glory of God," Hermano Sebastián said, until all in the small congregation, including the children, raised their hands, and Manuel felt himself moving back and forth with the group, a pressure on the base of his throat, a struggle.

His arms shot up and outward. The barrier at the base of his throat relaxed its grip. Manuel spoke. He inhaled air and exhaled words. The words gushing out of his mouth had tapped that deep ache inside him. Lulu, he said, over and over again. As more words tumbled out, he felt the stillness of the room. After a moment, other voices joined him, then began to thin. He inhaled and exhaled and stopped speaking. He looked around at the group and found Tía beaming at him.

He did not feel that she should be smiling at him. He did not feel as if he had done anything to be proud of. He had not been touched by God, he'd been ruined by loneliness, by the ache for his sister, and for what she meant to him. He was embarrassed for himself, and for the congregation members who smiled so broadly at him. He was fake, chueco.

Hermano Sebastián walked the two of them home. Manuel listened intently to their conversation, but there was no mention of what Manuel had just done. Tía thanked Hermano Sebastián for escorting them home and told Manuel to get washed and ready for bed.

He lay in bed, teeth scrubbed, in a clean night shirt, and waited for Tía.

She sat by his bed and picked up his hand. "My little one, when we speak that way, we are filled with the Holy Spirit. We do not know what God is telling us, other than that He is with us. But with you, I do think he is telling us something different. My sweet one, you are getting ready to talk to us. We are here, ready to listen. Now sleep. Good night."

She kissed him on the cheek, he placed his arms around her neck, holding her there until she gently removed his arms.

"I knew you could talk."

CHAPTER FOUR

Thursday morning at school Manuel matched shapes with their labels. He added sticks to more sticks and wrote down the total. He played with the puppets and told stories in his head with the puppets, who he named Lulu and Manolito. The two of them went to the zoo and wondered at the animals. The two of them took the red car to the beach and wondered at the ocean. The two of them went home and found their parents, waiting for them, this whole time. They had been mischievous, trouble-making children, but now that their parents were so happy to see them, nobody was angry anymore. Jessica watched him move the puppets around. She smiled and nodded at him. Like Manuel, she didn't speak either. Manuel wasn't sure she could. He wondered what her parents were like.

Of course, he knew he had parents. But he had no idea where they would be. He had no memory of their faces. Waves landed on the beach, he soared in his father's arms, a warm towel around his wet body, that's the best he could remember before the sunlight went out.

Lulu he could remember. He could remember her hand in his. He could remember walking alongside her, looking up at her. Laughing with her. Jessica tapped on her desk, encouraging him. He smiled back at her, and this time the story in his mind was about two kids in school, playing hide and seek.

* * *

Miss Woods was out that week. Manuel noticed this because the classroom felt different, more scattered, disorganized. With Mr. Reed alone, there was something uncomfortable, and an unfamiliar scent. Ileana was absent, too, and Jessica was in her wheelchair near the flag and abandoned there for the morning. Manuel played with his puppets nearby, while Mr. Reed worked between two desks.

Mr. Reed moved Jessica to a table and began working with her. Manuel concentrated on his math problems. A few moments later Manuel heard a pencil snap, and Jessica made a cry.

Mr. Reed scraped his chair roughly against the wood flooring. "That's exactly what I mean," he said, in exasperation, stalking off to a far corner of the room.

Manuel looked around and Jessica was crying. Tears squeezed out; she blinked them away and looked at him. He glanced at Mr. Reed—the door to the classroom slammed angrily shut.

Manuel patted the little girl on her back. There, there, there, he thought at her. He's a creep, we all know that. Miss Woods will be back. Jessica nodded her head in rhythm with his pats, as if she could understand what he was trying to tell her. He retrieved his puppets and sat beside her.

She had been working on math problems and fiddled with the still-broken pencil. Manuel stood and had picked the pencil from her hand to go sharpen it when Mr. Reed returned. "Leave her alone, Miguel!" Manuel dropped the pencil and returned to his place by the wall with his puppets, slate, and reader.

Who was Miguel?

He glared angrily at the teacher who had already turned his back to him.

He picked up his reader. Mr. Reed walked around the class. He turned the page. He would be fine here with a picture book and the reader where two children always explored a foreign world as if it were ordinary. Even the colors they were painted, the cheeks, the hair, were of a strange and different quality. Manuel rubbed at the pictures to make sure the ink didn't wear off.

He wondered how much candy Beto would sell this week. He wondered what Beto would spend his money on. He wondered what he would spend his money on. There were only three people in this world he wanted, only one person whose face he could remember. Would forty-seven cents help?

This classroom should have a radio, he thought, and they could listen to music, or La Palabra de la Biblia, or La Palabra de Dios.

Mr. Reed motioned to sit by him at the wobbly, oval table. "Bring the reader."

Manuel wished he were anywhere else. He put the puppets back on their stand, he picked up his slate and reader, he glanced around the class as if someone would save him.

"Hurry up," came the teacher's voice.

Mr. Reed grabbed the book and noisily flipped through the pages. He stopped at a picture of a strange-looking baby, so pale with yellow hair and red cheeks. "Today, let's get some work in, Miguel."

Manuel glared. He smelled of cigarettes and something

else. Manuel realized the sickly sweet smell came from Mr. Reed.

Mr. Reed said, "This is a baby boy. Say it, bay bee."

Manuel glared.

"Boooooy."

Mr. Reed put a heavy hand on Manuel's shoulder. Manuel squirmed, but the hand gripped harder, keeping him in place.

"Again," he said, "after me. Bay bee."

Peludo, at another table, echoed, "Bay bee."

Manuel glared at the pages, felt the grip on his shoulder, squeezing, squeezing. Mr. Reed had done this before, and all he got for it were a couple of tears Manuel blinked away before anyone could notice.

"Boy!"

Manuel wriggled under his grip. Peludo said, "Boy!"

"That's you, Miguel, a big ol' baby boy." Mr. Reed gave Manuel a final, powerful squeeze and pushed him off his chair. "Let's go, everyone, let's not be late for lunch."

Manuel rubbed and rubbed at his shoulder. Mr. Reed rushed them out of the classroom.

Peludo, smiling, waved and said, "So long!"

He knew he was in the chueco class—he knew this meant there was something wrong with him. Even his lunch pail was a subject of mirth. Beto, upon the first dozen or so occasions would comment, "Where you gonna work today, man? Are you gonna pick fresas? Maybe some sweet chabacanes? Simón!"

While Beto and others went home for lunch, Manuel wandered the playground. Today he sat on a swing swaying sideways. The air was cool, but the sun's rays warmed his face. He watched a teacher walk into the main office. He scanned around. City Hall was there in the distance; he kept his eye out for Beto in case he hadn't already left down the dirt road. Wildflowers had begun to spread out alongside. Manuel suspected that Beto only went home because all the other kids did, and that it was a good way to sell candy. Beto's mom was nice enough when Manuel visited, but there was a look in her eye as if she were weighing the food Manuel ate, and how much it subtracted from what was there for her and her family. So very different from Tía, who smiled and ate and dished out more beans. Manuel decided he liked her beans, and it would be very nice to walk home and have a hot tortilla. But that was not to be.

Rocking on the swing, little signals of hunger started up. He looked down at where his feet scuffed in the sand. How had he ended up out here without his lunch pail?

He went back to his classroom which stood apart from the main school building. There looked like a stream of smoke coming from one of the windows. Manuel rushed ahead.

His classroom door was unlocked. He raced in, glancing around expecting to find Mr. Reed and Jessica. Jessica waved at him. She was trying to move her chair, but the wheels were locked. Where was Mr. Reed?

Manuel moved to unlock the brakes. Jessica gripped his wrist. She sniffed, emphatically. Manuel looked at her and nodded. He smelled that sickly sweet scent again, but more powerful was the smell of something burning.

As he turned to investigate, Jessica propelled herself in the direction of the door. When he was sure she was outside and safe, he went to see if he could find what was burning.

Across from the bathroom were the clothing rack and cubby where students stored their coats and satchels. Smoke was curling under the bathroom door. Different from cigarette smoke. Like something had caught fire. He pushed to make his way in. It was locked. Was Mr. Reed in there?

Manuel pounded on the bathroom door. Pounding and pounding and pounding until he realized this would make no difference.

He ran to the front office.

There was always one lady there, her hair streaked with gray and tied neatly into a bun at the back of her head.

He dashed behind the front desk, held her hand, and pulled.

"Hey, hey, young man, what do you think you're doing?"

He pulled her hand again, insistently. He took a deep breath. It was time; he had something to say: "Help," he said. "Help. Please. I think," he cleared his throat, "there's a fire."

"All right then," the woman said, standing nearly twice as tall as Manuel, and followed swiftly in her long legs behind him as he ran.

Mr. Reed sat at his desk. The smell of smoke, of burning, had dissipated.

"Gerald," the office lady said, by way of greeting.

"Harriet," he responded.

"This young man seems to think there is a problem." Manuel listened to her tone of voice. This woman *had* to believe him. She had followed him, after all, didn't that mean she believed him?

"Oh my," Mr. Reed responded, his eyes clear and innocent. "What does he 'say' is the problem?"

Now Manuel could tell that the office lady was cross by the slanted movement her eyes made. "Have you been drinking again?"

Mr. Reed continued, "Whatever that dirty little Mexican said is a lie. He's known in this class for being a dirty little liar." Reed's eyes narrowed in his direction, with a look of scorn and contempt.

"Dirty little Mexican." Is that what Manuel was? What did that mean? He was little, but he was never dirty, Tía made sure about that. Mexican? Mejicano, did he mean? But the way he used that word was as if he were some kind of piece of filth, like a potato that had gone rotten and disgusting, filled with maggots.

"Gerald, that language is appalling and unacceptable. I realized Miss Woods is out this week, but I had no idea you were still here *unsupervised*." She stepped into the bathroom, then back out, scanned the room, picked up a pencil and a piece of paper and scrawled a note in writing Manuel was unable to decipher.

She gave the note to Manuel. "Take this to Principal Hansen." She looked at Gerald. "It looks like you were smoking and drinking in the children's bathroom." She folded her arms in front of her. "I enjoy a good story. Now tell me, how did something catch fire?"

Mr. Reed stood, angrily slamming the book down. He grabbed the note out of Manuel's hand and said, "I'll go get Mr. Hansen. We'll be right back."

The office lady pursed her lips and nodded.

Manuel walked over to the window to stare at the playground. Children were returning from lunch. He still hadn't eaten, but now he had no appetite. He was excited and proud. He kept his eyes open for Beto.

He saw, instead, Mr. Reed walking across the yard, to the office, then past the office. He kept walking. Manuel tapped at the window and called at the office lady to come see, but she was busy opening and closing cabinet doors.

* * *

45

That evening at supper Tía had a special treat: a pork chop that was so tender it fell off the bone and onto his freshly made tortilla. She patted his hand, "I know you can. I knew you could. Not everyone believed me! Now, when Beto waits for you in the morning, ask him in. Let us pray."

He listened to the prayer of abundant thanks and gratitude. As he listened, he prayed to Lulu. For a horrible moment he was gripped by the thought, what if it had been Lulu in that wheelchair, what if she were in a wheelchair right now? No, no.

Tía's prayer ended. She sat down across from him as he ate. "Of course you can talk," she said. "I knew you could speak. God told me you would talk when it was time. Today it was necessary."

"More beans?" she asked.

He shook his head, she smiled. "Little one, now you can answer me. 'Yes, please, Tía,' or, 'No, thank you, Tía' or whatever. Just something."

"No, thank you, Tía."

She nodded, approvingly, then stroked the side of his face. "Now you can speak to me, to Beto, to your teachers. It is time. Can you do that for me?"

He nodded, then corrected himself. "Yes, Tía."

He looked around the room and saw the stove with its immaculate handles and hissing griddle, the open cupboards where Tía stored her flours, spices, and chiles. The cuckoo clock that ticked and moved back and forth. The curio cabinet. Everything was still, everything was the same.

"I can talk," he said, looking back at her. "Thank you, Tía. That was good." She kissed the top of his head.

In the morning when he stood to peer out the window, there was Beto by the gate, kicking at the dirt.

Manuel went out to the front, banging the door. Beto

looked up, and Manuel waved him in. Beto shook his head and said, "Nah, man, come one, we're late."

"Come. In," Manuel said.

Eyes wide, his thick eyebrows higher than ever, Beto unlatched the gate and walked up the dirt path.

"Hey, you talking now?"

Manuel nodded his head and added, "Yeah."

Beto clapped him on the back. "That's great, man, that's great! Wait, does this mean I got to make room for you in our conversations?"

Manuel smiled and said, "Yeah."

* * *

When the two of them got to school, the lady with the gray-streaked hair took him aside. "You're going to a regular class-room now," she said. While Beto played with the other children on the playground, this woman escorted him down a hallway and through a door. "This is Miss Otis." She was brunette with a stiff, elaborate hairstyle. "Say good morning to her."

"Good morning, Miss Otis," he said.

The woman smiled. "Welcome, Manuel. I'm going to sit you up front. I look forward to getting to know you better."

Manuel smiled. Beto talked all about his first-grade teacher Miss Otis.

At the April assembly he stood on stage and peered at the faces in the audience. If Lulu were there, she would see him. She would wave and scream and jump up and down. He scanned all the students. Lulu wasn't there.

The woman with the hair neatly streaked with gray presented Manuel, among others, good citizenship certificates. Beto teased him about it all the way home.

"They give good citizenship awards for opening your mouth, now? I shoulda won one every month, simón!"

Tía kissed the top of his head repeatedly and propped the certificate up on their kitchen table for weeks and weeks.

Although Manuel had his voice, he did not have the words to tell Tía about Lulu. He did not have the words to ask about his parents. Where were they? Where were they all?

CHAPTER FIVE

I n May the mustard grass had sprung all over the hills, the matilija poppies spread wide their white petals and their puffy yellow hearts. Tía made syrup and canned jam from the nopal fruit. The houses and gardens in Palo Verde burst with colors, red, purple, yellow. She had planters of fuchsias and gardenias on her shaded porch. Mimi whistled back to the birds that were so near, yet so far.

Every day Manuel wanted to talk about Lulu. He wanted to tell Tía what Lulu looked like, how she laughed, how she made him feel warm and safe. Every day, he wanted to ask Tía about his parents, where were they, would they return, did they know where he was, why didn't they visit? Every day. And yet, at even the thought of telling her, that same silence that had descended when Lulu said goodbye returned and choked the words at the back of his throat.

He spent Saturdays helping Tía launder, fold. Iron, deliver. Feed the hens, clean the animal pens, rummage for eggs. Sometimes she'd take him on her rounds, other times he'd spend the day with Beto and a bunch of other kids, Peludo, and Kiko, scrabbling through the clumps of dirt, hiding out in the foliage. Laying low during the heat of the day, then running around again. Trekking down to the Los Angeles River, building dams with debris, watching the water make its way around, through, then finally topple their constructions.

Beto's mom scowled at them for asking for water and scolded them for bringing dirt into the house. Sometimes, so bored, they played school with the girls, Kiki, Chavela, even Peanut, and the girls would rap Manuel's knuckles when he wouldn't answer their questions right and laugh and laugh. He didn't mind, though, it didn't feel like anything at all.

He liked the evenings the best, when it cooled down, Tía made him bathe, and there was supper, waiting for him.

Manuel always knew when Tía had gotten a letter from her son: she smiled as she bounced around the kitchen, the letter displayed prominently above the curio cabinet. After supper she would read parts to him over and over again. "Ma, I wish I could be at home with you right now, sitting at the table, eating all the tortillas and chile rellenos I could hold." And, "Say hello to Manolito for me." And especially, "I miss you, your loving son, Antonio." Out of one letter tumbled smooth, glossy pink pebbles. Tía kept them in her apron pocket for weeks until they, too, joined the other gifts in the cabinet.

He had learned to write in school. He could write to his family. He needed an address.

One night after walking down to the arroyo and back with Beto, Manuel came home and there were two strange men sitting at the kitchen table, heads bowed, while Tía prayed. He stopped in the doorway.

Were they taking him away again? He would run to Beto's, he would hide behind his house, he would beg Beto to hide him, he would.

"Come here little one, come meet our guests," Tía called,

finishing her prayer. "They're going to be sleeping in your room tonight, while you sleep in my room."

They wore shabby but clean clothes. They nodded and smiled at him shyly. The smaller one asked him his name and age and Manuel told them, to head bobs of approval.

At supper the men spoke of Nayarit, and Tía nodded encouragingly. Of Zacatecas, and she smiled. Of San Francisco, and she shook her head. "I don't know. But I'll have tortillas for you in the morning."

The men and their bundles were gone in the morning, before Manuel awoke.

"Who are they?" he asked.

"They're far from home. They're looking for work, they had to leave early to catch the train north. God bless them, God protect them," she said.

She put her coffee cup down and said, "You have something they do not." Tía's smooth dry hand covered his small one and pulled him along.

She brought him back inside her room, pushed the mattress of her bed aside. She pressed at the wooden flooring. She lifted a small panel of worn wood, set it aside, and searched around. From the hole in the floor, she removed a small metal box. Fascinated by the hiding place, by the treasure box, Manuel sat down next to her.

In the palm of her hand, Tía held a small key. She twisted it in the lock, opened the lid of the metal box, and picked up a stack of papers. Manuel caught a glimpse of a photograph of a young woman holding a baby. A photograph of a young man in uniform, serious and important. A different man from the framed smiling photograph of her son. Tía found what she was looking for, removed it from the box, and closed its lid.

She said, "This is a very important piece of paper that is

yours. That is why I take care of it and keep it here. When you get older you will take care of it. You will use it as you need it."

She handed it to him.

The paper was folded. He opened it and noticed that it was creased from folding and unfolding. The paper had an unfamiliar sheen to it, and a gray and murky color.

She read it to him, in school language, in English. She said, "Certificate of Live Birth."

"What does that mean?" he asked.

"Your birth certificate, my dear. Look, here is your name, Manuel, your last name, Galvan. Your middle name, Victor."

He made a face and looked at her. "Who's Victor?"

"You didn't know you had a middle name? Do you want me to call you Victor?"

"No!" he laughed.

Tía traced the words on the certificate with her finger as she read to him. "Here is your mother's name: Filomena Vigil de Galvan. Her nationality: Mexican. Her race: Indian."

Manuel felt a buzzing in his body, a wiry cord of electricity humming within. She was real, she had a name, the woman who had hugged him with a warm towel, he didn't imagine it all, he didn't dream it all.

"Here is your father's name: Gustavo Galvan Andrade. His nationality: Mexican. His race: Indian."

The man who lifted him up from the waves. His father. He had a name. Gustavo Galvan Andrade.

He buried his face in Tía's arm. He didn't want her to see him cry. Tía waited.

After a moment, he wiped his eyes with the backs of his hands and looked at his own name. He read: Manuel Victor Galvan. Nationality: US. Race: White.

Tía said, "Those men don't have this. This says you are a

US citizen. This is a very important piece of paper. Do you understand?"

He nodded. It held his parents' names. It said they lived, they were real. This piece of paper was a promise—he would find them one day.

She said, "This means you are a US citizen. Like me, you were born here, you belong here. Those men are trying to start a life here. They were born in Mexico."

"They don't belong here?" he said.

She shook her head. "That's not what I meant. You have a right to live in this country. Those men do not. Those men can get taken away."

Manuel spread his birth certificate on the floor, attempting to flatten out the creases. No one could take him away, but he had been taken away. He and Lulu had been taken away.

"Why would they take me away?"

"All I mean is that you belong here."

Even though Tía was soft and warm and she took care of him, this was not where he belonged; Tía was not his family.

"Why did they take me away?"

"Who, little one?"

"The people before they brought me here. Why did they take me away?"

"I don't know, son,"

"Where are my parents?"

She looked stricken. "I don't know, Manolito. Oh, my dear, of course you would ask me about them."

"Where's Lulu?" he said.

"Who's Lulu?" she asked.

"Was Lulu born here?" he asked.

She covered his small hands with hers. "Who's Lulu, little one? Who?"

"My sister," he said, and held his breath. *Please, please,*

please know the answer. Please please please tell me where she is, where they are. Please, God, please Tía, please Lulu.

"I don't know. Up until this moment I didn't know you had a sister."

"I have a sister. I have parents."

Her mouth was set firm and hard. "They told me... something else." She held his hand, and silently prayed. Manuel looked at her, the thick graying hair splayed on her shoulders, her bowed head.

"Give me wisdom, Lord of the universe, grant us both grace," she said. "Manuel, you were brought here to me because you were alone in the world. The orphanage that granted you to me, brought your certificate, and nothing else." She made a pitiful face. "They told me you were an orphan." She shook her head. "That your foster parents were moving out of state, they weren't able to take you with them. Brother Sebastián, he was looking for children like you, who needed us, our congregation. He didn't tell me anything else, not how or where. Not that you had a sister." She looked at Manuel. "Is she older or younger?" she asked.

"Older."

She nodded to herself, as if deciding something. "All right. Lulu. Manuel, I will find out. I promise I will find out what I can for you."

Did Lulu have her own piece of creased paper? Was she safe? Was she alone? He said, "If my sister wasn't born here, what could they have done?"

"Son, let me see what we can find out."

Could Tía and Hermano Sebastián find his family? Could they all come here?

Throughout the summer there continued to be men who arrived late at night and left early in the morning. She would find his family, and they would all live here together. Maybe, even, his parents would build a home here, right next to Tía's.

* * *

During the week when he left his room, he usually went straight to the kitchen table where Tía served him a mug of atole or warm milk with one of the sour cream cookies she stored in an airtight container. This morning, the kitchen was still. He went around the back to visit the chickens, where he could be sure to find her most times, but she was not there.

Unusual, but not alarming. She might be at a client's retrieving or delivering laundry—but the shopping cart was on the porch.

"Manuel." It was her voice, coming from his room.

He opened the door.

She sat on his mattress, stripped of bedding. Her short brown legs jutted straight out from her dress, her right hand clenched and unclenched. Her left hand covered something.

"Manuel." Her face was hard and sad. Angry and soft. All those things.

She lifted her left hand. There was his savings, his pile of coins. He had no idea what to do with it, so he simply hoarded it.

"Did you steal this, Manuel?"

"No."

"Did Beto steal this?"

"No."

"Gather it up and bring it to me."

She stood, wiped her hands against her apron, and said, "Bring that into the kitchen."

She washed her hands in the sink, poured him a glass of

cold milk, and set it down in front of him. She handed him a glass jar, saying, "Put the money in that."

What was she going to do with it? He put all the coins in the jar, then shook them around to help them settle. The coins made a fun sound, clinking against the glass, but the look on Tía's face shot down any thoughts of joy or delight. He looked at her, feeling abashed and ashamed, but not knowing what was wrong.

"Is there something wrong?"

By the very nature of keeping something from her, was that what was wrong?

"Wash your hands," she told him, "before you drink your milk."

Manuel stepped to the sink. He heard Tía praying under her breath. She sat down in her chair as he sat down to drink his milk.

"I am trying to help you, and to listen to you and to under-stand you, as best as I can, my little one. I am going to be honest. Some people, people I don't listen to, before you could speak, told me you're not all there, that something's missing. They thought that because you didn't speak for a long time. When they gave you to me, they told me that you had never spoken. When I met you and realized that you wouldn't say a word, it wounded my heart to think that something had hurt your soul so deeply that you would not speak." She stood, went to the sink, wiped her hands on a dishcloth, came, and sat down again. She looked so brown and kind and full in her dress and apron, a dress he had watched as she stitched it together herself. An apron he had seen her launder dozens of times. From the well-worn fabric to the familiar scent of her dish soap to her plump arms. Everything spoke of comfort and familiarity and affection and now he was terrified, speechless again.

He had done something really bad. Those coins were

somehow really wrong, and now she was done with him. She was going to send him away.

"God touched my heart to bring you with me. I thought God would touch your heart and open it to me. But what do I know of God's plans? Brother Sebastián told me we do not know what can happen, we can only do our part, our share, our work. And that night you spoke in tongues! Brother Sebastián and I, we both knew God had opened your heart. That in time, you would open your heart to me."

Manuel felt a pang of shame. He had allowed them to think it was God. It had been him, he, Manuel. He had imitated those around him, it wasn't really speaking in tongues, it wasn't really being touched by God, it was pretend. He regretted making them believe, fooling Amparo and Hermano Sebastián.

Is that what had he done? No, the jar of coins stood accusingly in the middle of the kitchen table.

He had enjoyed the tinkle of the coins as they jangled together; he had enjoyed being with Beto, being important, and Beto's pride in collecting, redistributing, and counting the money over and over again. As their piles grew, so did Beto's dreams, in a ridiculous oversize fashion, of cars and mansions, of slippers and housekeepers, of showing his dad who Beto really was.

Manuel had smiled as Beto recounted his daydreams and wondered if this collection of pennies, nickels, and dimes could possibly bring him any closer to Lulu. But somehow, Amparo could!

"Please don't send me away."

Not again. Not again. Not again. Not again.

"I do not send little boys I love away. I do not send little boys away. Even if I know they will grow and leave and forget me, I will not forget them. You are with me, Manuel, for as long as you need me," she said. "Now, I am going to ask you a question, and I need you to tell me the truth. I cannot abide liars. You must tell me the truth. Did you steal this money?"

"No."

"All right, then, where did you get it?"

"Beto and I earned the money," he murmured.

"What?" she asked softly.

He cleared his throat and spoke a little more forcefully. "We earned it. We made tips," he said.

She sat down heavily and pulled him onto her lap. "That," she said sternly, "is too much money for tips. That pays for a lot of washing."

"Then candy," he said. "Beto invested it. One days he's gonna be rich, and I'm gonna find Lulu and my parents." What did his parents even look like? He didn't remember any more.

She made a face and pulled him close. "I know, I know you are looking for Lulu, and we are too. We are, Manolito, I just haven't had any news to tell. Tonight, Hermano Sebastián will tell you what he knows. And I will talk to Beto in the morning."

The jar sat accusingly on the table. "You can have the money, Tía," he said, pushing it toward her. "For you."

"No," she said coldly. She shook her head. The coins glittered in the jar. Manuel wondered at the fact that they could cause so much trouble for him.

That night Hermano Sebastián, Amparo, and Manuel sat at the wooden kitchen table. It all felt very serious and now Manuel was nervous.

They clasped hands, and Hermano prayed, "Lord of the Universe, with the wisdom of eternity behind us and eternity before us, touch my heart so I may have the words for this small boy, and touch his heart, so he may have the ears to hear our words with grace. Lord, give me strength to be gentle, give me the strength to be forthright. Give us all the strength that our hearts may be kind, loving, and filled with forgiveness when necessary. Bless us in our search for what is right, in Thy name, Thy will be done."

Hermano Sebastián clasped his hands in front of him and looked at Manuel. "Son." He sighed heavily. "It hurts me to say this because you are so young to be carrying this burden. But I want you to appreciate God has placed you in the care of this good woman, who I know loves you like her own son." He cleared his throat. "Manuel, I do not know what happened to your sister. I cannot find your family. We have been reaching out to the people who helped bring you to me, and brought you to us, to their organization. They tell us you were alone when they found you."

"But I have a sister," Manuel's voice trembled.

Hermano Sebastián bobbed his head. "We believe you, son." Tía squeezed Manuel's hand. "The terrible news I have for you is we cannot find her, or your parents. We can only speculate."

Manuel's heart pounded in his chest, a thrumming sound rushed his ears, he felt mist descending on his eyes, he began to shake with the cold.

Tía moved to him, rubbing her hands against his bare arms, shaking her head against Hermano Sebastián. "Wherever your family is, I know they love you. I know they miss you."

"Our people have suffered in so many ways," he said.

"He doesn't need to know all that now," she said. "He doesn't need to know everything."

"But you are safe with us here, in Chavez Ravine," Hermano Sebastián said.

"As much as you miss them, I am sure they miss you. As much as you love them, I am certain they love you," Tía said. "I'm sorry."

Manuel was silent. When Tía said she would find out, he

had believed her. And now the mist gathered and choked his throat, compressed his chest with rage.

* * *

The following morning Manuel did as Tía had requested and invited Beto in. "Good morning, Doña Amparo," Beto said, taking off his wool cap. Manuel noticed Beto's ears looked even wider without his cap.

"Sit down, Beto. Nice to see you this morning." She slipped a plate of biscuits and butter in front of him. When they were gone she gave him two more. He slowed down over the fourth, then wiped his mouth contentedly, and remembered to say, "Thank you, ma'am."

"Tell me about Manuel's money," she said.

Beto's mouth dropped open, his eyes darted between Tía and Manuel. Manuel's stomach flopped around.

Recovering, Beto said, "What money?"

"The money he's hidden under his mattress. How did he get it? Did you give it to him?"

Did Beto give it to him, Manuel wondered, and almost immediately thought yes, yes he had. His pennies would have never exploded into this amount without the glee of Beto's candy scheme.

"Well," Beto hedged.

"How much money do you have, Alberto?"

"Well." Beto squirmed, his eyebrows knit together, his eyes now focused on the immaculately swept floor.

"Does your father know about this money?" she said, softly.

Beto's head snapped up. "No!" he said. "No, he doesn't." Beto made an angry face at Manuel, and Manuel's stomach flipped over again. There was a vague sense about Beto's father, an unseated suspicion based on the fact that when Manuel ate at Beto's house the careless, happy talk stopped when the father came home and shifted its focus to Alberto Lujan Sr. Everyone swirled about him as he grunted to Manuel across the table.

"Is that how he talks to you?" he once pointedly said to Beto and made more grunting sounds. No one protested.

Tía continued, softly, "I shouldn't be the one to tell him, either. Now, Manuel has too much money; no matter how cute you two boys are, none of my customers are that generous."

Beto sat simmering, nearly seething. At last he said, "It's my money. I worked for it, Manuel helped me." Beto pushed himself away from the table and scrambled outside. Manuel trailed him all the way to school.

For a week afterward, Manuel waited outside Beto's home, until his mother came out, rubbed Manuel consolingly on the shoulder and said, "You better go along now."

Hermano Sebastián came to their home before the Wednesday evening service. The air was cool, signaling the wistfulness of fall, and everything Manuel pined for. He had a memory of weather like this, of being on a horse, of his father guiding the horse. His father had a straw hat, the horse was deep brown and walked slowly. These memories grew distant. But Lulu was flesh, like the word made flesh. She was real, and she had loved him, and she had taken care of him.

For another week, Beto refused to look at or acknowledge Manuel during recess. This put Manuel in the uncomfortable position of him now waiting down the road past Beto's home in the damp foggy mornings and waiting for Beto to walk down the dirt path to school. At last Beto would come down the path, his hair brushed hard to the side, slicked down, a glare on his face as hard as the lacquer on his head.

Manuel would not allow himself to consider the unimaginable: that his best friend in all the world would, like his parents and Lulu, abandon him. That was a menacing wave that hovered and threatened to break over him, take the air away. No, that would not, could not be. His family was gone; Beto he saw nearly every day.

One afternoon at recess as Manuel played tag with Peludo and Kiki, Beto came up to him, glaring at him angrily. Manuel, so grateful for the attention of his first and only friend, was thinking which words of greeting to choose when Beto socked him in the gut so hard Manuel landed on the dirt.

Manuel lay on the ground, without air in his lungs, gravel on the side of his face, an explosion of physical pain in his stomach. Beto leaned down over him. Manuel closed his eyes and braced himself for what would follow.

"What do you think my dad did after he heard?" he said in a low voice, through clenched teeth. "Took it all. Drank it all. Then beat the crap out of my mom and me. You did that." He wiped his hands against his dirty dungarees. "We're even now."

Beto turned to a clump of kids. "What do you think you're looking at? Get lost. My friend tripped, that's all." When the kids had scattered, and Manuel had caught his breath, Beto held out his hand and helped Manuel back up.

The next morning Beto appeared at Manuel's house, again waiting at the gate, a book satchel at his side, his hair firmly pasted down, politely declining Tía's offer of chilaquiles.

As the two boys walked up the path to school, Beto scuffed at the dirt beneath their shoes. "I want to let you know, no hard feelings, okay? Good. So, look, if I do have another great idea, I'm gonna do it on my own, 'kay?"

Manuel nodded. Something he'd heard in church. ¿De qué se beneficia un hombre si ganó el mundo pero pierde a su amigo? What doth it profiteth a man if he gaineth the world, but loseth his friend?

CHAPTER SIX

Soon after Mr. Reed stopped coming to school, Jessica's family moved away. Peludo eventually stopped going to school but hung around with Manuel and Beto. A group of them walked to Union Station to goggle at the Red Cars and trains. Manuel and Kiko half-pushed half-carried Ileana in her wheelchair so she could see, too. Manuel wondered where everyone was going, what they were all doing, if Lulu ever rode by, would she recognize him? Would he recognize her?

Weeks would go by, and he would realize with a jolt that he hadn't thought of Lulu the entire time. He wanted to hear from Tía or Hermano Sebastián more news of his sister, of his real family, but Hermano had made clear they knew nothing more. Over time he learned about Tía's family, how her father had moved to California from Texas, how her mother had been an Indian from Mexico, Zapotec, she said, how her son had enlisted in the Army. She was so proud of her son. A part of Manuel now resented the cabinet of souvenirs and letters. He was no one's son. He sent no one letters. He knew more about Amparo's family than anything of his own, and those images he carried, the waves, the towel, the swimsuit, and the faces of his family behind them, seemed fainter, less real.

His family was out there, somewhere. He never mentioned them to his friends, it would be like being a chueco kid all over again and being, like Ileana and Jessica, the focus of a weird fascination. Why were the girls missing parts? Why was he missing parts of his family?

* * *

By the time he was in sixth grade he was restless. When he could hear Tía snoring, he wandered at night. He heard the radio, sometimes the same music from different homes. On his walks he didn't exactly pray to Lulu, but now and again he thought of her, mentally telling her, "I'm in Chavez Ravine, Lu, where are you? Tell me." But he heard nothing in reply.

The letters from Toño came less and less frequently, but there were boxes of government food that Tía turned into casseroles. She and Manuel always attended the parades that welcomed back the young soldiers. When would Toño come home and have his parade?

Peludo told them about taking the red car to the beach. The boys were sufficiently impressed.

"You can take it all the way to San Pedro."

"What's it like?" Manuel was curious.

"I don't like it. Stinks of fish. Or, you get the right transfers or a lazy conductor, you can stay on it all day."

"Whaddya wanna do that for?" Manuel asked.

Peludo shrugged.

Beto related in elaborate detail the movie he'd seen the previous weekend, *King Solomon's Mines*. Manuel half-listened as Beto gave an avid and enthusiastic account about the hidden jewels, and particularly lurid attention to the booby trap, sealing them all in. He sighed heavily after the summary and said, "They had to leave the jewels behind. I mean, after all that."

Manuel recognized that dreamy sheen in Beto's eyes but barely grunted in response.

Beto and Manuel kicked at clods of dirt on their way home. Peludo mimicked animal sounds. Beto continued, "But, you know, they did have an amazing adventure, the whole other side of the world, you know?" Beto then looked sharply at Manuel, "Where do you go at night?"

"What do you mean?"

"I've seen you walk by our house at three in the morning. You and Peludo." Peludo nodded, then crowed like a rooster. "What're you doing? Casing the joint? You gonna rob us all? Steal our old sheets and our shabby rugs?" Beto laughed at his own joke, and Peludo joined him.

Manuel snorted, "Nah. Don't be crazy. Yeah, I go out. Just that, sometimes there's so much in my head I feel like I'm gonna explode."

Beto said, "I know, I know. Me too, me too."

The trio trudged past the shacks where the white bachelors, los viejitos, lived.

As if by silent agreement when the three loping boys reached the dirt road that turned left toward their homes in Chavez Ravine, the boys turned right. They followed the dirt road until it intersected with pavement, then road. They made their way to the pathway that lined the Arroyo Parkway, a gleaming highway, recently opened, and they followed the highway, while the mountains in the distance stood proud, snow on the peaks gleaming.

They crossed a concrete bridge that ran high over the roadway beneath them, waving at the cars that passed underneath. A couple of cars honked in greeting. They followed the sidewalks that skirted the hills, rather than climbing up.

Beto turned around every five minutes or so and looked behind them.

"Who's chasing you? Your dad?"

Beto gave him a dirty look. "Are you crazy? He'd keel over after three blocks. Or stop at the first bar and never be seen again. No. Let me ask you something, you ever been here before?"

Manuel shook his head. "How 'bout you?"

"Nah. Always wanted to but figured it's safer going out with you two. But, listen, if you've never been here before, how you planning on getting back?"

Manuel blinked. "Getting here's easy enough."

"Yeah, sure, cuz we don't care where we're going. But if you have a place in mind, you gotta know how to get there. That's why I'm looking behind."

The broken sidewalks they'd been treading had gradually given way to pristine walks and streets. There was hardly a car that passed them, and the roar of the busy highway was now a distant purr.

Manuel nodded, impressed by his friend's wisdom. "Who taught you that?"

Another dirty look. "Nobody. I was born knowing some things."

Manuel laughed. "Like what?"

Beto looked at him. "Like the world is wrong, and we gotta decide who we're gonna be."

Peludo nodded, encouragingly.

"How do you decide?" Manuel asked, skeptically.

"You wanna be a loser, or a winner?"

"A winner!" Peludo said.

Manuel sneered, "Everybody wants to be a winner. That's obvious."

Beto shook his head bitterly. "Nope. No, they don't. And they got a hundred reasons to tell you why not. God is the number one reason why people decide to be losers."

Manuel felt queasy. He didn't enjoy church, he barely listened. He thought about the gap of his family, not God's presence in his life. Tía, however, still prayed for him, for his missing family members, and he felt her love for him with the prayers she gave over his head. Her supper prayers exasperated him with their length, but he would never insult or condemn the centerpiece that propelled her life and gave structure to his. No, never. There was a scripture quote that said something like that, but knowing himself to be a bad Christian, he couldn't remember it to offer it to Beto.

"I dunno," was the response he managed. He felt profoundly disloyal.

"Look, all I'm sayin' is, you wanna get somewhere, you wanna be someone, somebody somewhere is gonna get hurt. Somewhere along the way you're gonna lie or cheat or steal. Why are you lookin' at me that way? And I'm not sayin' everybody who lies or cheats is a winner, shit, look at my pops. He beats me down just to be sure I'm gonna be a loser like him. Welp, I'm tellin' you, no, I'm not.

"You still lookin' at me that way, but think about it. Who can actually help losers the most? *Winners*, boys, *winners*. Instead you gotta railway trainload of blind, poor losers, dragging around other blind, poor losers. If you're a rich son of a bitch with gold rings on your fingers and fancy cars, then you're a winner, propped up, supported by, fed by, watered and raised by your flock of losers, and you want to keep them just as dirt ignorant as they started. I tell you, I was born knowing this shit. I can't understand why nobody else sees it neither."

Manuel tried to laugh off the intensity of his friend.

"Oh, now you go ahead and laugh! Think of the way we live. Now look at that house!"

They did. They gaped at a two-story house that had white gleaming columns, a front yard larger than their grade school playground. Manuel inhaled the scent of freshly cut grass.

"Damn if this isn't like the movies," Peludo said.

"What's that?" Manuel pointed to a statue of a short, strangely dressed dark man holding up a circle.

Beto said, "Heck if I know. Rich people have weird ideas."

"But they're winners," Manuel said.

Beto stopped in the middle of the sidewalk, exasperated. "Look," he said, gesturing forcefully with his hands. "You gotta choice about where you want to live? This house here or our shacks in Palo Verde? C'mon, that's not even a choice."

They kept walking. The sidewalks seemed bleached white, the houses appeared bright and newly painted, even as dusk approached. The streetlights twinkled alive. A car drove by them, slowed down as it passed, then sped off. Manuel and Beto followed the street as it curved around and spotted an empty park, with picnic tables under a pergola, swings, a slide, a merry go round.

The boys picked up their pace and paused as they arrived.

Manuel gasped. It was a carpet of green over soft rolling hills for as far as he could see. It looked nothing like the dry parched land around their home, that sprouted into wildflowers and weeds after downpours. This grass was deliberate, culti-vated, maintained. People made this happen.

Why here? Why not where they lived?

What would it be like to run and roll around on this?

"Come on!" Manuel said and raced Beto and Peludo up and down the hills, chasing each other, Manuel tiring quickly, with a stitch on his side. He avoided the picnic tables and sat on a swing. He marveled at the swing set. It was as if everything had sprung up brand new, just for them. He wondered if this was real or a mirage, a ghostly apparition, like Pleasure Island his third-grade teacher had read to them about, where lazy, pleasure-seeking boys arrived only to be turned into mules.

On the swings they pedaled high, to see who could fling themselves the farthest.

Manuel won repeatedly. That soft cushion of grass made him fearless. When bored with the swings they took turns pushing the merry go round as fast as they could, jumping on, hanging tight to the side, then letting it slow.

Dusk became dark, and the park became long shadows. The metallic scent of the carousel was on his hands. Manuel and Beto rolled onto the damp grass and looked up at the sky shifting into night.

Peludo said, "I wanna sleep here. Can we sleep here?" When he didn't get a response Peludo returned to the swings. Manuel heard the rhythmic creaking of the structure; he felt the prickle of grass blades at the base of his neck and the back of his arms.

"You're never gonna believe what I did last week," Beto said.

"What?" Manuel watched a wavering leaf and felt a light breeze, cooling the sweat on his face.

"I took my dad's car out for a drive. Swear to you. I put it in neutral, pushed it onto the street, and had a ride. I wanted to go far, but I drove down the hill and back. I guess I was worried about getting lost or getting into trouble. Doesn't sound like me, right? I need to pay more attention to the roads in the daylight, to memorize them for nighttime."

Manuel remembered what happened with the candy money. "Beto, what if your dad finds out?"

Beto turned his head in Manuel's direction. "I gotta make

sure he never does, don't I? Cuz no one would snitch on me, right?" Then added, "Besides, he's never gonna touch me again. Last time he tried, was his last time." Beto's voice was hard.

Manuel wanted to say, "Man that's rough," or, "Gee I'm sorry," but he didn't think anything he said would help right now. Instead he leaned back on the grass and inhaled its scent. It was probably time to head back. Tía might be wondering where he was. On the street a car meandered; they heard the rustle of family noises. A car parked nearby.

"Who lives here?" Manuel asked, as if to say, what species of people came and went as if this were the most natural of things? Huge homes, paved streets and sidewalks, a personal park, empty of visitors except for the three of them.

"Rich people," Beto said, matter of factly, without bitterness. "Winners, Manny. You bet your life I'm gonna be one of them. You bet your life."

Manuel thought of Tía. For some reason it occurred to him that she hadn't gotten packages or letters from her son in a long time. He wondered why that was. He looked up. There was a circle of haze around the moon; a science teacher had explained it was moisture in the air. The same science teacher had explained that seeing the moon in the morning was not a sign of end times, but a natural phenomenon. Manuel enjoyed the way science explained the world, like wood shop explained how joints fit together, how to make wood even stronger. He hoped electric shop would explain how lights worked. Science helped you piece things together, make sense of things. You couldn't get angry at the way mechanical things worked, they just worked, or they didn't, and you worked on fixing them. People were a different matter. He turned in Beto's direction, his eyes were closed.

Manuel said, "Let me tell you something." He told Beto about showing up at Tía Amparo's, about losing his sister, about losing his parents. As Manuel talked, Beto sat up, leaning on his side and concentrated on Manuel. Manuel looked up at the moon and explained about the birth certificate. How Hermano Sebastián and Tía Amparo had looked and failed to find anything.

Manuel stopped talking.

"Carajo," Beto said. The boys were silent for a moment. "Sometimes I hate my family, but, even then, I wouldn't..." He coughed. "What're you gonna do? What're we gonna do?"

They heard the swish of heavy footsteps on the grass. They watched the wind lift the tree limbs above.

"Stand up," came a gruff voice. Startled, the boys looked around.

"Stand up, I said." The voice belonged to a figure with a policeman's cap, and a flashlight in Peludo's face. Peludo gaped, drained of color, and hung tight onto the metal chains of the swing.

"I told you something, boy. Get off of that goddamned swing. You Mexis shouldn't be out after sunset. Here in Rosewood, we don't want you here in the daylight either."

Manuel thought his heart would leap out of his chest. What had Peludo done?

It all happened so fast Manuel didn't even have a chance to glance at Beto. Peludo remained on his swing seat, face slack, mouth open, horrified, in the glare of the flashlight, but hanging on. The officer stepped swiftly near him, banged his stick on both of Peludo's hands; Peludo dropped his arms and tried to scrabble away, falling to the ground, climbing on the ground, and the cop raised his stick.

He was gonna kill him, Manuel realized. He was gonna kill Peludo for playing on the swings.

He wanted to be ten years older, ten inches taller, fifty

pounds heavier, with his own night stick. He wanted to pummel this man.

Beto and Manuel screamed and shrieked. They ran to the merry go round and pounded it, shouting.

Manuel heard a sound he remembered with sickness and disgust his entire life. He heard the thud of a stick of hardened wood slamming against Peludo's skull. Again. And again.

CHAPTER SEVEN

I nside the Santo Niño church Manuel recognized faces from La Loma and Bishop, kids from school. It seemed as if all of Chavez Ravine tried to cram into the church for Peludo's funeral.

Miss Otis sat in the aisle in front of them. Manuel couldn't stop staring at Peludo's mother, a pitiless expression on her long-drawn face, seamed with lines, unkempt gray hair which trailed down to her waist, as if she knew this was how it all ended. She caught him staring at her and glared at him. Manuel turned away.

The priest had said Mass, and now began to discuss Peludo. Beto crossed over a few people and sat down next to Manuel.

Manuel felt sick. His guts had been a mess ever since the park. Peludo had lain at home, on a mattress in the corner of a room. Peludo had six brothers and sisters, and when Manuel and Beto visited, it seemed like people were constantly moving in and out. Manuel found it hard to look at Peludo, sprawled on the bed unmoving, his head thickly bandaged. But he visited, bringing jars of apricot jam from Tía. Peludos' mom said nothing in response to the token gift or his visit. Her mouth was a firm line. "Can I help you?" Manuel asked, and she said nothing. Did she blame them? Was this their fault?

She rarely sat in the chair next to Peludo's mattress. Beto did, instead, while he told jokes and the details of the last movie he'd seen; Manuel told him what was going on at school.

What had happened? How could Peludo be dead?

Beto grimaced, like they were thinking the same thing.

The congregation lined up for communion. There was no need for Tía to grip his arm, he wouldn't be going up. He patted her hand gently.

Beto didn't move, either. He said, in a stage whisper, mocking the priest, "God works in mysterious ways, all right."

Manuel wrinkled his forehead. Again he heard the thud of the nightstick against Peludo's skull.

"Why'd we let him come with us?" Beto muttered.

"Why'd we leave him on the swings, alone?" Manuel answered.

Beto said, "I am gonna make so much money they ain't never gonna touch me. Simón. Not a goddamn finger."

A man in front of them turned to scowl at Beto.

"It's church," he said, thrusting his chin at them. "You go be disrespectful outside."

The two of them shut up and watched silently as Peludo's family waved over the pall bearers. The Lopez brothers Tía had warned him about led the way, in long flowing jackets and high-waisted, flowing trousers. They were somehow both flashy and dignified.

Beto leaned over, "Gotta hand it to the zoot suiters, they got style."

* * *

For weeks after Peludo's murder Manuel went around with rocks in his stomach. One night as he and Beto watched City Hall, its red-light flashing, he told Beto maybe there was something they could do about that dirty cop.

Beto looked at him. "You're crazy. I told you I see things other people don't. That's the way the world works, Manny. He killed him. He wanted to kill him. It could've been either of us. And that cop didn't give a pedo."

Was that possible? To kill someone and not care?

That night on the steps to the porch of his home, he heard an unfamiliar voice coming from inside, and Tía's response. Her voice was tight, controlled. Manuel opened the front door, ready to greet her, when he stopped. Across from her at the kitchen table, in Manuel's place, sat a man in his mid to late twenties, dressed only in undershirt and underpants. A wan, worn face with a thin pencil mustache, hair parted on the side and slicked down with grease in a style different from the men Manuel saw around here every day, different from the teachers. There was something familiar about him.

Tía said, "There he is!" Her voice was now grateful and relieved. "I was wondering what you'd gotten up to, where you'd gone. You remember my son, Toño?"

Of course! But he looked so different from his photograph on the cabinet. Manuel eyed the undressed young man, sitting in what Manuel considered to be *his* seat. Here he looked diminished, vulnerable. On his right arm Manuel could see were letters in a thick Gothic script spelling our USMC. Under the letters were the head and shoulders of a fierce eagle.

Tía added, "I'm washing his uniform right now."

Toño gave Manuel a kind of salute, tapping his forefinger to his forehead, then tilting it in Manuel's direction.

Manuel looked at him blankly.

Tía continued, "Are you hungry? I kept some enchiladas warm for you in the oven."

Manuel said, "Thank you, Tía," then looked at Toño. Would he mind he addressed his mother this way? Did he resent his presence, the way Manuel resented him sitting in his seat?

"Wash your hands, then." As Manuel washed and dried his hands at the kitchen sink, he was shocked to see Toño drinking from a can of beer. Beer! In Tía's house! Which may have explained the stern look on her face, the edge and impatience in her voice. She pulled a plate out of the oven. She ladled a dollop of beans onto it. He sat down at the side of the table where she placed the plate, feeling slightly unmoored, unused to this new seating arrangement, as well as tired and hungry.

"How's it going?" Toño asked, appraising Manuel openly.

"Good," Manuel said, before shoveling food into his mouth. "How 'bout you?"

"I hit a snafu and now I am fubar," he said.

It was clear Toño hadn't expected Manuel to understand. Manuel examined Tía's son. He noticed there was a tattoo of numbers on Antonio's left arm, which stayed slack and still beside him.

Toño noticed Manuel's scrutiny. He offered his can of beer to Manuel. "Ever try this?"

"You come back and ask to stay here with me?" Tía raised her voice. "You follow my rules. No, he has not tried that, no, he cannot try that now here in my home. Manuel, hurry up and eat, and go to your room." To her son, "I'll bring you things to sleep out here. If I had known, I would have been ready."

Toño shook his head. "I told you I'm sorry, Ma. If you'd've known, you'd have invited the neighborhood. I don't want to see anybody like this." He picked up his left arm and dropped it, falling lifelessly back to his side.

"If you had told me, if you had let me know—I hadn't heard from you—"

"Look, Ma, we already argued about that. You wanna argue again in front of"—he looked at Manuel, pausing, as if he didn't know his name—"this one? Don't worry, I won't stay long. I forgot what hell it is to live with you."

Manuel was so shocked he stopped eating.

The glare Tía gave her son cut Manuel's insides. "I love you," she said, in a voice that was steel and sharp glass, "but you cannot speak to me this way, in my home, in front of this boy." She went into her room and closed the door.

Toño stared down the interior of his beer can, then glanced sideways at Manuel who started to eat again.

"How about you, my replacement, the model son? What are you up to these days?" Toño's glare was a challenge flung in Manuel's direction.

Manuel shook his head, uncertain, and angry at himself for being bewildered. Why did Toño give him a look almost as cutting as the one Amparo had given him?

"What have you got to say for yourself? Where you been tonight?" Toño insisted.

Manuel gathered himself, tilted his head back like the tough boys at school, as if to say, *why should I care what you think?* He looked at Toño's shirtless chest, there was a net of scars by the left shoulder. He looked away and said, "I was out with a friend."

Toño lifted his brows in mock approval and said, "A girl-friend?" He waited for a reply that didn't come. "In any case, you look fat and happy. My mom's a good cook. When I was away, I thought on her food most every day, until I didn't, cuz I didn't want to think about it. You know what I mean?"

"Sure," Manuel responded, trying to act disinterested. He knew about hiding wonderful things because recalling them only caused pain. That's what thinking about Lulu was like. That's why sometimes he didn't want to think about her at all. Or ever again.

Manuel cleared his throat and asked, "So where *you* been?"

Toño gave him a look as if to say, "What are you digging for, you clever bastard?" and instead said, "Here and there." He finished the last of his beer and, with his right arm, pulled up another can from the floor, opened it one-handed, then leaned back in Manuel's chair. Now Manuel noticed there were already two empty cans on the floor by the creaking wooden chair.

"You shoulda seen the look on their faces, Ma," he yelled toward the closed door. "Like I really was somebody."

She came out of her room with bedding and a dispassionate expression on her face. In Spanish she answered, "You were somebody before you put on a uniform."

Toño made a face. "To you, to me, but not to a bunch of strangers." Then, to Manuel, "I've been in the service, kid. Do yourself a favor and don't join when they come calling. Definitely do not volunteer. Not worth it." Then to his mother's door, "Did you know there was a Mexican who captured 2,000 Japs? All by himself?" Toño looked at Manuel. "He was from around here, you know, Los Angeles. Spoke their language because he grew up around them."

Manuel was thinking about something else. "What you said about war." He screwed up his face into a question mark. "You mean you get a choice to join or not?"

Toño shook his head and said, "Like most things in life, nah, not really. But you can be smarter than me. The Japs bombed Pearl Harbor and I wanted to strangle their necks!" He thumped his chest. "America! I wanted to protect my country. Die for my country! God's country!" He snorted. "That attack drained all the sense outta my head. I volunteered the next day. For God and country!" Toño drank more beer.

Manuel asked, "Where you been? How come you haven't visited your mom in so long?"

"Listen to the little man, listen to my replacement, all filled with pity and outrage over my behavior and comportment. I been gone, kid, and now I'm back. But not for long, believe me." He looked up and away from Manuel and scanned the kitchen. "The neighborhood looked worse than I remembered it. This place looked better, I guess. Nice room you got, now." Manuel felt the slap of another accusation. He continued, "I seen places that make this dump look like a castle, and places that make this dump look like a dung heap. I don't know where I'm going because I can't stay here."

Tía stood in the doorway.

In Spanish, he said, "Isn't that right, Ma? Be easier for everyone involved."

"No, you stay as long as you like, as long as you need to."

"That's what you say. That's not what you mean. Don't worry, I'll be gone by supper tomorrow night."

"I say what I mean. Palabra de Dios."

He smiled like she said something funny and repeated the phrase, "Palabra de Dios."

Wordlessly Tía set bedding on her kitchen chair, went back to her bedroom, and was about to close the door until she interrupted her movements and spoke. "Good night, boys." She closed the door.

Toño sipped at his beer, offered it again to Manuel, who took a sip, made a face, and handed it back to him. "I'm not sure you can tell, but I have a sneaking suspicion she's mad at me."

Manuel laughed.

"Pretty clear, eh? She get mad at you?"

Manuel made a face. He couldn't think of a time when she

got mad at him, not really. Beto's money? That was a long time ago. But it seemed Toño needed an answer. He nodded. "Yep."

"What about?"

"Mostly about church stuff," he lied.

"That's all right then. You can recover from that." He finished his beer. "Other things, not so much, not so quickly. Or never."

"What do you mean?" Was he talking about him? Did he know about his family? What had Tía told him? Were these things he was going to recover from, not recover from? Lulu, he wanted to see Lulu. Please.

"Look, she's mad at me for a lot of things. I shoulda written. I shoulda told her about this." He waved his left arm with his right hand. "I get it. The only way she knew I wasn't dead was cuz she hadn't gotten a telegram." He looked around the room, past Manuel. "I was hoping to save her some pain. I just gave her a dose of a different kind." He scratched his ear. "She wrote me and told me a little about you, what she was doing. You know, you showed up 'bout a year after I left." He sighed. "I sent her some money." He looked at Manuel. "That surprise you? We didn't have much money when I was here." His face changed. "Things sure look different, though, in the neighborhood. Not sure about it. Not like a good way."

He looked around again, this time over at the curio cabinet. "It slays me a little bit, she's got all that stuff there."

"I thought you sent it to her."

"Yeah, I know. I knew she'd like them." He drank more beer. "Honorably discharged." He put his beer can down, picked up his left arm with his right, and released his arm. It dropped to his side. He shook his head. "I still gotta figure out what I'm gonna do to earn a living. Believe me, it coulda been a lot worse. Coulda been dead, like two of my friends. Now that's rough. Yeah, I see you looking at my scars. My friend, he's got scars from here"—Toño stroked his throat—"to here"—Toño lightly touched the top of his thighs—"and everywhere in between, if you get what I'm saying. Definitely coulda been worse for me. This is bad enough."

The boulder weighed on his guts as Manuel thought of the cop, what he'd done to Peludo. Out of his mouth spilled, "Did you kill people?"

Toño looked at Manuel for a moment. Then looked away. "Not if I could help it, brother."

"Did Tía tell you about Peludo?"

"A little."

Manuel told him everything that had happened. The boulder within, seemed a little lighter as Toño sipped and listened.

"See the problem is," Toño said, in the voice of a young man who has traveled the world, "when you live in one place, you think the world is just like what you know. It's hard to imagine things are different. But things are really different outside of Chavez Ravine. I'm sorry, really sorry, to be the one to tell you this, but people outside of here hate Mexicans. It's a disease, really. They fucking hate us."

Like the officer in the park. "Mexis," Manuel said.

"That's right, and hell of a lot worse." He finished his beer. "But not when I was in uniform, man. No one served me shit then. Cuz I would shovel it down their own throats. But with this..." He tapped his shoulder. "I don't know."

The two of them sat there for a moment.

"Are you gonna have a parade?" Manuel had been looking forward to the day when all of Chavez Ravine would come out to celebrate Tía Amparo's son, the war hero, coming home.

"So the whole damn world can see me with this?" He tapped his left arm, and it swung a little. "Not on your life, little brother." Toño yawned. "I gotta hit the sack now, or I'm gonna die," he said. "You hit the john first, and I'll go after."

Manuel did as requested, then lay in his bedroom listening to Toño's movements. From the creak of the floorboards, the opening and closing of cupboards, he felt their visitor was either restless or looking for something. He wondered what it was like to wander with only one arm, one hand.

The next morning there was a platter with a few pieces of bacon remaining. The sofa was empty of Toño, the bedding stacked neatly, two dirty dishes in the sink.

Manuel raised his face to Tía. "Don't start, you. It's all right. We're okay. He had a good breakfast, and even left you some." She hugged him tight.

"What happened?"

"En todo estas menos en misa!" she said. "He's beautiful, my boy, isn't he? He'll always be my beautiful boy." She sighed, then looked at Manuel. "I'm glad you two met."

Manuel sensed she wanted to say more, but she just drank her coffee and watched Manuel eat.

* * *

It took a few days, over a glass of sweet iced tea, for Manuel to ask, "Is Toño gonna live with us?"

She cleared her throat. "He's grown-up, my boy. He went into the service a tall boy and returned a young man." She shook her head in a friendly but dismissive way. "I had hoped he would stay with me, but it's clear he doesn't want his mother around, watching over him, telling him what to do. He can tell himself what to do. You, too, will grow, and move out one day, start your life on your own, or with someone. Won't you like that?"

Manuel ignored the question. "Why doesn't he come here,

then? Go to church with you, or come over and help you work, or come over for supper?"

Tía bit her lip in that way she did when she was concentrating on a task, marking a hem line, feeding the chickens, running the clothing through the wringer.

"Lives don't go in straight lines, do they? You know better than most, Manolito."

She went to their ice box and pulled out the pitcher of cold tea, filling both their glasses. It was hot and sticky outside, they had been picking the remaining apricots. Later he would help her pit the fruit so she could stew them. She would turn the late-summer almost-rotting fruit into syrup and jams. The very last of the cooked fruit she would turn into empanadas.

He smelled of tree bark and was sticky with apricot juice. His arms were lightly scraped from the branches he had pushed against or shrugged aside.

"Where does he live, anyway?" How, he wanted to know, could Toño not see his mother? Manuel couldn't even remember his mother's face, if she were alive, if he could find her, he thought he might never move again.

"Enough with you, young man. Enough!" Amparo tapped him lightly on the head. "It's too hot to boil these jars—we'll do all that tonight. Go, shoo, go out with your friends."

* * *

Toño was an unpredictable presence, sometimes moody and resentful, sometimes lighthearted with both Tía and Manuel.

"What about Cano, is he back?"

"No, Son, he won't be back."

Toño frowned.

"Enrique?"

"Not yet. But Frankie had his parade a year or so ago. You should visit him."

Toño looked thoughtful for a moment, then nodded. "Of course he knows I'm back."

Manuel was disappointed about the parade, too. He couldn't help it. Tía's son was a war hero, look at his injury. Didn't that make him one?

He always brought a six pack of beer and slowly drank them all throughout the day and evening while he watched her cook, or, when feeling friendly, showed Manuel how to play poker and gently teased his mother about Hermano Sebastián. Manuel would smile as Tía shushed her son. What did he know about her? She had had enough men in her life, praise God, including her sons—Manuel quietly felt his face go hot when he realized she called him her son—and her late husband, God forgive him.

"You get all twinkly when you see him," Toño insisted, and Manuel smiled to himself, because she did.

"You boys! You two!" she said, impatiently, then served them apricot empanadas still warm from the oven.

CHAPTER EIGHT

1951

Manuel had stayed up all night, long after Amparo had fallen asleep, long after the collective symphony of the neighboring radios were silenced. He was agitated. He listened to the roosters crowing with the morning stars, he listened to the neighborhood noises, the rhythm of the evening, the late night, then the morning. The trains at night warned of their crossings. In a few hours the red cars would clatter in the distance, starting their morning rides.

He couldn't bear being enclosed, being inside. He pushed the bedding off. It was hot and miserable. The urges of his body still overwhelmed him. He ignored its demands and instead dressed and headed outside.

He wandered the streets, picking his way around the hills by moonlight. He walked down the dirt paths, winding behind homes, listening for the snoring of the occupants.

He could tell people by their shapes in the distance. Were they stumbling, were they exploring? Or were they out and miserable, like him?

A figure nodded, Kiko. "Hope you had a better night then me, Manny," he said in passing.

Some nights he heard Cisco serenading, wordlessly, from the water tower. The guitar hummed like strings in his heart. No Cisco tonight.

He walked and walked, through the unpaved roads, disturbing the dogs, setting off a racket on the corner of Jerry's Liquor Store.

He walked and walked, nearly to downtown.

He was sixteen years old, starting his sophomore year. A week or so back he heard a couple of white boys outside of shop talking about mechanical engineering.

That sounded right. That sounded good to him. He liked the word "engineering." Brother Sebastian, who still came around, still escorted Amparo home Wednesday nights even after he married, talked about God as Nature's engineer.

Yeah, nice.

He wanted to talk to Toño about this, but by now Toño had moved to San Diego with his girl, now his wife. Manuel had only ever been to Pentecostal weddings, and he was nervous and tense with the Mass, which seemed so foreign, and the priest, so distant. Whether Tía's mouth was tight with judgment about the church or her ex-husband—who was there!—Manuel couldn't tell. So Toño was lost to him, and even though Toño had paid for the phone to be installed and called once a week, Manuel knew that those calls were expensive and not a time to ask about this strange country called "engineering."

He'd talk to his counselor Mr. Owens about it, who would be helping him sort out his schedule and planning his time at high school. Mr. Owens had brown and gray hair swept to the right side of his forehead, a brown and gray mustache bristling over his top lip, and he wore tortoise-shell eyeglasses.

His eyes were compassionate, his tone friendly. He listened

patiently, with an encouraging smile, and nodded along as Manuel detailed his enthusiasm, and the things he could build. Bridges. Highways. Buildings.

"Have you seen the Stack, Mr. Owens? My friend took me, and there's four rows of highways, on top of each other. What would it feel like to build something like that? You know City Hall? Engineers build buildings even higher than that. Skyscrapers. That's what I want to do."

"I don't want you to waste your time in those math classes you'd have to take. They're way beyond your abilities. What I want you to do is this." His counselor pushed a dull sheet of paper toward him, with the schedule filled in.

He continued, "See, this is what you should be taking. This here will get you some basic math and reading skills, and this here will be sure you get a job—you know one that will pay for the babies you'll be bringing into the world." He pointed to the shop classes, wood, metal, auto.

"Yeah, but... what would I need to be an engineer?"

"Son, there are no Mexican engineers."

His face was kind, his tone was friendly, but Manuel didn't bother to lower his head to hide the scowl and contempt that swept across his face. He looked at Mr. Owens.

"What kind of engineers do they have in Mexico?" he asked, jutting his chin forward. He'd seen pictures of Mexico City.

"American ones, son." Still the friendly smile.

Could it be true? Manuel clutched his schedule and strode out of the office.

"I keep telling you you're a sap to be at that school," Beto said. Over the summer Beto had lied about his age and gotten a job as a valet. The uniform made him look five years older. He liked to tell Manuel about the women who looked at him all hungry, and the size of his tips. "I'm not gonna be here for much longer, man. I may move in with some guys from work. I can't decide. I wanna save enough to buy a car, but I'm not gonna let my old man put his name on the deed, and I don't think I'm old enough to buy it legally." Beto's eyebrows furrowed in that familiar far-off way. Then he said, "But worse, they're the saps at that school. Fuck 'em. They're gonna treat my friend that way? Fuck 'em. Whaddya gonna do, man?"

They were sitting on a dirt hill, watching the City Hall light flash. They could hear the noise of distant traffic and around them the movement of birds.

"The thing is," Manuel said, "it's like they don't expect nothing from me. Like I'm a fucking burro."

Beto nodded. "That's right. And I'm gonna surprise the shit out of all of them."

Manuel laughed.

"How 'bout you?" Beto said. "I'd say get a job with me, but I just squeaked in. I'm gonna wait to see if I keep my job before I move in with the guys."

"I dunno," Manuel said.

Beto and Manuel looked off into the distance. "Fuck them," Beto said, as they turned around and headed home. "Things are changing here, too," Beto said.

Manuel nodded. Peludo's family was one of the first to move out. Sarita and Amparo gossiped about who sold, and for how much, or how the renters had been kicked out so the owners could sell their land to the city. Amparo had said she was never moving. Good.

After her prayer and during their dinner of tacos of the nopal from the yard, Manuel told Amparo what had happened. She covered her mouth with one hand and silently shook her head.

"What?" he asked.

"No tienen vergüenza, descarados. There were engineers

on this continent, Manolito, before the Spaniards arrived. Before there were Americans."

This was the first time in his life Amparo had said anything negative about white people, ever.

* * *

This September morning Manuel had change in his pocket and grabbed the first red car running. The conductor nodded at him, and he remained standing and gripped the rail. The tram was cold though, and the wind whipped through his ears, so he huddled in the best-protected corner. The spire of City Hall towered in the distance; they approached Union Station, then downtown was behind them. Laborers filled the tram now, women the shade of Amparo, men in clean white shirts and deep brown skin. Out of habit, Manuel examined all the women—working women in practical clothing, no pretty girls, no one Lulu's age. How old would she be? Nineteen? Twenty? Would he even recognize her if she was standing across from him?

At the end of the line the conductor asked if he needed a transfer, Manuel nodded, took the slip of paper, and hopped on another car, heading south.

The air was fresher, not like downtown Los Angeles. The sun was up to his left, shimmering on the gray sea. He could smell salt in the air.

A memory that he had returned to so often, he was afraid of rubbing it away, surfaced, leading to glimpses of others: the warmth of sun, the tenderness of emotion, the spray of the ocean, a ride on a horse, a faceless mother; his sister, telling him to be brave and good. He had given up praying to Lulu, he had given up believing God would lead him to his family. He didn't believe in God, who did?

He stepped off the tram in San Pedro, buffeted by cold air and the stench of the canneries. He headed up a hill, where he shivered against the temperature. He sat on a bench and stared out over the sea.

He hated them all, everybody at the joke schools he attended. Teachers without a whisper of hope to Manuel about his family. Mr. Owens, with his lies. Toño with his distance, San Diego—so far—why? Hermano Sebastián with his wife and family—What did Manuel have of his family?

"Tía" Amparo. Sometimes he even hated Amparo. He hated his need for her, her pity and abundance and comfort and presence. He hated needing all that! If he ever prayed again, it would be to say, "God, take this pain from me. Take this need for anyone, for everyone, away from me."

He hated everyone and everything.

In the distance Manuel spied a stream of men heading purposefully to the docks. Manuel followed them. Their hats and caps made him wish he had brought his own as the wind whipped through his ears. He caught up to them, and he noticed they were men of all ages and shades. Some were grim as they headed along, others made jokes with one another.

"Where you all going?" he asked the man with a gnarled face on his right.

"Fishing, son."

"All of you?"

"Fishing for work."

Well, then, so was he.

A man with a gray-banded felt hat in a blue serge suit stood above the scores of men, reading in a high reedy voice from a clipboard. Manuel followed a clump of men who were moving up the rampway onto a ship. He was sweaty with excitement and anticipation; nobody paid any attention to him at all.

"You," another man in a suit and a black felt hat called out at him. "You're not twenty-one. This way." He had a red face, fierce eyes, and pointed Manuel in the direction of a stairwell.

The stairs spiraled downward, and Manuel found himself in a corridor where men were standing about, some were smoking cigarettes, others talking with each other. A heavy hand descended on his shoulder.

"The fish get fresher every day," a voice said. Manuel wriggled out of the grip of a sturdy pale man with dusty brown hair under his fisherman's cap and brown freckles across his face. "I'm Nick. I hope you packed a pair of gloves. No? We're gonna unpack this cargo, we're gonna be here for as long as it takes." Nick looked around, no one paid them any attention. "What's the pay?"

Manuel shook his head.

"You speak English?"

Manuel choked on the words that came out. "Of course I speak English!"

"Good, kid, I was a little worried there. What're they payin' you?"

"I don't know."

"Next time, you want to know before you start, got it?" Nick looked him up and down and shook his head. "When you get paid, get yourself a decent pair of gloves and steel-toed boots. You don't want to know the damage I've witnessed."

Manuel nodded.

"They tell you what we're doing?"

Manuel shook his head.

"You see why I asked if you speak English, kid? It's like you're dumb or something. Anyways, we're unloading banana trees from the ship onto this moving carpet." Nick roughly patted the table that ran the length of the corridor. "It's not moving yet," Nick said, as if Manuel had voiced his doubts.

"We do that 'til the ship is empty, and then we collect our pay. Got it?" Manuel nodded.

"Good," Nick said. "Look, this is your spot right here." Nick moved away from him and down the line, greeting and positioning other men.

Most of the men were gloved, but jacketless, in their undershirts and works pants, and it made Manuel cold to look at them. He himself looked out of place, but he brushed away the discomfort. He nodded at the men to his left and right.

A sailor winched the cargo doors open one after the other; with a screech of mechanical apparatus grasping for traction, the conveyor belt began to move. With a rush of movement, the men leaned into the cargo pods and gripped a banana tree, nearly as long as Manuel was tall, heaved it onto their backs, and dumped them on the conveyor belt.

Manuel hadn't moved, but now he leaned into the hold, fumbling for a handle on his rigid, green-tipped tree. Getting the load onto his back was harder than he could have anticipated, and hauling it to the conveyor belt, a few feet away, seemed interminable. The tree felt like it weighed more than he did. He glanced around to see if anyone paused before they dug into the cargo for another tree; instead he was surrounded by enormous massive unceasing movement. He reached for a tree, hoisted it this time a little more easily, and carted the tree across the few feet to the conveyor belt. The belt itself was already stuffed with trees. With additional effort he threw his bunch on top of that.

This was the way his morning went. There were welts on the palms of his hands, his shoulders; his arms and back ached. He glanced at the men around him and kept working as long as they did. Every now and then one of them would lean against the far wall and smoke a cigarette, once getting yelled at by Nick to get back to work. There was some kind of mechanical problem with the belt, which stopped completely.

"Okay everyone, slow down, slow down!" Nick bellowed. "Belt can't move if it's too heavy," which resulted in Manuel crouched with his banana tree waiting for a gap to open up.

The morning had started cold and now with the movement of the men and the machinery, the workspace was warming up, growing hot and stuffy. He stripped his jacket off, then his shirt. He sweated through his clothing in a way that warmed him and chilled him. He was proud of his labor, until he pictured himself as a burro. But he didn't dwell on that because he spotted a green banana that slipped onto the floor, and Manuel watched it writhe and wriggle and scramble away. What was that? He watched the men down the line kick at squirming green bananas. What was wrong with them?

Manuel looked closely and realized they were snakes, slipping out of the banana trees, tumbling off the conveyor belt. He jumped back, scowled at his skittishness, then went back to the hull for the next banana tree.

Two trees more and this time as he hauled it on his back it felt as the damn tree itself had hands, with one crawling across his shoulders. Another damn snake?

He flung the tree with the others. The hand still moved, more tentatively now, across his back. Manuel shook himself free of the hand. There, at his feet lay a massive, hairy spider. He glanced down the line: the men nearest him were watching him, waiting for his response. Manuel ignored them and the spider and headed back for another tree. This time he shook the trunk hard, like the men alongside him had been doing, before he hoisted it onto his shoulders.

When the containers were emptied and the assembly belt halted, Manuel looked around to see what was next. A heavy hand pounded his back, sending a shiver of pain down his spine. Nick said, "This is an early day. Let's make sure you get your money, son."

Nick pulled Manuel ahead of the line, and Manuel heard some muttering behind him, but nobody confronted Nick, who pushed him in the gap in the line, just as the man in front of them held his payment in his hand and stared hard at bills. The man behind them grumbled.

Nick turned to him, a hatless, shivering white man who said, "Wait your turn."

Nick shoved him hard into the line. "You change your tone when you talk to me. Understand?"

The man muttered something.

"Louder," Nick menaced.

"Yessir."

Nick nodded, mollified, then turned to the cashier, a gray-skinned man who smoked a cigarette out of the corner of his mouth.

"Same again for this one," Nick said. The cashier counted out bills between his two hands and shoved them at Manuel.

Manuel stared at the dollar bills in front of him. Twenty dollars. How long had he been hauling and scrunched and aching? He looked at the wan sun over the gray waters but was disoriented and couldn't sort out the time in his head. He stood there dumbly until Nick again pulled him aside.

"That's a lot of money," Manuel couldn't help saying.

Nick laughed. "Not good enough for the union," he said. "But bet that's plenty good enough for you. You plan on being back tomorrow, right?"

Manuel shoved the bills into his pocket and looked at his hands. They were blooming with blisters that would explode soon. Manuel had twenty dollars in his pocket, and he was already hoping for twenty dollars tomorrow. Was he coming back? Of course he was. "You bet!"

"That's right," Nick said. "Good kid. But you're really gonna need a pair of gloves. Come with me, I'll show you where you can buy a pair."

Manuel followed Nick, who cut swiftly through the dock. Now that they were walking and Manuel wasn't using all his attention to figure out how to do his job, he took a moment to look at Nick. He had to walk swiftly to match his pace: Nick was bigger than him, both taller and broader. His muscular forearms were stained a deep brown, while his neck was thick but pale and freckled like his face. A few of the men they passed nodded at Nick, a few others touched their caps.

Away from the docks, Nick picked his way over to a main street.

"Wait, first let me buy you lunch," Nick said. "You like Italian?"

Manuel had no idea what Nick was talking about. "Yeah, sure."

"You ain't never had Italian like this," Nick said, turning into a doorway. "Tomorrow you bring your lunch. I have to admit I was impressed you didn't pass out—you gotta bring food to make it through the day. I mean, you don't want to spend your money here every day." Nick waved at a woman who sat at the back of the room, then prodded Manuel into a corner table. The chairs were uneven and the table wobbled.

"Two, Sarah," Nick called out.

As Manuel's eyes adjusted to the light, the woman set two bowls in front of them and handed them silverware. The food had an unfamiliar scent, but whatever it was prompted the suppressed hunger within him to roar. He slurped it up. A broth with tomatoes, garlic, fish, and seasoning he couldn't identify. Out came rolls, the two tore at the bread and wiped their bowls, soaking up the liquid at the base of the bowl.

The waitress set down two glasses, unscrewed a jug, and

filled them with red wine. Nick drank half his down, she poured more. Manuel sipped at his; it was sharp and bitter. After a couple of more sips, he felt warm inside. What would Amparo say if she knew?

She brought out a platter of noodles and two plates. Nick tilted half of the platter onto his plate and motioned for Manuel to do the same. Out came more rolls.

Manuel ate. The noodles were slick with oil, sprinkled with breadcrumbs and pepper.

Throughout the meal Nick prodded Manuel. What did he think of the spaghetti? Where was his family? How many kids did he have?

At the last question, Manuel realized he was being teased; he felt flush with anger, embarrassment, and wine.

"Slow down, kid, more's on its way."

What more?

She retrieved the empty platter, then returned with another dish. Six neatly grilled fat fish, their blank eyes staring up at the ceiling, slivers of garlic shoved into their bodies, surrounded by boiled potatoes.

"You know what kinda fish that is?" Nick quizzed him.

Manuel shook his head.

"Anchovies. Small, tough, and wiry. Anchovies made this port what it is," he said, stabbing a fish with his fork and putting it on his plate. "You're an anchovy yourself!" he said, laughing at his own joke. "You got lucky today, you know that? They don't always hire like that, usually you gotta know someone."

"What about tomorrow?" he asked.

Nick shrugged. "It depends on who's docking. The union doesn't like us when we do this, ya know. How did you know to come today anyways?"

"I just followed all the guys."

Nick nodded, knowingly. "The thing is, if you get a chance,

you really do want to be a union member. Problem is, it's you gotta know somebody to vouch for you, who's worked with you for a while."

"You're not a member?"

Nick's face shut down with a mean look. Then he called the woman over for more wine. "Nah," he said, "but I can look out for guys. I can look out for you."

By the final forkful, the last swig of wine, Manuel felt himself alive. He was not a donkey, he was an adventurer, traveling out of his neighborhood, discovering the great mysteries of San Pedro. Meeting Nick.

The server cleared the plates and brought two small dishes. Ice cream.

"How much is this gonna be?" asked Manuel, suddenly terrified and protective of the bills in his pocket.

"Now you don't go worrying about that. More wine! I invited you, kid. When we're recovered from this feast, we're gonna go buy you some gloves and boots. The boots though..." Nick looked reflective. "That might be too big a step for you right now. Too steep. But you gotta have the gloves."

After the meal Nick stood and stretched and Manuel did the same. He watched him set down two dollar bills and two quarters on the table.

Out on the street his new guardian led him to a storefront with fishing supplies in the window. Nick frowned. "I forgot they're still closed for lunch. No matter. How'd you like the wine?"

"Fine," Manuel said, feeling dizzy, he assumed from the large meal and the sun in his eyes.

"Come with me, kid, and meet people just like you." He put his arm on Manuel's shoulder and pulled him through an alleyway and into another doorway. Again, the interior was dark.

"This is Manny," Nick called out. "First round's on him."

Manuel shot Nick a horrified look.

"Come on, you can at least buy me a drink, after the lunch I just paid for!"

"Yeah, sure."

Nick held up two fingers to the bartender, who poured brown liquid into two shot glasses.

"Suade," Nick said.

Manuel repeated, "Saw oo jay."

Nick knocked his back, and Manuel felt the eyes of the bar on him. He did the same.

He controlled himself against sputtering and gasping, years of keeping his thoughts to himself helped him with that. Nick clamped a heavy hand on his back and said, "Good kid!" and flashed another two fingers. The bartender poured two more shots and growled at Manuel, "Two bucks."

When Manuel hesitated, Nick added, "You take care of me, I'll watch out for you tomorrow."

Manuel dug into his back pockets and pushed two dollars onto the counter. He didn't care if Nick was going to pour it down his throat, Manuel held onto his glass—never wanting a refill, not wanting to spend another penny.

Nick turned away from him and talked with a much older man at the bar. Manuel picked up his shot glass and moved toward an empty table, feeling himself stagger, feeling the fatigue.

His limbs ached, his arms and legs, his back radiated with pain, the blisters popping on the palms of his hands hardly mattered.

He had felt rich, and now, two dollars no longer his, he felt poor. He needed to leave soon. How much were those gloves going to be?

He wanted to be back at the docks tomorrow.

A much older man perched on a stool in the corner looked at him and shook his head.

Manuel struggled not to feel offended. What the hell did that guy know about him? Nothing. What could he hold against him? Nothing.

Manuel could hear Nick's voice rising; Manuel left his shot glass on the sticky table and headed outside.

The air was cool, dusk was settling in. Manuel looked up and around and tried to navigate. Where was the red car? He picked a direction.

CHAPTER NINE

Manuel sat and waited as Amparo lit the stove, filled a saucepan with water, and as the water warmed, threw crystals into a wash basin. When the basin was ready, she set it on the wooden table in front of him, along with a handful of clean rags.

"This is going to sting a little. Soak your hands in the water."

The seasoned water did sting, but in a way that soothed his hands.

"Does your back hurt?"

Manuel nodded. Amparo rummaged in the kitchen and brought out two tablets and a glass of water to him.

"Take this," she said. And he did.

She went back to the sink and used her molcajete to crush together some things Manuel couldn't see.

When she said to, Manuel removed his hands from the water. Amparo dried each hand tenderly, delicately, with one of the rags. She dabbed the white concoction from the molcajete onto the popped blisters, then gently but firmly wrapped his hands with the rags.

"Keep your hands spread, try not to close your fists," she said. "We need to get you a good pair of gloves, son."

She stood behind him, kissed the top of his head, and hugged his shoulders. Amparo stood again, leaned over him, and kissed the crown of his head lightly. "Money costs us so much, it's true. And yet, unlike the lilies of the field, we need to toil." She stroked the back of his hands. "What about school, son?"

He shook his head. He had that familiar choking feeling in his chest and his throat, but he spoke through it. "They make me so mad," he said. "I just don't see the point."

"You are so young, Manuel, and now you decide to work with men." She gathered her materials. "You will be in the world of men," she said. "I don't know that world."

As she washed up, she said, "Many women worked at the port during the war, doing all those jobs young men had done. Then the young men came back, and all those women lost their jobs. Doña Filomena's daughters." Amparo hung the dishtowel on a hook. "You're going to need gloves. If Tiburcio were still here, he'd lend you a pair." Tiburcio and Hermelinda, their neighbors, had shocked the neighborhood a few months ago by selling their property to the city and moving away. Their home next door was abandoned, the yard lay barren. "Let me think," she said.

Manuel's hands felt soothed; his back had been tense, now he relaxed his shoulders. He watched as she made herself coffee. She made him feel warm and welcome and he resented that he needed that feeling. He hated that he needed her, needed anyone. But right now, he felt the warmth of his hands spread up his arms and down his back, warming the muscles that had tortured him on the jolting ride then the long, dusty walk home.

"That's all yours, Tía." He meant the money he had left on the table. She regarded it neutrally.

"Because people are moving out, my work is less. The money is less. But even so, education is a gift. Toño almost graduated high school, but he enlisted." She sat at the table. She drank her coffee and thumbed through her Bible with gilt edges. She pawed at the pages as if reading through her fingertips. When she finished her coffee, she washed the cup and saucer and set it on the drying rack.

"I'm going to bed now. Your hands will feel better in the morning."

"Thank you, Tía," Manuel said, in a low voice, then stopped. His gratitude had no beginning and no end, and he had no way to share the jumble of thoughts in his head with her and now he was angry about that.

"Good night, son," she said.

He sat at the wooden kitchen table, keeping his palms open, although with the force of his anger and confusion he wanted to clench them. That idiot counselor, that awful Nick, the pain of the blisters of his hands, that ache within him like a gaping maw that nothing could feed or fill.

The poultice on his palms soothed the pain. The tense muscles in his arms, shoulders, and back slowly relaxed. He listened to the late neighborhood sounds, he knew them well enough, the train in the distance, the dogs barking, the small signals reminding him it was time to wander freely.

He glanced at the money on the table, where he had left it, where Amparo had left it. He had brought home fourteen dollars.

The next day in place of the money was a packed lunch and a pair of used gloves; Amparo was already gone by the time he awoke. He scooped them up. Amparo's name should have been Milagros. Always these everyday miracles.

Manuel wanted to stay away from Nick, have nothing to do with Nick, but how was he supposed to get a job? That same day when he followed the crowd of men, when he got to the man with the clipboard, he was asked for his union card.

He left the line, bitter, and tried to find where he'd worked before, but it had been a different ship, and no one let him pass.

He felt cold and angry and unprepared, no boots, and the wind from the shore whipped through his thin clothing. He hadn't thought about that. He'd thought he'd get straight on an assignment and be sweaty and starving and aching by the end of the day, but he'd stay away from Nick and come home with a fistful of money and give it to Amparo, like an offering, a gift for everything, everything he couldn't put into words, and all he would do today would be to stand here and shiver.

He was just another stupid Mexican.

To hell with it. He walked to the lighthouse he'd seen. He'd never seen one up close—he'd walk there, then go home, and figure out what he'd do tomorrow and the day after that.

He made his way through the crowd of milling men, listening in, but not understanding the languages. The scent of canneries was thick and heavy; he had seen Mexican women stepping off the red cars, uniforms immaculately covered by their aprons. He scanned them reflexively, looking for a trace of his sister. He made his way up the docks, and spotted Nick in the distance, the knit cap low on his head, a thick sweater over his broad chest. Manuel watched Nick as he spoke expressively to the man on his left and made his choice.

"Hey Nick," he said.

"My little anchovy, it's not a good day for you, kid." Nick looked him up and down and shook his head disparagingly. "You gotta listen to me, kid. No gloves, no boots, you're gonna lose fingers and toes. Maybe that doesn't mean much to you, but I enjoy my fingers, and the places I put 'em." The two men laughed, lewdly.

"I got gloves." Manuel pulled them out from under his arm and waved them at Nick. "No work today?" he asked.

Nick shrugged. "Sometimes there're enforcers out there. Sometimes not. There's always work, kid, there's always ways around whatever they got running. I was just taken by surprise."

"What about tomorrow?" Manuel asked, insistently.

Nick turned to the man on his right, a man with craggy wrinkles on his cheeks and forehead. "I'll be seeing you, Gus," he said. The man nodded and walked off toward the hill.

Nick leaned back against the railing, folded his arms across his chest. "What do you want, kid?"

"Work. I want to work."

Nick nodded. "You don't got the equipment, you don't got the strength, you sure as hell don't got the union card. What do you wanna do about it?"

Manuel thought. "Whatever it takes."

Nick nodded. He opened his thick coat, pulled out his wallet from the inside pocket. He plucked a number of bills and handed them to Manuel.

"You're my investment, kid. You got your gloves, now go buy yourself boots like I told you. Be here tomorrow, ready to work at five a.m., and I'll get you in." He clapped Manuel heavily on the back and walked off in the direction of his companion.

Manuel felt the wind rip through his clothes and tangle the hair on his head. He stared at the money: seven ten-dollar bills.

His heart thudded with dread and excitement.

For one brief thrilling moment, he thought of taking the money and giving it to his Tía; of course, he'd never be able to come back here, and the docks would be forever closed to him.

He trudged off, pushing the money into his pocket, clutching it tight, and headed in the direction of the stores Nick had pointed out to him earlier.

Nick told him he was his supervisor, but it seemed more like he was a recruiter, putting himself in charge of who qualified for what non-union job. Meaning Nick decided whether or not Manuel worked that day, and, if he did, Nick demanded a kickback. Ten percent, unless Nick was pissed, then it was 15 percent and no work for another week.

It didn't take Manuel long to catch on. After a few weeks, Manuel realized Nick had a system of bringing in new blood like him, taking money off the top of their wages and insisting on meals once every few weeks or so. Manuel got the sense Nick's sole paid gig was recruiting boys like him and skimming their wages. It bugged him, but what about it? He wouldn't have a job without Nick. When Kiko, impressed that Manuel was a working man now, wanted to join him, Manuel brought Kiko with him. Nick gave them both a dirty look and didn't hire Manuel the entire week.

"When I want someone, I'll let you know," he scowled.

Nick maneuvered things for him, and Manuel moved around in different stop-gap capabilities: loading, unloading. On the days there was no work, Nick would either send him home or offer, once again, to buy him lunch. Manuel avoided the lunch offers a few times until he realized it only angered Nick and delayed Manuel's next assignment. He accepted once every half dozen or so times.

It became routine, Nick would buy him an enormous meal that seemed never-ending, and then insist on drinks afterward. Manuel paid for the drinks, pretended to finish his, then left them all.

Manuel's goal was to stay out of trouble, pocket the money. He just didn't know what was next. His money from work was coming in fast, but it seemed to be leaking out swiftly all the same. Nick took his cut, "a finder's fee," he said pointedly, each time he plucked the bills straight out of Manny's hand and expected a couple of drinks.

He grew accustomed to bars. The truth was drinking made him only sporadically happy, feeling joy-infused for a brief moment, a fleeting sense of warmth toward his brethren. But most of the time he felt miserable, dull, dizzy, maudlin, obsessed with Lulu, with his family, a wretched cast-off. He might as well pour the jugs of wine, mugs of sour beer, and bottles of brown liquid straight down the urinal.

How did Nick survive this life? If Manuel was a burro, a beast of burden, Nick was a bull. Manuel had seen him lift other men off the ground with a shove of his arm.

Manuel gave Amparo most of his money. As their neighborhood thinned out, people in his neighborhood were bitter against each other: those who wanted to remain blaming those who sold their homes; those who sold their homes cruel and mocking, according to Amparo. The Sanchezes had moved out, bragging about how much they'd made on the sale of their property. Amparo said the sons would make quick work of that money.

CHAPTER TEN

1955

Three years went by. Three years of watching the Mexican cannery girls, sleek and untouchable and laughing as they disembarked and headed to their jobs; three years of listening to languages similar to but different from Spanish and picking up some Italian and Portuguese; three years of bringing money to Amparo and keeping some for himself. Three years of being an adult, with the blisters and the aches and the body muscled and hardened and filled out to prove it.

He gave Amparo money, he bought himself sharp clothing, he considered buying a motorcycle like Beto. He made more money than Beto which made him feel a bit superior, and uncomfortable. He bought Amparo a nicer sewing machine, and a TV set and everybody came over to watch and, for a while, thought they could come over and watch even when no one was home.

During those years he went from swinging on red cars all the way to the ocean air to riding buses that deposited him near the docks. From a lookout he could see the ocean, the boats, and, over on Terminal Island, the stacks of now obsolete red cars, rusting, eaten away by the salt air.

Three years went by, and it was clear that what Nick did for him and others, placing them, taking a kickback from their wages, then placing them again, profited Manuel in the short term, but made him look like a scavenger to others.

* * *

Manuel worked, and his muscles filled, and his body lengthened. Manuel worked, and he brought money to Amparo. Manuel worked, and he dreamed of being in the union, a crane operator, a welder even. He was never going to be an engineer. But he could still do something better than this. To build. To make.

He had to figure out how to get into the union. He'd rather that money went to them. He didn't care if they were grifters like Nick said they were. He'd rather they smoked fat cigars and drank bourbon with his money, rather than Nick taking his cut.

He hated that man. Nick made him feel mean and cheap and, around women, crude and ugly. But he liked the money, he could do the work.

What else was he going to do?

Toño had moved back to Whittier with his wife Cristina, a round and bubbly woman who gushed over Manuel and filled her home with smiles. Even Toño, who easily descended into moody sullenness, smiled back. Manuel watched Toño cradle his twins; it moved him and pained him. To be a father, to have a father.

Amparo occasionally left on Thursday mornings to help care for her grandchildren. Manuel felt small and petty, and abandoned. He shook his head at himself. He could have gone too, but that made no sense. He didn't belong. God knew he wasn't Toño's or Cristina's responsibility. Amparo returned in time for Sunday morning services.

The number of parishioners may have become fewer, but they were hardy. Amparo spent some time organizing rent parties for those being forced out of their homes in Chavez Ravine, those who rented or squatted, or lived on the generosity of others.

More and more families were moving out, while other families refused and began to protest. What they were being offered, they said, wouldn't buy them a home in the hills. What they were being offered wouldn't replace Chavez Ravine. They were being pushed out, the protestors said, because they were poor Mexicans.

"I don't like that kind of talk," Amparo said, and Hermano Sebastián nodded vigorously. "But sometimes, sometimes, it's hard not to agree."

Amparo and Hermano Sebastián nodded and prayed with the young protestors, and they were among the group of people who were fighting to stay exactly where they were.

As this went on each day on his way to the bus stop, Manuel passed a store front. Sometimes the lobby was crowded with brown faces, sometimes it was empty. The sign read: Horace Romero, Notary Public, Income Taxes, Inmigración.

Today in San Pedro there was no work for non-union men. Manuel watched Nick begin to talk to a group of disappointed men with speechifying bursts of anger. Those outbursts usually ended up with some poor scared soul getting roughed up, bruised, or damaged. Manuel walked up and down the streets, past the restaurant where Nick had taken him the first day; it was too early in the morning, it was still closed. Manuel passed the houses with their hanging laundry. Everything was so tight and close together. Did the people like it like that? Not like

Palo Verde or Bishop, where the houses and dirt paths scattered in different directions—except now with fewer and fewer people.

Every day, he began to think, how much longer would he and Amparo live there? Waiting for the bus alongside others, he thought about Palo Verde. He knew the senses of his neighborhood in his bones, the colors of the shrubs, the flowers, the animals, their smell after a swift dense rain, or scents of cooking, the music from other radios during a dry hot evening. The colors of the hanging laundry, the bold but fading lettering on the liquor store, the way the paths turned to rivulets after the rains. How dirty some of the homes were; even the white bachelors had moved up and abandoned their shacks.

He hopped a bus and stood alongside a dapper Black man in a gray felt hat, who moved to give Manuel room. Where did he work? What kind of job did he have? Manuel hung on as they jostled up and down the streets through downtown. A group of older women (Chinese? Japanese?) got on.

At Union Station Manuel found himself without direction, following his feet home. Until they stopped outside of Horace Romero, Notary Public, Income Taxes, Inmigración.

He peered through the heavily lettered door. The lobby was empty. Now his thoughts were pangs in his heart. He pulled at the door and walked through.

Bare white walls, wood floors, half a dozen folding chairs leaned against the counter.

A heavy man, who seemed slightly out of breath, walked to the counter. "Help you?" he asked. "Le puede servir?"

"Can you help me find someone?" Manuel said.

"Normally, not really, kid. But, as you can see, business is kinda slow. Why doncha come in, have a seat, and we can talk."

The office was a side room next to the counter with a wide wooden desk covered by manila folders and papers. A gray file cabinet behind him was stacked with folders. In wire baskets there seemed to be printed forms, different forms in each basket.

There were colorful Mexican calendars, from Rosario's Market, Saucedo's Carnicería, Rogelio's Mercado. He and Amparo had been to Rogelio's plenty of times. The black phone on the desk rang. The stout man with thin black hair brushed slick across the top of his head, whom Manuel assumed to be Horace, raised a palm to Manuel, picked up the phone, and spoke rapidly and softly into the receiver. Manuel tried not to eavesdrop, but it was difficult to avoid the fact that there was a bill collector on the other side of the line.

Hanging up, he said, "Shouldn't of answered that one!" The pale man wiped his hands on his thighs, held out one hand across the table, and said, "Call me Horace, by the way. Now, what pretty girl ran out on you?"

Manuel shook his head, snorted.

"Don't be shy. You've got the looks and the build of a total heartbreaker. Girls love that decent honorable shit. What happened? Did you two-time her?"

"Not a girl," he said. "My sister. My parents."

"Ah. Okay. That's just bad luck."

The man adjusted papers in front of him, picked up a pad and a pencil, took a deep breath, and said, "So. Tell me what happened."

Manuel told Horace Romero everything.

Horace listened closely to what Manuel said, jotted down a few notes on a crowded note pad, and listened some more. Halfway through Manuel's monologue, Horace threw his pencil down, slouched back in his chair, his face drooping. When Manuel stopped, Horace leaned forward, his voice soft.

"Son, there is no easy way to tell you this. First thing I'd assume is that your parents were picked up and dropped into

Mexico. They're not coming back. They'd be denied entrance at the border—their papers were probably stamped 'deported' to make sure they'd never get back in."

How did this man even know?

As if reading his mind, Horace said, "How do I know? That's easy. Los Angeles was at the heart of it. They kicked it off right there, across the street, at Placita Olvera in '31. Later they got my cousin Tony. My wife and I visit him during Christmas. During the Depression they got tens of thousands of us. Mexicans, I mean. Pretty rough during the Depression. Between that and the TB you'd think they were trying to kill us off."

A spark, a glimmer, like a light inside a home during a storm was a beacon of gladness, a wound being soothed. They hadn't abandoned him. They had been *taken away*. Everything swirled inside of Manuel, as if he had been turned inside out. The man across from him kept talking.

"You know, it worked in different ways for different people. Some were actually paid some money to leave and given free freight to Mexico. Others were told their benefits would stop. A bunch got on and left, even if their kids were citizens... My cousin Tony?" Horace shook his head. "Real bad for him and his kids. Their kids didn't go to school anymore, you know? The other kids made fun of them, they didn't speak Spanish, they'd gone to school here, in English. Real pochos. A shame, a terrible loss. And those kids, truly, ni de aqui ni de allá. You know, my wife and I, we don't teach Spanish to the kids. We want people to know our kids belong here."

"What about my parents then, my sister, Lulu?"

"What year did you say?"

Manuel said, "I was born in 1935. I remember being with them, being with my sister, then there's some gaps. Then I moved in with Amparo Valenzuela, who kind of adopted me."

Horace nodded, scratched on his pad. "So sometime after 1935, and you moved in with Mrs. Valenzuela when?"

After Pearl Harbor, Toño had enlisted. After then. "1942?" he said.

Horace nodded, grimly. "Maybe '38 or '39? That's a little late for 'repatriation' or the cleansing of this country of Mexicans, but there were parts in this state I heard where they'd just pick you up off the streets and send you to Mexico." He shook his head. "No time to gather your things, no time to tell your family, you were just gone. Didn't matter if you were a US citizen. Missing. Disappeared. It happened here, I know it. And I know in the '40s Los Angeles wanted to ship train loads of us to the heart of Mexico. World War Two interrupted those plans. Guess they figured they could use the bodies in the military, instead."

Horace's words in his ears, in his heart, in his chest hit him like a fifty-pound weight. He cleared his throat and asked, "They could still be alive?"

The man across from him shook his head, shrugged. "Sure, son, they could still be alive. Any idea where they went? You ever been to Mexico?"

Manuel shook his head.

"It's a big place."

The two men sat silently.

Manuel said, "My sister was with me. I didn't go to Mexico, neither did she. Do you think you could find her, at least?"

"What do you got to go on?"

"Her name's Lulu. My last name's Galvan. She could be twenty or so. I'm eighteen. She's older than me."

Horace scribbled that down. He nodded. "Let me think about that. I don't know. Here, take my card. Drop by in a week or so, or call me. Where do you live?"

"Palo Verde, Chavez Ravine," Manuel said.

Horace grunted. "That's gonna be prime real estate—I know some of you are trying to stick out it, but as they say, you can't fight City Hall! Ni modo." He shook his head.

Manuel clutched the card and walked out of the office. There was a buzzing in his ears, a tingling in his hands and arms, and the sun on the street was too bright. He stumbled back into the office, now empty, unfolded a chair, and sat in it.

He leaned forward and put his head between his legs, something he'd learned from work when they felt light-headed from too much labor and too little food. He closed his eyes and breathed. He heard Horace's heavy steps move toward him, then retreat.

Both light-headed and heavy-limbed, Manuel waited until he could trust himself to walk without stumbling. For the second time he made his way out of the office door. He walked home, to Amparo's home, kicking at the clods of dirt like the angry child he'd once been, shaking his head at the years of not knowing.

He glanced back at the tower of City Hall, turning green in the light of the setting sun.

He walked with a buzzing in his ears and confusion in his heart. He walked, considering that the woman who had loved him and sheltered him had lied to him. Lied to him by not telling him.

It was all an ache. All a confusion. All a misery.

Everything was confusion, and everything was clear. Everything was different, and everything was wrong. In this country, God's country, his country? Sure, the teachers could hate you, the counselors hate you, the cops, hate you, but this? Pick you up and throw you away? Was it possible here, in these United States?

CHAPTER ELEVEN

Manuel felt that odd tightening of his throat, so long ago and faraway but immediately familiar. Choked by salt water, drowning, dying.

He would not drown, he would not die. He fought back against it; he was no longer a terrified boy.

He stalked past the abandoned shacks of the bachelors, past the water tower, past Jerry's deli. How come no one ever told him? They claimed to be looking for his family, but his family was gone. Gone far and who knew where and, if Horace was to be believed, never to return. Did they know, all this time? All this time, Amparo telling him his family loved him and was looking for him—consoling him with lies. Lies that he believed.

He was going to ask Amparo, "Why are Mexicans so fucking stupid? Why are we fucking burros and pendejos and idiots who believe in God and the future and this fucking country?" The anger surged through his veins, bringing blood to his face, his arms and fingers tingled with the righteousness of it all. "This fucking country. This fucking country."

Instead of his family, his parents, his sister, Amparo was a kind of pathetic consolation prize with her scripture and her meetings and her hermanos this and hermanas that.

He was too angry for tears.

And this place! Palo Verde, with its birds and its flowers and its people fleeing, the homes falling apart, the unpaved roads, the goats, the chickens. To hell with them, to hell with them all. To hell with Tía. And he would tell her so.

He stormed onto the porch, wrenched open the door filled with wrath, ready to pound the table and walls with his fists.

Amparo sat at the table, still.

Her hands had been pressed to her face; she moved them, glanced at him, then covered her face again. Her reading glasses were on the table, on a piece of official looking paper.

He sensed that she had been crying.

"Tía," he said. "Tía, what is it?"

She shook her head, her mouth shut, her lips trembling.

He picked up the paper, read it, and read it again not understanding. He looked at her. "An eviction notice? But you own this house."

"Yes, I own this house." She looked at him. "It doesn't seem to matter that I own this house. That I chose not to sell to them."

He scrutinized the announcement. Public housing. Weren't they part of the public? "How much time do we have?"

"It doesn't say."

What did that even mean?

"People have left, son. But not the Arechigas. Not the Vargases."

This fucking city. "We'll fight, Tía, we'll fight this."

He stepped gently toward her, pulling her gently into an embrace, to comfort her, while his heart thudded and pounded and pumped the fury that swirled and circled within him.

* * *

In the morning he heard Amparo's shopping cart trundle down the dirt path. When he'd started at the docks, he lost track as to what her daily schedule was, the different ways she supported herself and him. He gave her most of his earnings and paid little attention to the changes in the neighborhood. And here it was, the neighborhood thinning, selling out, and, finally, their eviction notice.

He should have been up and down at the docks already, but what did it matter? Earn money to give some to Nick to earn the right to earn more money—give money to Amparo so she can lose the home she owns free and clear.

He pulled out his metal box of precious thing and retrieved his birth certificate, creased from years of examination, pondering, wondering.

Lose your parents. Lose your family. Lose your home.

Beto had it right. He hoped that Beto would be a winner. He'd like to know at least one.

He left his room, washed up, walked around the kitchen table. He opened the oven door and there, sure enough, was a platter of food for him.

After breakfast Manuel washed up. He looked around the home that Amparo kept so clean and tidy. He went out to the shed and cleaned out the chicken coops. He tightened the swinging door that was tilted off its axis.

He wanted to walk to the notary public's office. But what could he have found out in less than a day?

He took a walk. He walked around his neighborhood, more than half emptied out, unusually quiet. Families had left, taking their colorful birds that sang from their cages, taking their goats and chickens. It was a different place, now, from the one he had grown up in. City Hall towered indifferently in the distance.

After a week of solid work and a week's wages to give to Amparo, he had a free day, and as soon as he was up, he walked to Horace's office.

Closed.

He waited at a diner, sipping a cup of coffee until it was cold, getting a friendly refill from a friendly white waitress who then ignored him.

He left her a generous dollar tip and walked back to Horace's store front. This time the sign was flipped to open, and he walked in.

There was a scattering of people in the lobby. An older couple was seated against the wall, the man so far country he still had his straw hat, gleaming a pristine, shiny yellow. The woman next to him sat in a simple gray suit with a black sweater around her shoulders. Across from them a young man, possibly related, wore crisp, clean jeans, oiled-back hair, and a clean white T-shirt. Manuel had seen young men like that before. He resented them. They seemed to have time and money and leisure enough to be bored. It struck him that he resented them all here, right now.

By the time Horace waved him in, there were three people waiting behind him, another family, the couple decades younger with a small girl in a frilly pink dress.

Manuel walked into the small side room.

"Have a seat," Horace said.

Manuel did. The man across from him looked harassed and impatient.

"I hate these cases," he said. "I hate everything they mean." He rubbed his mouth. "Let's talk about why you came here in the first place. Look, I could tell you a bunch of pretty stories, pay a private investigator, go to Mexico, dig for yourself, but they're all manure." Horace tilted his head at Manuel, then righted himself. "The short story, son, is your family's gone. They're gone. They were dropped somewhere in Mexico. I mean we don't even have a clue where! You have any idea the manpower it would take to investigate a country the size of Mexico? We're not talking thousands of dollars, we're talking tens of thousands of dollars."

Manuel felt his stomach drop to the floor.

The man scratched the back of his head. "I won't even tell you to go yourself, that would be pointless. The truth is, son, the people I've helped before knew where their family was exiled. Often it was where they came from. They'd get letters from them, you know?"

Manuel didn't know.

The man continued, "And even then, there's not a lot I could do. Once your passport's marked 'Deported' you're done. Finito la cantata."

"What good are you, then?" Manuel asked.

The notary shrugged. "Fair question, what good am I? Sometimes I help people get their US-born kids back up here. Whole damn thing is, you used to be able to immigrate the parents, you know? Not once you've been exiled from this country." He paused, "Son, you came in knocking on my door. I'm being honest with you and warning you. There are people out here who might tell you something different, but all they'll want is your money."

Manuel looked around at the shabby surroundings. What had he expected?

He knew the answer to that. He had had hope. What a worthless emotion, hope. It only ground the glass deeper into your wounds.

"I guess I wasted your time," Manuel said. He looked at the ground. Maybe he could go to Mexico. Maybe he could go on his own and look for them. He and Amparo had been back and forth to Tijuana. Could he do that? He wouldn't know where to begin, or how.

"Another thought," Horace continued. "You put ads. Newspaper ads looking for them in the Spanish papers down there and up here." He scratched his ear. "One problem with that is you get a lot of pretenders." He shook his head. "You get a lot of people who want to separate you from the little money you have." He made a face. "It's cheap but unreliable. Going to Mexico's more reliable, but there's no guarantee your family's where you're looking."

Horace stood, and Manuel felt that he was being dismissed. Already! And nothing had been done.

"Wait," he said, resolutely staying seated, "Wait, what am I supposed to do?"

"That's what you gotta decide, kid." Horace remained standing and ticked off the points on his fingers. "One, hire somebody to go down to Mexico and investigate on your behalf. Two, go down yourself. Or three, put ads in all the papers that you can afford. Four, you got the money, I got a guy who can investigate. But most of us don't have that kind of money."

Manuel moved unhappily in his seat. He had no idea what to do next. It sounded like it was hopeless. He said, "How much do I owe you?"

Horace shook his head. "It was a consultation. You need something from me, let me know."

"There's another thing I want to ask you about."

Horace grunted. "Fine."

Manuel handed him the eviction notice.

Horace read and nodded.

"Yeah. Ni modo, kid. Like I said, you can't fight City Hall."

"Nothing?"

"Short of tying yourself to the building."

"Thank you," Manuel mumbled and walked back out and onto the sidewalk filled with passing pedestrians and the exhaust of bus fumes.

* * *

Beto and Manuel sat on a hill facing City Hall in the distance. Like Manuel, Beto had grown long and lean, but more filled out. His thick eyebrows were just as expressive. While Manuel was hard and muscular, Beto was soft. Manuel was dark, Beto was light-skinned. So much so he had talked his way into working the floor of a car dealership, explaining the advantages of different models. His hope was to be a real, honest-to-God car salesmen. "You ever buy a car, Manny, you talk to me first. The things we get away with!" He made a low whistle.

They could hear the traffic coming from downtown; one of the abandoned homes nearby was surrounded by honeysuckle, and Manuel could smell its scent from where they sat.

"To think, to some people $10,000 is practically nothin'," Beto said. "To think, to us, and all of here in Chavez Ravine, it's like a fortune. But it's not enough, man, not enough." Beto shook his head. "Once, just once, my dad talked about Mexicans being rounded up at Placita Olvera. My mom gave him a look and he shut up." Beto snorted. "That's why I remember. He usually ignores her." Beto gave him a sideways look. "Where you two gonna go?"

Manuel was so immersed in his dead end with Horace, it took him a moment. "I dunno, Tía says her church is fighting the evictions. They got lawyers."

Beto snorted. "I'll tell you right now, they don't got money."

Manuel nodded.

"I told my dad if he let me manage the money, I could make something of it." Beto laughed. "He looked like he wanted to smack me real hard for saying that, but he couldn't. Not since I hit him back."

Manuel said, "I don't think I could ever hit my dad."

Beto said, "Well, I hope yours isn't a pendejo like mine."

"I don't think I'm ever gonna know." The young men were silent for a moment.

Beto sighed. "We'll be moving. I wanted to let you know. My pops found a place in Bunker Hill. Yeah, we'll see for how long." Beto looked sideways at Manuel. "Sorry, Mano."

That was the moment Manuel realized Palo Verde, and all of Chavez Ravine, was dying.

CHAPTER TWELVE

A week later he returned to the notary's office. This time the waiting area was empty.

Manuel flopped down in the seat across from Horace. It seemed the same stack of papers was there.

"What can I get for $200?" he said.

Horace, his face made wider and paler by a thoughtful frown, said, "For $250, I can put ads in the papers, both languages, run 'em for a couple of weeks, maybe even a month. I can set up a post office box. I can write it so you don't get a bunch of crazies answering. I can write so if someone knew them, they knew you."

The two men spoke some more, the notary writing notes down on his yellow pad, asking more questions, then putting his pen down.

Manuel pulled a wad of fives and tens out of his wallet and counted out $195. The notary wrote him a receipt, leaving him a balance of $55.

"You check the *Examiner* and *La Opinion* on Monday. You'll see it."

Monday before getting on his bus, he picked up two papers. He searched through the columns at the back of the page. At last, he spotted it in the *Examiner*.

"WANTED: information on the whereabouts of Gustavo and Filomena Galvan. Please identify names or sexes or number of children. Please write to—" and there was a post office box address. Horace had said it would run for three weeks, and to give it a month, at least, if it didn't pan out.

Manuel didn't want to think what then. He had given the man all his savings. But what had he been saving for? There was nothing ahead of him, only more of the same.

The wind blew through the bus window and ruffled his hair as they continued on to San Pedro. He watched the Japanese women get on at their usual stop, the moreno businessman get off at his stop. Manuel wondered who he was, looking so calm and peaceful. He wondered who those women were, where they went on their days.

All these things he thought about in order to not think about what he had done, what he hoped had been set in motion. It was hope that gutted you in the end.

On Wednesday night he joined the Bible group to write letters to Mayor Paulsen to help change his mind. On Sunday he followed Amparo to the annual Church Fest, where small Protestant churches congregated and shared. This year Iglesia Pentecostal de Dios were hosting.

He walked alongside Amparo, in her homemade dress, finely stitched, pressed, perfectly fitted, a subdued gray paisley print. She had made sure his black trousers were clean and pressed. He had polished his shoes to impress her and ironed his own shirt and jacket. He watched as she smiled at the members of the congregation who greeted her, the women, younger, older, Amparo's age, in their well-tailored, home-sewn dresses, skirts, blouses. Cinched waists, wide skirts. Hand-stitched hemlines right at the knee. Manuel paid attention to the young women with their bright dresses with floral prints. Dainty ankle socks or delicate hose. Tiny hats, some with veils. The men, like himself, in their dark slacks and white shirts, shiny patent leather shoes.

This might be the last time they gathered in His name, here near Chavez Ravine.

Amparo led him through the well-scrubbed, well-appointed crowd, pausing at an exclamation, "Manuel!" or "Manolito" or "Manolo," where Manuel would allow himself to be pawed, admired, praised, scolded, cajoled, implored to return to the regular service.

And of course, the omnipresent Hermano Sebastián, who appeared a little older since Manuel had last seen him, a fuller face, wire-rimmed glasses exaggerating thoughtful brown eyes. He reached his hand out for Amparo's, and the two came together in a close hug, the greeting of preference in this church. An outstretched hand, pulling each other together, a brief contact or embrace, a "Dios te bendiga" or "Cristo te ama," and the two retracted, smiled, and began a conversation.

"Our prodigal son!" Hermano Sebastián proclaimed, giving Manuel a hug as if he were a boy of ten. "So happy to see you here with our beloved Amparo today." He introduced his much younger wife and the baby she held in her arms.

Manuel smiled at the young woman who fussed with her baby. Amparo exclaimed over the baby's growth and the beauty of the young mother while Manuel followed his own thoughts.

As the crowd entered the sanctuary, Amparo steered

Manuel to her seat, nodded and smiled as she passed her friends, introduced herself to the new faces, the visitors from other congregations, and seated herself. Manuel squeezed in next to her.

They stood and sang during the procession of pastors. They stood and prayed under the leadership of a visiting minister. They remained standing and sang "Solamente en Cristo," and then they were bidden to be seated.

Reflexively, he searched for Lulu. He doubted he would recognize her if she sat down beside him. Still, he kept his eyes open for a woman a little older than himself. Although, how could he even tell their ages?

The church's minister stood and gave a long hearty welcome, listing all the congregations, listing the names of the visiting churches, Pentecoste Israel, Iglesia de Dios San Gabriel, on and on as if answering Manuel's question, where did they all come from?

A minister from Iglesia de Dios Stockton stood. In Spanish he read, 'Beloved, I urge you as sojourners and exiles to abstain from the passions of the flesh, which wage war against your soul. Keep your conduct among the Gentiles honorable, so that when they speak against you as evildoers, they may see your good deeds and glorify God on the day of visitation.' In his Texican lilt he continued, "Are not we all sojourners? Are we all not in exile? The lands we have left behind us, the lands we will leave. Some of us in our midst facing exile right now."

Manuel noticed the nodding and murmuring. Amparo gripped his hand.

"And yet, here we are. And Peter tells us, very clearly, what is our duty. To remain honorable. To abstain from evil. For others to see that our goodness glorifies God."

More murmurs and nods of assent.

He stood for the prayer. He sang with the hymns. Amparo's face was so bright and happy. He squeezed her hand; she patted his arm. What he wanted was to feel something. Some light, some joy. That was his prayer, if he had one. It had been years since he prayed to Lulu.

Another pastor stood and gave a prayer of gratitude. It was a preaching convention up there! The next sermon was about the end times, how some of us had thought the previous war was a sign of the end times, but how we all know He will come like a thief in the night. No one knows His hour.

Unlike their eviction notice, thought Manuel sourly, which came in broad daylight.

Another hymn, then time for silent prayer while the congregation passed the donation baskets. Amparo's envelope was ready; Manuel dug a few dirty bills out of his wallet, and waited, ready to for his turn. Was that what they were here for? What was *he* here for? Beto had called them all losers, following other losers. He was here for Tía. He had an obligation, a duty, to her.

The young woman was aisles away when he first saw her dress, a burst of yellow sunshine. She shimmered in it, her skin a silky golden brown in contrast. She passed a basket down one aisle, bobbing her head at the members, moving to the next aisle to await the basket's return.

Who was she?

After the music, the hymn and the prayer, this church's pastor, Hermano Nuñez, thanked the young people from Iglesia de Dios Goleta, for their help.

She was from Goleta. Where was that?

The final pastor, Hermano Sebastián, stood and spoke. He welcomed the congregants, from near and far. He praised the depth of their faith, and their determination to gather together.

During his sermon, Manuel's thoughts wandered to the woman in the yellow dress. Closing his sermon, Hermano Sebastián asked the congregants to stand in prayer.

"Lord, God of the Armies, Lord God of the Universe, bless all who have gathered here in your name, to do your work, your bidding. Guide us all, guides us as we face our daily challenges, our daily obligations of caring for one and another. For loving one and another. Bless us in our daily journey to live the lives you have gifted us." He paused. "Bless us all, as we congregate to share our joy in Your magnificence. Bless us all, as we part, and go our separate ways. A special supplication, dear Lord, for all those in Chavez Ravine, and for Pentecostal Iglesia de Dios, as we go in search of a new home for our worshippers."

Amparo gripped his hand. There it was. Their church was moving as well.

* * *

Manuel caught a glimpse of the yellow dress as the crowd of congregants made their way toward cups of punch. The yellow flittered in and out of his line of vision like a hummingbird: when he headed in its direction, it set off elsewhere.

Manuel sipped his tamarindo, tangy, not too sweet. A large group, most of whom were strangers to him, were talking to each other. He leaned against the courtyard wall and half-listened to the conversations around him before joining the jostling line of men and women for the buffet.

So much food! Chile verde with pork and chicken, black mole, green mole, yellow mole. Five different kinds of tamales, including sweet tamales with walnuts and Mexican chocolate. Arroz con pollo, enchiladas, someone had even made chilaquiles. Black beans, pinto beans, refried beans, beans a la olla. Gorditas filled with beans and cheese, or butter and beans, or cheese and meat.

Across the room and pushed against a wall, Manuel spied a table laden with desserts: gelatin desserts stuffed with canned fruit, banana cream pies, lemon meringue pies, white powdered sugared polvorones.

"'Christ is the bread of life,'" the man behind him quoted a sermon Manuel had often heard. "'That we will never be hungry again.' Thank you, Lord, but not right now!"

Manuel smiled while a group laughed.

Women and a few men served the food, Amparo as well, behind the table ladling out the ensalada de nopalitos she was so proud of. She had scavenged the cactus paddles during the week, trimming them of all needles and tough skin, and brought a huge casserole dish filled with the tangy salad, garnished with red onion slices and tomatoes she grew herself. He overhead threads of conversations, how some people were fighting the eviction notices, while others had given in.

Manuel peered around for the yellow dress, did not see her serving food, could not see her in line, nor at a table.

By the time he had rounded off his platter with Mrs. Romero's flour tortillas, covering and keeping his food warm, he saw her at the end of an aisle of tables, already surrounded by young men. His feet set off in that direction. He squeezed between tables, murmured "con permiso" multiple times, then sat next to one of the young men surrounding her. He set his plate down, introduced himself to the young man on his right, who was intent on scooping flecks of pale orange rice onto his corn tortilla. The young man grunted.

He looked past the young man to get a better look at the woman in yellow. Her deep black hair sleekly waved to the right above her forehead, then dipped low and long where it curled into her jawline all the way down and around her shoulders. She smiled attractively at the boy to her right, while tearing into a piece of fried chicken. She wore pearl stud earrings, which emphasized her delicate earlobes. Was she with that man she was sitting next to? He wasn't paying much attention to her. Maybe, maybe not. He looked very young, and she looked very much like a woman. The woman of his dreams, and he didn't even know he could dream so extravagantly. She looked at him, and Manuel, feeling caught, looked away. He tried to swallow his mouthful of ropa vieja, and instead began to choke.

Sputtering into his napkin, unable to breath, he thought, *I am not going to die here, at Tia's church, before ever knowing her name. I am not going to die.* He heard noises around him, and a young voice commanding, "Help him, Bobby!" then a pounding on his back, out came the chunk of meat, onto his plate, and he gasped for air.

The man who had pounded on his back grabbed Manuel by the shoulders and turned him around. He said, "You had us worried there, viejito."

Manny shook his head with self-conscious embarrassment and displeasure but forced himself to smile at the ironic use of "old man."

"Sorry," he said, "and thank you. I'm Manuel."

"I'm Bobby and that's my older brother, Roland." He pointed to a young man wearing thick, black-framed glasses over his lean nose, who had a lazy look to his face and a smirk for a smile. "And that's my big sister, Lizette."

Ah, Lizette of the lovely eyes, and hair, and shoulders and arms. Lizette.

The woman in yellow, now Lizette, made a face at her brother. "You're not supposed to ever mention a woman's age," she scolded.

"I'm sorry I interrupted you all," Manuel said. "Pleasure to meet you."

Bobby said, "Hey, you brought some excitement along. Never saved a man's life before." The table laughed and Manuel felt his face go hot. He nodded then paid attention to the food on his plate. Between bites he glanced around. He felt like he was a member of a crowd scene in one of those movies he occasionally accompanied Amparo to watch, those where there's a crowded dance floor in an elegant night club. That's how Lizette's presence made this church basement feel.

"Which church are you all from?" he asked, knowing the answer.

"Iglesia de Dios, Goleta," Roland answered.

Manuel looked around at the table, their faces, intent upon his own, settled on Lizette's and said, "I've never heard of Goleta, where is that?'

"See, I told you," Roland said. "These people in Los Angeles know only Los Angeles, like there's not a world outside of them."

Lizette said, "But we don't know much out of our own high school, Roland, so what are you complaining about?"

"That's not true! Hollywood this, and Hollywood that. Rita Hayworth this, Gilbert Roland that." Then to Manuel, "You ever see any movie stars? Susan Hayward? Kim Novak?"

Manuel looked at them, peered around at the rows of tables and chairs and said, "Around here?"

They all laughed.

Roland began talking about the movie stars he'd want to see. "Elizabeth Taylor. If I saw her, I think I could die happy."

Bobby interrupted. "Goleta's just past Santa Barbara, you know where that is?"

"Sure," Manuel lied.

"Farming town, near the beach. It's not bad."

Roland nodded. "It's all right, I mean, at least the Mexican part isn't too bad."

Manuel took a bite of the rolled flour tortilla in his left hand and shoveled another mouthful of food in while listening to the group talk about people Manuel didn't know. Then about what they were going to do with the church bus that broke down just as they got here.

Roland said, "We stopped three times on the way down here, and I don't want to get stuck in the night on the road. No sirree. I've heard about these Los Angeles cops."

The memory of the cop in Roseville still burned him.

"There's plenty of mechanics here," Manuel said. "Easy, let me find someone for you."

Manuel hunted through the dining tables and buffet table for Isaac, his age, who had dropped out of seventh grade to help his father at the auto shop, stopping to accept the slice of pineapple banana cream pie Hermana Gladys offered him. She patted her hands together and said, "I like seeing you here, Manolito. So does your Tía. This is such a hard time for all of us and you're a good boy. She is so proud of you."

Is she? Was she? Would she be?

A good boy, the phrase echoed, but he couldn't place it and pushed the thought aside as he went outside, looking for Isaac.

While Isaac and his dad worked on the church bus that looked as if it had been driven thousands of miles over thousands of years—the tires were terrifying, the rear and front lights miswired—Manuel helped with the others stacking the chairs, folding the tables, pulling off the tablecloths, sweeping up. Whatever Lizette was doing, Manuel watched, but not too closely. He didn't want to her to be conscious of his attention. He just wanted to enjoy watching the way her arms and torso moved, the way she frowned at a task or laughed at a friend.

She was a star in a Friday night movie, and he had the pleasure of watching her.

A crowd had gathered around the worn church bus; Manuel watched Lizette in a group of other young women. She laughed long and deep and Manuel was suffused with pleasure in her laughter.

What was he thinking, dreaming of her?

He was a slab of mud, surrounded by sweat and dirt and ugliness.

She lived by the sea and wore dainty things and laughed with dainty women. He was seaweed.

He lived in Chavez Ravine with its dirt roads and rundown homes. And even that, for how much longer?

She lived in the exotic town of Go le ta. Cerca de Santa Barbara. Foreign, exotic, glamorous and glorious.

He stepped away from the crowd and went back down to the basement. Roland sat at the remaining table, leaning over a slice of pie that he was devouring quickly. The room was empty of women, and Manuel caught an air of furtiveness in Roland's dessert. As he approached, Roland looked up guiltily, then, realizing it was him, looked back at his pie, finished the last bite, swallowed then belched with a display of pride and sense of accomplishment.

"Does Lizette have a boyfriend?"

"My sister?" Roland made a face of horror against the suggestion, mashing his fork against the remaining crumbs on the plate.

Manuel went up the stairs more lightly than before. There was a sliver of a smile on his face. Maybe Goleta was closer than he thought.

On the street Isaac and his dad removed their heads from the guts and underbelly of the bus while the driver pushed the passenger door inward, seated himself fussily in the driver's seat, and turned the key.

Nothing.

Isaac, the dad, and the driver started shouting conflicting directions at each other; Manuel watched Lizette.

Manuel heard the bus's engine roar, with a gust of dirty exhaust sailing into the crowd: Lizette laughed and hugged a friend.

This was how these gatherings ended, the food packed up and redistributed so everyone had something with them at home, the older men and women gathered in the courtyard, gossiping, flirting, children scrabbling around the basement and sanctuary, the smell of old wood and cold stone in the air.

All the visiting congregants would go back, taking a Sunday drive through dirt roads, scenic roads, dusty roads to Stockton, Lompoc, Bakersfield, Goleta.

Small groups hugged and waved at each other; a handful of people Manuel knew started up the hill back to their homes in Chavez Ravine, the peak of City Hall pointing them in their direction. Like a guiding star, Manuel had thought as a child. Now, as one of the countless pastors had mentioned, he was a man, and he put aside childish things. Now he saw the building loomed as if to demonstrate its power over their lives.

Amparo and the neighbors stayed and chattered and smiled and gossiped or flirted with the new faces who they would see next year. Manuel heard condolences about the congregation moving. But to where?

Lizette now wore her own pair of white lace gloves, with a shiny yellow purse in the crook of her arm, and her other arm through that of the woman in the floral dress. Her friend? A cousin?

He felt his tongue grow thick, his legs and arms go numb, but he trudged forward. He couldn't tell if the look on his face was a horrid leer or a sad smile, but he made it anyway as he made to say farewell to Lizette.

"Con permiso," he said to her friend, then, "Are you two sisters?"

The friend laughed and said, "Primas."

He prodded himself to keep speaking, but now he felt all his burro parts blending into one tonto, the perfect idiot.

"Lizette," he attempted. She looked at him, curious, an arched eyebrow. "I would like to visit you and your brothers, your parents, in Goleta."

"Would you?" There was a smile on her face, but he didn't feel she was laughing at him. "Handsome men are always the boldest. Look, Manuel, you'll be disappointed. My brothers never really gather all together, except for this weekend. And my mother"—the girls looked at each other—"won't be there either."

"Can I visit you on a Saturday?" Manuel tried to ask as smoothly and as debonair as possible, just like men in shiny suits spoke in the movies, with confidence and swagger, knowing the girl they adored adored them back, but it came out as a cough and Manuel was embarrassed. The bus horn sounded, and the clusters of idling people scattered, regrouped at the car entrance.

"You are fresh!" she said. The bus honked again. "We need to go."

Manuel said, "I need to see you again."

Lizette looked at her companion then back at him and said, a slight smile at the corner of her mouth, "My father's name is Felipe Ojeda. He's in the phone book." She pulled her giggling companion along and pushed past him.

Isaac came up to him and slapped Manuel on the back, as he watched Lizette board the bus with the brother and cousin.

"That was not so easy, but it's done," Isaac said. "I just hope they get tires on that old bus, and soon. I told the driver to go real easy on turns and curves. One skid..." Isaac shook. "I hate to think of all those girls splattered against the windows."

Manuel glared at Isaac. "Don't say such a thing!" He was horrified. "Can they make it home?"

"Sure, sure," Isaac said, "but after that—they better take care of the bus."

The bus backfired black smoke and stirred up clouds of dust as it drove off. She had called him handsome.

CHAPTER THIRTEEN

All week long, Manuel floated on the memory of Lizette, the yellow dress, the warm skin, the way she had half smiled at him, the way she had called him handsome. "Am I handsome?" he wondered, inspecting himself in the small bathroom mirror. Taller than when he left high school for the docks, his arms, and legs long, lean, and muscular, his face—was his face handsome? A long nose, high cheek bones, all burnished by the sun. To himself, he looked like a man without a sense of humor. Like Toño—a man with serious things on his mind. Building things.

He laughed at himself.

Would he call her today? That was the game he played with himself, ever since he dropped into Jerry's corner store and dialed Goleta information for Felipe Ojeda's number. "Home or farm?" the operator had asked, and he'd requested both. Was it too soon to call, or was he too nervous?

What he did know well enough was not to tell Nick anything about it, he'd turn Lizette into something ugly and vulgar.

And then there was the notary. What he wanted to do was to visit Horace every day, but he stopped himself. He limited his visits to Saturdays, when the docks were still and Horace's lobby stuffed with humble and miserable-looking people. Brown like him. He probably looked humble and miserable too. What kind of options did he have?

He'd poke his head in, and Horace would look at him, shake his head, and Manuel would leave.

The time waiting for a response, any kind of response, made Manuel feel as if he were a child again, a child who has no idea what time is, where the direction of time flows, how long hours and days are.

At work Nick said, "He took your money, man. That's all he did. That's all you've got to show for it, a coupla ads that set him back ten dollars maximum."

Two weeks later, when Manuel finally decided to call Lizette, both numbers rang and rang and rang. Ni modo, he thought.

He made his way to the notary and sat in the lobby, even after Horace shook his head at him, and instead insisted on waiting to see him. He penciled his name on the piece of paper on the clipboard and waited, along with the others, trying not to spend too much time wondering at and examining the girls who came and went.

But Horace had helped with the eviction notice. He had also helped the Arechigas and the Lopezes. He got Amparo an extension, a filing, a court date.

But what of Manuel's family?

Why hadn't anyone answered the phone at Lizette's? Was that really her father's name? Had she set him on another wild goose chase? He sat sullen and miserable, Nick's words repeating in his head, waiting two hours until a young man led him into Horace's office.

"How can I help you today, Manny?" Horace asked, scratching the back of his neck, his thinning black hair stiff with gel and brushed sideways across the top of his skull. The even, almost gentle tone he used goaded at Manuel. Nick was probably right, wasn't he?

"You could help me by giving me back the money I already gave you. You been sittin' here the whole time, and I got nothing to show for all that money. You think it's easy for me to scrape that together? You want me to tell how many crates I needed to move, how many days of work that was? And you sit here all nice and clean and unbothered. And I've got nothing at all for those $250. I say, give it back."

Horace took a deep sigh and pushed his swivel chair back from his desk.

"I always tell myself not to take these cases on. I always tell myself, the last time is the last one. Sit down, I'll be right back, I got plenty to show you."

Manuel sat, then stood angrily, then sat back down again. He gnawed at a rough patch of skin on the back of his thumb, until Horace appeared, smooth, unruffled, with a tray of envelopes.

"There's nothing worth sharing with you, yet. But since I clearly didn't explain things well enough to you, here, see for yourself."

Manuel picked up an envelope addressed to a post office box.

"Dear Sir," the letter began, "I can help you find your loved ones." He looked at Horace. Why had he kept this away from him?

"Keep reading," Horace said.

"Last night, in a vision, I saw them clearly. If you contact me, I am sure I can find them for you. The landscape was familiar..." The letter writer gave his name and phone number.

Manuel opened another. "Dear Sir: I have the gift of second sight, and am well-skilled in finding people others cannot."

And another. "Dear Sir: God told me to write to you and offer you my gifts as a sign of His love..."

And another. "Dear Sir: In these trying, desperate times, I am willing to offer you a lifeline and find your beloved people. Since childhood I have had the ability..."

Manuel looked at Horace. "All these people can find my family?"

Horace shook his head and sat down. "So what do you need me for, am I right? No, Manuel, none of these people can find your family, but they can promise you that they can. And they will claim to look, to talk to God, or the spirit world or the occult, and ask you for offerings on behalf of your family, or have you pay them to remove a curse, or have you pay them for the right prayer, that is somehow just on the tip of their tongue. They won't, of course, put it so boldly. They'll make recommendations, suggestions, and tell you where you can find the right piece of jewelry to conjure your family together..."

Horace sighed, and to Manuel he now appeared tired, sad, even. "In English, in Spanish, they have no plans for a family reunion. They only want to separate you from your money. And when it runs out, it will be at the precise instant that they are on the verge of a great discovery. And they will wheedle, threaten, act so dramatically, that you will ultimately do something reckless to get your hands on that last bit of money.

"Then they will disappear, and you will remain, much, much poorer, and certainly in worse shape than you are now."

He poured all of the letters into a cord-handled paper shopping bag. "Here, these are yours. Enjoy." He handed the bag to Manuel. "What you are paying me for is to follow up with a credible contact. We're going to run the ads again. If, within three months we hear nothing, we can talk about what we might do next." Horace now glared at Manuel.

"You know, I did this because of what happened to my uncle. I've done this before for others, and two or three times had some success. I didn't make any promises to you, Manny. You're paid up for the ads ahead. Probably just more of the same. But I am not giving you one cent back. I thought I was doing you a kindness, and now, well, frankly, young man, I feel insulted."

Manuel stammered. "I didn't know. I didn't understand."

"I hope you do now."

Manuel made his way out of the crowded lobby, his face hot and flushed and walked home. He'd check in with Beto, Beto would find a way to make him laugh about this.

Partway up the hill, he stopped. There were tractors, land movers, dump trucks, a lot of dust and noise.

The bachelor shacks were gone.

Manuel moved faster, almost running now, past a few of the newly abandoned homes, past Kiko's, past Jessica's. There was his home, intact, quiet. He walked by and headed to Beto's.

The gate was ajar and the front door open.

Manuel walked up the worn path, up the rough steps, and peered inside, where he had sat at the dinner table with Beto's mother, the reluctant hostess.

The room was empty of furniture. There was debris in the corners, an old, stained rug left on the floor.

Beto and his family were gone.

Manuel was dizzy. The landscape of his life had changed. This was the real world.

CHAPTER FOURTEEN

Manuel continued to drop by the notary's. The ads had stopped; the letters from psychics and fortune tellers continued. Saturday afternoon without much to do, Manuel peered into the office. Horace nodded at him and called him over.

He handed Manuel an envelope. Manuel pulled the letter out of its sheath and read:

> To Whom It May Concern:
> I do have some knowledge of Gustavo and Filomena
> Galvan. I would also very much like to know what
> happened to their children, Victoria, and Manuel.

There was a phone number listed above an address in Bell, and the letter was signed Jean Shiro.

Victoria? Victoria? Manuel's heart started pounding. Victoria. That didn't sound familiar. Her name was Lulu. Who was Jean Shiro?

Horace said, "I think this is promising. I think this is what you've been waiting for." He pointed to his phone.

Manuel called the number. A woman answered the phone. "Is this Mrs. Shiro?"

"This is she." She spoke like a white lady.

He looked at Horace, then away. "You say you knew Gustavo and Filomena Galvan?"

"Yes."

"Do you think we could meet and talk about them?"

There was silence on the line. After a moment Manuel said, "Mrs. Shiro."

"Yes, I suppose so. Why else would I have answered?" They agreed to meet next Tuesday afternoon. Mrs. Shiro gave him detailed directions, which Manuel scrawled on a pad Horace had handed him.

"Congratulations, Manny," Horace said, patting him on the back. Manuel found himself covered in nervous sweat.

"Thank you, sir, thank you," he said.

"You let me know what turns up," Horace said, holding out his hand.

Manuel stared at it a moment, then shook it, too long, then made his way through the crowded lobby.

He didn't know what to do with himself. He didn't know how he would survive until Tuesday afternoon. Maybe he'd catch a movie at the Orpheum?

He walked over to Union Station to see if the trains ran to Goleta, and what the cost was. He stopped at the Greyhound bus station to see how long the ride took and how much it cost.

When he settled on the bus line and time, he'd call Lizette's home from a diner near Union Station—his diner, the one that let him sit at the counter and stare at his mail, where he could walk home, if he wanted. He looked across the street over at Olvera

Street, with its Mexican toys and clothes and food. He thought, what if he were looking at them with new eyes? What if, instead of seeing cheap Mexican souvenirs, Lizette would see it as charming, as proof that Los Angeles was not so unaware of the world?

Lizette was too beautiful to be with him, not even a union worker, a scab, working whatever scraps Nick gave him. He needed to do something else, anything else. Anything legal.

He could have finished high school, at least. He could have tried to be an engineer. Instead, he was nothing.

He was part of a world that was ugly and built by force with grunts and sweat and injuries. A man who worked alongside him last month had his arm broken when a crate came apart while they were lifting it. Manuel had no idea what happened to him, his dark face contorted in pain as others carried him off the job site. And to where?

Manuel opened the phone booth and put a coin in. He dialed the first number the operator had given him. No answer.

Maybe he was a fool, maybe Lizette had played him for a fool.

Manuel sat at the counter and ordered eggs, ham, grilled onions, and potatoes with a cup of coffee. He had a strong sense of pride in being able to sit at a counter that had been wiped down, just for him, handed a menu card, just for him, and a guy or girl behind the counter paying attention to his order. His. No one else's. Like he mattered.

Probably his tip mattered, but that didn't make any difference to the feeling of pride that lived within him when he sat and ate.

Manuel chewed his food, thought on the stories the notary had told him about Mexicans. He remembered that one of the many times Nick had dragged him to a bar and insisted Manuel pay that there had been a sailor there. He told stories of beating up zoot suiters and pachucos during the war.

"Why?" Manuel had asked.

The sailor just laughed, "You had to be there. But if you were, you'd probably get a beating too." Nick and the sailor laughed while Manuel seethed.

After his meal he went back to the phone cabinet and called the second number. This time a voice answered, breathless.

He said, "Hi, Lizette? This is Manuel."

Silence. Did she forget him already? Was she giving him the run around? Was it all some kind of wicked joke?

"Hey Manny, it's Bobby—Lizette's not here right now."

Manuel cursed himself for thinking it was Lizette's voice he had heard. "When will she be there? I'd like to talk to her."

"She's not around, gimme your number, Manny, and I'll have her call you back."

"When's a good time to call her back?"

"I dunno, man, she's always got something going on, you know? We got church all day tomorrow, she's got church stuff tonight—maybe... maybe Tuesday night?"

"Thanks, Bobby. Please let her know I called."

"Will do. You know what they say, you save a guy's life, you're responsible for him."

Manuel snorted before hanging up. Was that the right way to do it? Would Bobby mock his mistake to Lizette? More importantly, would Lizette know how little he knew about anything? He felt stupid again, the warm sense of pride in sitting in this diner, paying his way, vanished from his chest.

* * *

Tuesday morning Manuel navigated his way to the address on the envelope, following the bus directions Mrs. Shiro had given him.

In this neighborhood the sidewalks were paved and even. The yards were still misted with dew in the cool morning, and Manuel smelled fresh cut grass and juniper. The Shiro home looked similar to the house on its left and right. Bungalows with shallow covered porches, a long drive leading to a garage far in the back, circular window high above the door, and a large picture window facing the street. The Shiros' yard was different from the others, not simply a plane of grass, but filled with plants Manuel didn't recognize, with trees and shrubs pruned elegantly. Manuel's anticipation prevented him from recognizing the beauty, but he registered that something was different here, calm and harmonious.

A woman opened the door to him, a Japanese woman, he guessed. She seemed similar to the women he had noticed on the bus, but she was older and stern looking. She dressed in a tidy dress, stockings, and cotton slippers. The shoes paired at the entryway surprised him. But frankly, the look she gave him made him take a deep breath and steel himself, as if she were going to scold him.

That wasn't going to stop him. Nothing would stop him.

"You came about the letter," she said, accusingly.

Looking at her, even though they had spoken on the phone, he was jolted by the way she talked. She looked like a Japanese lady but sounded just like a white lady.

Manuel said, "Yes, Mrs. Shiro."

"Call me Jean," she said. "That's what most folks do. Take off your shoes."

He did, feeling disoriented by her request, worried about the socks underneath, and set his pair with the others. He stepped into her home, right into the front room. The home was quite extraordinary to Manuel. It was carpeted, from the doorstep onward and for as far as he could see to his right and left and through the hallway. A few more steps in and on his left was a shiny wooden dining table surrounded by eight upholstered chairs. He noticed that the house smelled different from what he was used to. Not unpleasant, just different, as if there were spices he didn't know or an unfamiliar perfume or soap.

There was a glass case filled with porcelain figurines. There was a large grandfather clock with a shimmering gold face ticking loudly. There was a fireplace, and on the mantel framed photographs, too far for Manuel to make out. There were two wide and deep sofas covered in thick fabric but soft to touch, and where Mrs. Shiro, Jean, told him to sit. Mrs. Shiro must be quite wealthy, he thought.

"I can get you a cup of coffee or a glass of water, if you like," she said. Manuel did not know this woman, or her ways, and the words seemed to be an offer, but the tone made it sound begrudging. He shook his head. Horace had helped him with this meeting. Don't look like you're asking for something or wanting something. You're just there for information. Whatever you can get. And thank her.

"Thank you for writing," he said. "I don't want to take up too much of your time. I'd be very grateful if you could tell me a little, or all, of what you know about Filomena and Gustavo Galvan?" he asked.

Jean grimaced, hovering above him, then sat heavily down across from him.

"We used to live next to each other, in the apartments over on Slauson, and our daughters got to know each other. We got to know each other. They were a very nice couple, Filomena was a darling thing, with dimples you could swim in. Her English was good, but of course not as good as Victoria's. That's normal."

Manuel felt a weight on his chest and his throat tightening.

He knew Slauson. That close? They had been that close? He cleared his throat and Jean looked at him.

"Victoria is?"

"Filomena's daughter, of course."

"And her husband?"

"Gus?" Now Mrs. Shiro smiled. "Like my husband, he was a hard worker! You know we'd all done picking or canning, it's what people like us could do, you know. Gus, though, he knew how to have fun. He could pick up any instrument and play it, and before you knew it people were moving, or singing, or dancing."

Manuel felt a jolt of surprise. He, himself, couldn't play a single instrument.

Manuel's mouth was dry, and his arms itched. "Could I have a glass of water?" he asked. She frowned as she stood, then returned with two glasses of water and a small plate stacked with pale cookies.

"I made those," she said, in the same way someone else might say, "Eat, if you dare!"

After swallowing half the water in one gulp, Manuel at last asked, "What happened to them?"

Mrs. Shiro's frown deepened. "They went away."

"The family moved?"

Mrs. Shiro shifted in her plush sofa, pulling at a dark green cushion and plumping it without responding.

"Do you know where they moved to?"

She looked at him, cocking her head with angry amusement. "Do you know why I responded to your ad?"

He shook his head.

"Because I want to know what happened to them! What happened to them? One morning Filomena and Gus are there, heading off to work, I walk the daughters to school, while someone comes to her home to take care of the little boy."

Manuel felt a pang.

"I went to their school that day, I picked up Jenny and Victoria. We went back to their place, but Filomena was not there, the young girl who took care of the boy was there, and she told me she would wait for Filomena to return."

Mrs. Shiro looked at Manuel sternly. "But they did not return." She picked up a cookie, placed it on a saucer, and perched the saucer on her lap. "By nightfall the girl knocked on my door. She didn't speak English like Filomena, but Vicki, Victoria, asked me if I knew where her mother was, where her father was, and all I could hear was the little boy in the apartment crying like a nightmare."

Manuel's throat was dry; he drank the rest of the water. "What did you do?"

She shook her head. She ate the rest of the cookies and swept invisible crumbs from her skirt.

"Did they come back?"

Mrs. Shiro glared at him. "There's that young girl who's not much, and whose English is worse, there's my Jenny, Filomena's daughter Vicky, and their son Manolito, a small boy who won't stop crying. Everyone came into my tiny apartment, then my husband came home. Too much noise for one tiny place!"

"What did you do?" Manuel asks as calmly, as quietly as he possibly can. His throat is scratchy, his chest is scratchy, it's as if he will die. He will die. He will, just not right now. He has to know first.

"We did what good American citizens do," she said, primly. "We did what good, upstanding people in this world do, when they think the world is organized, orderly, and just. We called the police. When I told her this, the young girl slipped out the door and left me with the children. Now the children are all crying, my daughter as well, and when the police arrived the two officers who wanted to know if we are all citizens."

Manuel watched her face glower with the memory. "Citizens! My husband looked for our paperwork and I went to Filomena's apartment to find theirs. And I did—I find the children's birth certificates and show the papers to the police officers who huffed and puffed a bit."

Jean Shiro stopped.

"And then?"

She shook her head angrily.

Manuel realized she was angry at the memory, not at him. "What happened then?"

"The officers told us that they will have to take the children to a social worker, or to foster care, or something like that. And my husband nodded his head, and I started arguing with all three of them." She shook her head. "And my husband took me aside into our tiny bedroom and tried to calm me down and said this is for the best. He said, 'What if Filomena and Gustavo are dead in an accident, what if something terrible happened?' and I said, 'Something terrible *did* happen, or they would be here right now!' I argued with my husband, I don't know for how long. A long time. I wanted to keep the children with me, at least for that night, until we could find out what happened. It's simple, it should be simple. But I couldn't do this on my own, I needed my husband to agree, and at last he finally agreed!"

Here is the secret of his life, he thought, told by this angry woman.

"Then my daughter started crying, 'Mama!' We stepped out of our bedroom." Jean paused. "All the children were crying, the officers told us they have to take the kids. My husband and I argued with the officers. Only then did my husband say we would take care of the children. The officers said no. This is a matter of national security. And they took the children away."

The neighborhood was silent. Manuel heard the thumping of his heart.

"What did you do then?" He examined the plush carpeting at his feet. He purposefully tried not looking at the woman who sat across from him, the emotion on her face was terrible. She left the room.

He did not expect police officers. He could not remember any other officers in his life, except for that time with Peludo.

Jean was gone for a while. He stood and scanned the room, the photographs, the porcelain in the display case, the cookies on the fine plate, as if there were any more clues here in this silent room. A man and woman in kimonos, he assumed this was Jean and her husband. A young girl with a dazzling smile and glasses, he assumed this was their daughter Jenny. The young girl, older, in a cap and gown. Same glasses.

He wanted to shatter that.

Mrs. Shiro returned, sat down, apologized, and began to talk again.

"You think—You say to yourself, this is America, this is the country where we do things right. Or at least tries to do things right. That is what I believed. We knew not all things are right, we all knew that—my husband, Filomena, and Gustavo. We had all been in strikes together, and there was head knocking and injuries and violence. But afterward you think to yourself it was a kind of mistake. A misunderstanding, the police didn't understand that it was people they were supposed to be protecting, people like me and Filomena, on the street, not the people hiding in their buildings, hiding behind blankets of money and banks. You make excuses for them. If they only understood the truth, it would all be different." She looked down at her hands in her lap.

"There must have been a mistake, there must have been a misunderstanding, I thought, when the children were taken.

The next day, all that week, I went to the station, the one that was near us, and I told them who I was looking for. At first, they said nothing. I stayed there. Then they said that the children are with social welfare. I went to social welfare. I waited. An afternoon. A day. Days. And then they said, they said..." Jean Shiro struggled to compose herself. "They said since I am not family, they do not have to tell me anything at all, ever." She clenched and unclenched her fist.

"And the parents?" Manuel whispered.

"They never returned," Jean said. "They never returned."

"What did you do?"

"I looked for them," she said. "I looked for that babysitting girl. And I thought if I could reach the children, I could keep them for Filomena. If I could keep the children, I could find Filomena and Gustavo. I kept waiting for letters from them, for letters to tell me where they were, and what we could do. I couldn't find her. I talked to neighbors. They didn't know. But then, you know about Pearl Harbor, right?"

Manuel nodded, Toño had enlisted. There was a problem with the Japs, Japanese. Like this lady?

"I had been looking, talking to people for over a year. I tried looking for the children, but they really wouldn't tell me anything. Ever. After Pearl Harbor happened, things happened to us. Shameful, terrible things that my husband and I try to forget. Things about this country, you probably don't know, never heard of, never thought of, but people like me, we know."

Manuel said, "What do you mean?"

"What happened to Filomena and Gustavo was a warning. I should be grateful, we should be grateful they let us keep our children. After Pearl Harbor Americans hated people like me," Jean's voice was stern and commanding. "Japanese people, Issei, Nissei, all of us, Buddhist, Shinto, Christian, all of us. Strangers scowled or worse at me and my daughter on the street. It was terrible. But what happened next was worse."

She picked up a cookie then set it back, shaking her head. "It is so strange. I can sit here in my comfortable house. You like this sofa? We found someone to make it, just right, Mexican fellow, made it just the way I like it. You see this carpeting? Ridiculously expensive. Ridiculous. I wanted it. You see." She took her house slippers off and rubbed her feet across the carpeting. "For three years we lived in a barracks with dirty wooden floors where the wind and rain and snow got through the cracks in the wood. We lived there with dozens of others, just like us in the only way that mattered to Americans. We had Japanese blood in our veins."

Her face was dispassionate, disconnected.

"They told us to pack a single bag and get on a bus, and first they housed us like livestock at the Santa Anita race track. To this day I won't drive by there, swear to God. Then they put us on a train and another bus and by that time even the men are nervous, biting their lips, sucking their teeth. We didn't pack any food because we could only take one bag per person!" She shook her head.

"You don't want to hear this. I don't want to tell you this. It has nothing to do with Filomena or her children. It's just that, I think that what happened to Filomena and her family told us everything about this country. We just didn't want to recognize it."

"I don't understand."

She shrugged. "No one does when I go on like this. My husband doesn't, my daughter doesn't, they want to put it all behind them, forgotten. I can't forget."

Now her eyes were sad. "You look just like Gustavo," she said. She stood and left the living room. Manuel wondered if he was supposed to leave, if this was her way of making him go, but he waited. He gnawed at the cookie, but it tasted of nothing. He got up and stepped into the kitchen, refilling his glass of water. The kitchen was white counters and cupboards and a gleaming white and chrome stove. From the window he could see the paved driveway, the garage, and the neighbor's home, with its blinds shut against the outdoors. He returned to his seat on the sofa, this time taking time to inspect the photographs on the mantel.

Jean Shiro returned, holding a snapshot in her hand. She said, "I'm sorry this is all I have. I'm sorry I'm not any more help." Her tiny frame maneuvered him to the front door. "I've given myself a headache, I need to lie down now." He was so surprised he was unable to ask another question or thank her again. He walked down the concrete steps in his socks, his shoes in one hand, the photograph in the other.

A younger, slimmer version of Jean smiled brightly, tilting her head against that of a pretty Mexicana with deep dimples and perfect teeth. What he assumed to be Jean's husband smiled casually, standing next to Jean. Standing at the far end was a solemn-looking man with only a hint of a smile on his long, lean face, darker than the rest, his hair combed back in the style of the day.

Change the hair and it was like looking at himself. He sat down hard on the curb.

For the first time in his life Manuel had a photograph of his parents.

CHAPTER FIFTEEN

When Manuel told Amparo the story and showed her the photograph, she began to weep. "How much pain, son," she said, "they have in losing you."

She dried her face. She propped the picture up, inspected it. "He is certainly your father," she said. "Look at his eyes, that nose! Those strong arms. He has a sparkle, too! Look at your mother, how sweet she seems. God brought this to you."

He covered his face with his hands as she began to pray. To him, God was dead. What did his parents think, without him and Victoria? What did they believe?

Amparo prayed, thanking God for the abundance of this sole snapshot, and Manuel couldn't help thinking it was so much, and so little.

Wednesday morning as he stood at the docks waiting for his assignment, he realized he hadn't called Lizette. He ran off during lunch, found a phone booth. The phone rang and rang and rang.

After work outside of the notary's, he made another call. Again, the phone rang and rang and rang. Each ring was like a death knell. He had blown it. He had ruined his chance with her.

* * *

At the notary's Manuel signed himself in, but Horace waved him on through.

"How did it go?"

Manuel held the photograph out to him.

Horace let out a low whistle, then nodded to himself. "I had a feeling about that one. Good for you, Manny. Good work."

Manuel watched as the notary bit into his ham sandwich, mayonnaise leaking out of the sides, dripping onto the desk. The notary mopped it up with a paper napkin. He grunted.

Manuel said, "My sister's name's Victoria Galvan. I wish I had a picture of her, too."

The notary chewed another pepper and stuffed the last of his sandwich into his mouth, then patted his face with his handkerchief.

"But you've got something there with your sister. Victoria Galvan. You think she was two, three years older than you?"

Manuel said, "Victoria. And I should've asked Mrs. Shiro."

"Easy to slip out of your head, easy to choke it, after all this time, I imagine. You can call her and ask. In fact, you should." Manuel felt like a fool as the notary continued, "So let's say, two to four years older than you, a spread." He looked at the ceiling, moved his lips around, blew through them. "This would require digging through public records, county services."

"What do you mean, county services?"

"Looking through marriage certificates, death certificates, adoption papers. No guarantee she's even in LA County, though, so might have to expand the search. And, again, no guarantees."

He wrote a figure on his pad and pushed it toward Manuel. "Half to start. The second half to keep things going. Absolutely no guarantees. Can't make you promises for things I can't control."

The figure was $2,500.

"You might as well ask $10,000," Manuel said. "I don't have anything like that."

"I understand, kid. That's my rate. We could get lucky, we could come across her info sooner, rather than later. But it could cost that much, and there's no guarantee." Horace looked at him pointedly. "I wanna be up front with you. I don't need your money, but that's how much it would cost. That's what I'll do it for."

Manuel stood. "Is this the only way?"

"It's the only way I know," the notary answered.

He called Lizette for a week. It was Roland who finally answered. "Nah, she ain't here, Manuel," with a devastating finality. Manuel hung up.

* * *

He was a slab of mud that worked with other slabs of mud, loading and unloading banana bunches, crates. His arms and back ached and his mind blurred. Lulu was Victoria Galvan? His sister's name was Victoria Galvan.

He read the papers, *La Opinion*, the *Herald*. He went to Terminal Annex on Alameda, near Union Station, and got a post office box. Despite what he had told Amparo, like the notary, he put ads in the papers. Fresno, San Francisco, San Diego. He didn't have $1,000, but he had money for ads.

He continued to work on the days Nick deigned to tap him for it. He hated working for this brutish man, and he despised himself for being too chicken shit to stand up to him or quit.

The port had been a way out of school, but Manuel didn't see himself there forever, couldn't see himself at Nick's whim for years to come. Even if he didn't get into the union; there had to be something else for him.

He just didn't know what.

Within days the post office box started to fill with letters, in Spanish and English, similar to those the notary had shown him.

Manuel took thick bundles of envelopes to the diner, flipped through them, opened them up. He set aside those that were clearly grifters, the psychics, those mentioning God or visions, to the side. He figured if God wanted to announce his sister's presence through visions, God might as talk directly to Manuel.

Each day after work he stopped at the post office. Each afternoon he felt dread and anticipation argue with each other as he opened the brass door with his key and retrieved a few envelopes, or saw nothing there at all.

He sat at the diner with a cup of coffee or an RC Cola and opened and read the letters. He had a particular disdain for the psychics, for those who referenced God and visions. He hadn't realized there were so many ways to separate him from his hard-earned money, the labor of his back and arms and legs, and stiff neck and aching head. Who knew that there were so many Victoria Galvans in the world?

There were a couple that said they knew where she was, or who she was. He started with the letters that claimed to be her and pulled out a roll of dimes and headed to the phone booth.

It seemed forever for the call to go through, for a voice to pick up, a voice barked, "Yeah?" then yelled for "Vickie!" then silence.

He was hung up on.

He called back. This time the person at the other side picked up quickly.

"Hello?"

"I'm looking for Victoria Galvan."

"Speaking."

He asked her parents' names.

"Plutarcho Gomez and Chepita Raigoza."

"Wait," he said, confused, "What about Galvan?"

"Oh," she said, "That's my second husband's name."

He hung up in frustration.

Another Victoria Galvan spoke only Spanish. He learned from her that she had six younger brothers and raised them all in Zacatecas.

No one he called mentioned missing or looking for a younger brother. One by one, he called the culled candidates. One by one, they revealed themselves to be the wrong Victoria Galvan.

* * *

Amparo came home late that afternoon, after the sun had set. Manuel sat listening to a baseball game on the radio.

Amparo had framed the unexpected miracle of a photograph, and it sat in their living room. Manuel glanced at it each time he entered the room, and he spotted it now.

She stepped into their home and looked at him in the lamplight. Neither of them said a word, but Manuel swiftly pulled the shopping cart up over the steps, into the home by the kitchen counter area.

She placed a piece of paper in front of him.

FINAL EVICTION NOTICE, he read and looked up at her.

He said, "We will fight this. *I* will fight this."

"How?" she said. "How are we going to fight this? Our church has done everything they can. People have taken their money and moved, others are staying and fighting." She looked at him. "People are selling out here. We've been told to move, Manolito, you know that," she continued, as if not hearing him. "It seems the first people who sold got the most money. Maybe I should have then. How was I to know?"

"Nobody knew."

"My friends and I," Amparo said, "we weren't going to move, but even you can see we have no choice. Do you know how much they're offering us?"

Manuel shook his head.

"$7,000."

Neither spoke. Manuel looked at the worn wooden table that he had known since childhood. He looked at the wooden floor, the door to a room that was once a closet, but that friends of Amparo had added on and built his bedroom. He had watched them, then helped them, sighting the boards, chalking the edges, pounding, then painting. That was years ago, now. He glanced around the kitchen. This world he had known since childhood.

"But where would we go?" he said.

Amparo sighed. "Toño's. I've been talking to my son. We can live with him and his family in Whittier. You would decide where you would go next." Manuel nodded. "Sooner or later, son, I will sell the house. I can give you the money. You can take it and find your family."

He shook his head. "No. I can't take your money," he choked on the words. "I can't."

She stood and walked behind him. Manuel felt her arms on his shoulders, her head on him. "I will give this to you."

"It wouldn't be right. It's not right. I can't."

He stood and hugged her, the side of her face pressed

against his heart. He held her; Tía smelled of butter on freshly made flour tortillas and cinnamon coffee.

He whispered to her. "You have given me so much. I can't take that, too."

He hated money then, with all his being. He hated what it represented, he hated its lack.

He stepped away from Amparo and picked up the framed photograph of his parents between his hands.

He looked at their two uneaten plates of food on the table. Amparo swiftly picked them up and placed them in the oven.

One day, he'd be hungry again.

One day, he'd stop thinking that his life was a cruel joke.

"Thank you, Tía," he said. "God only knows where I'd be without you."

"Only God can care for you," she responded.

"No, Tía, that would be you."

CHAPTER SIXTEEN

Manuel slipped into Jerry's store and made a call. This time someone answered.

"Hello?" The voice was sweet, liquid.

"Lizette? This is Manuel. From Los Angeles."

Silence.

"Manuel. How lovely to hear from you. How are you?"

Was she teasing him? It was so hard to talk to people over the phone. "I'm good. No, actually, a lot has been going on here. I'd like to tell you about it, in person, if I could. I was hoping"—he let it all out in a rush—"I could take the bus and visit you and your family this Saturday?"

They both let his words hang in the air. It was forever. She could say no. She should say no. But all he wanted was to see her face again.

"Whatever for?" she said, her voice light.

"To assure myself you're as beautiful as I remember."

She laughed.

"The bus gets there at ten, and then I'll take the three-thirty bus home. I can meet your family."

Still no answer.

"What do you think, Lizette? Mi reina?"

"I think," more silence, "I can show you downtown Goleta. My brothers and I will be at the station waiting for you, Manuel. G'bye."

Thursday Manuel spent the day unloading and stacking crates and thinking about the Saturday to come. He kept the picture of Lizette in his mind, beautiful and radiant, her skin clear, her teeth so white and even, a smile only for him.

He was planning on keeping all his Friday pay for his expenses, in order to take Lizette somewhere nice, somewhere she deserved to be taken.

Something, certainly, better than the diner at a café counter.

He needed a better job. He admired the shipbuilders at the docks. He was mesmerized by the welders in their thick masks protecting against the sparks. It didn't even have to be at the docks. Bethlehem Steel was inland. A union job. That's what he wanted. He'd reach out to Beto—he always knew someone.

Another job, Lizette, Amparo, their home—there was too much going on in his brain.

On Friday at the docks, it was barely possible for him to hide his impatience with the hours ahead of him. He put all the energy he had into his work. Today instead of unloading from the docking port, the cranes swung containers over them at a quick pace.

The crane teetered, the container swung wide, a cable snapped, and the container arced above the men who scattered or crouched as the cargo landed with a heavy thud on a bed of mud. Stunningly, no one was hit.

"Our reflexes are getting too good for that crap," a worker muttered to Manuel.

Standing in line waiting for his pay, Manuel off-handedly

asked Nick, "You know, we could have someone double-check the fittings for the crane, I mean, how much more time would that take? Maybe the crew is tired, or lazy..." The look on Nick's face stopped him. Nick called him out of the waiting line and pulled him to the side.

"You got a problem?'

"No," Manuel sputtered. "Just, you know, a coupla guys got hurt a while back. It was a relief no one did today when that crate slid off." That's all he was saying.

At the end of the day the pale, green-edged man behind the cage counted out bills and pushed them toward Manuel. Nick had come up alongside him, picked up all his cash out of Manuel's hand.

"Taking a collection for those fellows who got hurt," Nick said, with a smirk.

Manuel tried to laugh, thinking it some kind of bad joke. Nick wouldn't be giving any money away, he'd be using it at the bar, and later for one of the girls who worked the men at the bar. He'd seen it plenty of times.

He made a move for his money, and Nick stepped back, laughing, shoving the bills deep into his jacket.

"Knock it off, man," Manuel said. "Give me my money." He had a date with Lizette.

"Your money? Your money? Where you think you'd be without me steering this your way?"

A group of men paused to watch them.

Manuel said, "You already get your share for that."

"Yeah, well, things change." Nick watched him. Hell, he was testing him. What was the test this time? Manuel was sick and tired of this. All he wanted was his pay, to head home, to dream of Lizette, and to see her, tomorrow.

"Come on, man," Manuel said, feeling fury begin in his chest.

Nick backed up, "You been sucking on my titty for the last three years. This is the membership fee."

All the rage in his body against this brutal man who stole his money to drink and screw, all the incoherent frustration in his heart from a dead-end job unfurled in his chest. His arms shook in anticipation, and with the roar of the men behind him, Manuel inhaled, leaned, and charged against Nick.

He hated this animal. His force surprised Nick, who staggered back and tried to regain his footing.

The shouting of the men surrounding him, their energy was on his side. Now all their bitterness and venom targeted Nick. The shouts gave him hope, strength, and ferocity. He reared up against Nick, his mentor, his traitor, buried his fists in the solid gut, blocked Nick's punches at his face and chest. He hated this man. He hated so many things. Amparo's eviction notice, her useless congregation, and City Hall who looked down on them all. He hated knowing his parents were gone, gone, gone. He hated this, his life.

With each thought, Manuel threw a punch that staggered Nick, over and over again.

An impact and stars—Manuel didn't see the fist, only felt it against his face and the crush of bone beneath. He stumbled back into the line. Someone pushed him forward. He tried to protect his jaw when Nick pummeled him in the gut. Manuel knew he could not fall, he could not fall, or Nick would kick him on the ground and keep on kicking, and keep on kicking through the blood and the snot and sweat streaming on his face, until he was dead.

Nick was every scrap of pain or misery or ugliness he had faced. He would obliterate the man. He would obliterate it all.

Nick was down on the ground, bleeding, and Manuel would have kept kicking, but the men pulled him away.

Manuel was breathless. How had their positions changed? How had *he* come out on top?

The men made way for him as Manuel headed back to the pay cage. "You dig through his pockets," he said, tilting his head at Nick on the ground. "I want my pay."

The pale, green-edged man behind the cage counted out his wages again and said, "Don't come back, you hear?"

Manuel nodded his thanks. Hands clapped his back again and again as he headed out.

It was on the bus home that he passed out, waking only when the driver jostled him, "What? Are you drunk already? This is your stop, man." Manuel startled awake, waved his hand at the driver, and slowly made his way off the bus and up the dusty road home.

He didn't remember the trek home when he woke up. He didn't remember undressing himself, or washing his face, or lying down. He awoke in his room, the white drapes moving with a breeze, the sounds of Amparo's movements in the house.

He blinked. Of course he wasn't going to work today. He patted his right pocket to verify his pay was there—except he wasn't wearing his work pants, of course. He rolled over to get out of bed, get dressed, get breakfast, and was stopped by a wall of pain that was like the weight of a shipping container on his skull. He rolled onto his back, and even that made the pain ripple through his head, down his shoulders, and the rest of his body.

He spent a moment taking inventory. He looked at the knuckles of his fists, found them bruised and scabbed. He gripped his head and prodded for the tender spots; finding too many of them, he just lay there, blinking up at the ceiling.

Despite the pressure on his skull, the bruises on his hands and body, he felt like his world had shifted, and only for the better. Sure, no job, but he could find something. Only an idiot like him would have stayed where he was for as long as he had with that idiot's Nick's ugliness staining him and draping over him like a violent shroud.

He was gone, he was spent, he had left. The docks were over to him. Over.

He touched his face and groaned. His face throbbed, his nose stung. How could he even present himself to Lizette?

Amparo came in with a mug of atole and handed it to him.

"Careful," she said, shaking her head. She prodded parts of his face as he grimaced, then nodded. She checked his skull.

"Take a breath."

He did.

"Anything hurt in your chest?"

He shook his head.

She said, "You are going to be okay, then."

"I have to get going, I'm going to miss my bus." He needed to get on that bus, he needed to see Lizette. He tried sitting up and the pain in his head pulled him back down on the bed.

"That bus has already taken off, Manolito. Today is Monday, Manolito. When you came in Friday night—you made me think of the animals on the road."

"That bad?"

Now her face tightened. "My prayer group gathered Saturday morning. Amalia came back later that day. She knew how to take care of you. She fixed your nose."

Manuel groaned in embarrassment.

Amparo gave him two tablets from her apron pocket. "Take this now." She touched his head lightly, kissed his cheek, and said, "You can't escape me so easily, son."

Something else weighed on him. Lizette!

* * *

When he could get out of bed and walk, the first thing he did after getting dressed was walk to Genaro's Liquor and use the phone there. Jerry winced at him in greeting, his face was that bad.

Lizette's number rang and rang and rang.

He debated whether he should just show up, but he decided against it. Jerry nodded at him as he returned each hour, until, at last, someone answered.

"Hey, this is Manuel. Can I speak to Lizette?"

He heard male laughter. "Manuel, this is Bobby. I really don't think you should." Manuel heard voices in the background. Bobby continued, "I mean, if you are planning on staying alive, I think you should stay as far away as—"

"Give that to me," Manuel heard Lizette's voice in the background, then, on the receiver, "Who is this?"

"Lizette!" Manuel's heart thrummed. "It's Manuel, from the church." Silence. "In Los Angeles." Had she forgotten? "I was supposed—"

"Yes, yes you were. You were supposed to be here that Saturday morning, an entire week ago, and me, como una mensa, was sitting here waiting for you, until I was sitting here worried about you, and now you call, as sweet as honey, as cool as an ice box. Who do you think you are, Manuel?"

He leaned against the store wall, as if she was the one who had punched him in the gut.

"I'm sorry," he said, softly. All those dreams of his, vanished, evaporated. He was nobody, and she was everything. He didn't have a job. He soon might not even have a place to live. Who did he think he was to even dream of Lizette?

"You're sorry. Well, dammit, so am I. I thought I liked you enough to get to know you better. Let me tell you, mister, there may be a lot of things wrong in Goleta, but no Mexican or white boy here has ever stood me up."

He was working his way through her last statement. How many boys had she dated? What did that all mean, and then he realized she had said she wanted to get to know him better. That gave him hope.

"Lizette, it's a long story." Crap. He should have walked to Union Station. He could tell Jerry was listening in. Not that there were many people he'd have to tell. He should have thought about this more. He lowered his voice, "Parts of it are embarrassing. I don't want to tell it to you standing here, talking to the wall. I'd rather tell you in person."

He wanted to see her face, that was what he wanted. And if she didn't want to see him again after that, so be it. "And that's why I'm calling. To apologize. A couple of things happened," he was thinking of his face, "so I can't make it this Saturday, but next week?" He couldn't admit, right now, that without a job he could make it any day of the week. He couldn't face that, right now.

"I'm not letting you in unless you tell me something."

Manuel twisted as far as he could from Jerry and spoke low into the phone. "A big fracaso at work. I thought I was doing the right thing. When you see me, believe me, Nick, the other guy, deserved what he got."

Silence. At last she said, "Listen, Mr. Los Angeles, you write the date on your calendar and memorize it. Because if you mess this one up, I never want to hear from you again."

"I will be there, mi reina," he said.

CHAPTER SEVENTEEN

He worked as a day laborer a couple of days, alongside older and rougher looking men. The docks had toughened his body; he knew how to keep his head down, follow directions, do his share. He dug trenches, he mixed concrete, he tore down shacks and hauled rubble. For now, for now. So that he had some bills in his wallet, so he didn't show up to Lizette's as a bum.

On Friday Amparo had laundered and pressed his best shirt and pants. Saturday morning he shaved, dressed, inspected his face in the bathroom mirror. It was fairly healed up, some scratches, a little discoloration practically blended into his dark skin.

Amparo had gotten up early, as always, and packed him a lunch. He hugged her before he stepped out to walk to the bus depot. "Dios le bendiga," she called out.

His heart was beating and aching in anticipation.

He ate his bean burritos on the ride and watched the sea every time it appeared. He wondered how close to the water

Goleta was. Arriving at the depot answered his question—he could still see the horizon of the water in the distance.

As the bus pulled into the depot, he unfolded the slip of paper where he had painstakingly written down her address, and the directions of how to get to her home, but when he walked out of the bus, there she was, an arched eyebrow and the beginnings of a smile at the corner of her mouth. Golden skin that looked like silk to touch. She wore a soft pink dress, cinched tight at the waist, delicately tailored at the bodice, revealing the soft curves of her chest, and a delicate gold-colored necklace. The skirt blossomed outward, giving Manuel no idea the actual shape of her hips or rear, but none of that mattered, of course, because all he could see was her face, her lips the same color as the dress.

He almost missed the last step, absorbed as he was in spotting her, and he definitely missed that her brothers stood alongside her. Had he noticed, perhaps his appraisal wouldn't have been so obvious, his pleasure in her appearance so evident.

He wanted to hug her, lift her off her feet, and kiss her like he saw in the movies, like she was the leading lady in the movie of his life.

As he approached, grinning madly, her expression changed to scrutiny.

"Is this," she waved at his bruised face, "what you needed to explain to me, in person?"

Bobby and Roland laughed, and Manuel's heart shrank. "Yes, but," and there he couldn't stop himself, "I thought it would be just the two of us?"

Her brothers laughed again, while she looked at him, and shook her head. "Come on," she said. "Bobby's driving."

The four of them piled into the front seat of a rust-colored flatbed truck, Lizette between her brothers, her legs covering

Roland's, to avoid the gear shaft. Manuel squeezed in tight against the closed door.

"Figured I give you a tour of the town," Bobby said. Roland grinned at Manuel, flashing his white teeth, perfect, like Lizette's.

"Never had an entire welcome party," Manuel said, trying to catch Lizette's eye, who stared out toward the left.

Bobby drove them by their old high school, their old elementary school, the main street, and the hardware store where they bought supplies. Manuel paid little attention to the tour, but watched Lizette as best he could. Her legs were crossed primly at the ankles, her toenails painted pink, the strappy sandals stark white.

Bobby stopped the truck with a jolt. "Here we are," he announced. Manuel opened the door and scrabbled out, glancing up and down the main street. Roland pointed at a diner named Rice Bowl, the signage written in Chinese-style brush strokes. They stepped into a busy restaurant, all white tile and chrome.

Lizette led them, snagging the far corner at the counter. He moved to sit on her right, she pointed to her left. Roland sat next to him, and Bobby on the other side of her.

"Pork chow mein," Bobby called out.

"Make it two," said Roland.

Manuel felt he could catch his breath now. He glanced around the diner, with its off-white walls, slight grubby floor. Roland and Bobby were both dressed in gabardine pants and white T-shirts, very different from the Sunday clothes he'd first seen them in. He glanced at Lizette. She leaned on the counter, her arms folded in front of her, the fingers of one hand tapping impatiently.

The soda jerk set a glass of pop in front of her. "Thanks, Joe," she said to the Chinese man who served her, taking a delicate sip. She looked at him, and he felt evaluated, then she smiled. "You like Chinese food?"

"Not sure."

"Let me order for you, then. Two chicken fried rice, please." She turned to him. "You want a coke?" He nodded. She called out, "And another Coke, please." She turned to him. "Now I'm ready for this story." She raised her eyes skeptically. He could feel Roland and Bobby's eyes on him.

Crap, how had *he* not been ready for this? He had been so busy thinking about seeing her.

"I been having some problems with my job. I been working on the docks for three years, nearly four, since I was sixteen." He didn't tell them how he felt pushed out of his high school, how he impulsively left. "Loading, unloading, anything that needed doing. The money was not bad. Good on good days." Lizette watched him so intently he got distracted. Her eyes, so brown, so big, staring straight at him! He cleared his throat. "This Nick guy, he would get me the jobs, and take a piece of my money. Every time." He heard Roland grunt. Bobby made a face and shook his head. "Every time," he repeated. He hadn't told Amparo about this, he figured it was, you know, the price of admission. He hadn't told Beto. He was embarrassed. Staring at Lizette, he couldn't stop himself. He talked about the work, the trolley rides which turned into bus rides, the long stretches of no work at all.

Out came their orders. Roland and Bobby began shoveling noodles into their mouths.

"Then I met you." He paused. Lizette smiled a very tiny bit. "All I could think about was getting my money and bringing you something nice, taking you out somewhere special." The smile remained. He looked down at his plate of food, glazed looking, over unfamiliar shapes. It smelled savory, in a way that made him hungry, and he looked back at her.

Lizette nodded. "It's good, I promise. Then what?"

As Bobby and Roland ate, Manuel explained that afternoon. How when Nick took every last dollar bill, something exploded inside him. "Like he took it away from my Tía, and you," he said. "And we started going at it. In the end he was on the ground, and I got my money back. I made it home. I don't even remember how. And the next thing I knew, I woke up on Monday." Lizette watched him. She hadn't touched her food yet, and neither had he. He said, "Standing you up was the last thing I ever wanted to happen."

On his left, Roland guffawed. Manuel was immediately mortified. He had practically forgotten her brothers were there.

Lizette said, "What a horrible man. It's a good story. Taste your food before it gets cold."

Bobby and Roland started talking over them, something about their farm, their dad. Manuel couldn't say what the food tasted like. He was sitting next to Lizette, her legs crossed next to him, a shiny white purse on her lap, while she ate her food and sipped her Coke.

When the brothers were done eating, they crumpled their napkins onto their plates. Bobby said, "I suppose that was a long way of telling us you don't have money to pick up the check."

"He's not paying for you two," Lizette scolded before Manuel had time to respond. "Pay up. Then take a walk."

"We won't be far," Roland said, setting some bills on the counter. "In case this bruiser gives you any problems," he said, winking at them both.

Manuel paid for their food. The two of them walked up and down the main street of downtown. Lizette pointed out the landmarks of her childhood, the library, the post office, the hardware store. They sat down on a park bench. He inhaled salt air, mixed with her hand soap.

"Now I have seen Chavez Ravine, and you have seen Goleta." She said it like a challenge, and Manuel smiled.

"I like what I've seen so far," he said.

She snorted. "Roland and Bobby want to run the farm someday. It's so much work!" She briefly covered her face with her hands. "I think it killed my mother. I don't know it for a fact, it's just what I think." Manuel reached for her hand, her golden skin as soft as he imagined, felt a tingle through his body, and squeezed. He didn't even know if his mother was alive. He couldn't tell her that now.

She continued, "Bobby's really good at all the ins and outs, the animals, the crops." She pulled her hand away from him. She turned to him and lifted her chin. "I don't want to live and die in Goleta," she said. "There's nothing here for me, I know it. What about you, Manuel? What do you want?"

Lizette, with her huge brown eyes, the delicate lashes, the expressive mouth. He wanted her.

"I want whatever you want, mi reina." Gently, he put his hands on the side of her face, so soft her skin! He pulled her gently toward him and he kissed her, lost in the sensation of her lips, with traces of Coke. He continued to kiss her in full daylight in the middle of the park where even her brothers might be watching and his whole body was on fire. She put her hands on his as she pulled back.

"You don't want to miss your bus home," she said, laughing. "I asked Bobby to drop you off. No use in all of us crowding into that heap again. Next time, I want you to meet my dad."

All the bus ride home Manuel relived his few hours with her. Over and over again.

"You make me believe in God," he wanted to tell her, the thrumming in his body, the humming in his chest, the volts of current charging through his limbs. Alive, alive, alive!

* * *

From the bus stop he walked his usual way up the hill to Palo Verde. Chavez Ravine had been emptying out. He and Amparo were among the handful who stayed. There was a dull pang in his chest that not even the day with Lizette and her family could quell. He and Amparo were still here, but for how long?

He turned a corner and saw Toño's delivery truck in front of Amparo's house. The neighborhood was still, not even birds sang. The houses beside them, once sheltering Amparo's friends, the Vascos, the Casares, their neighbors, were empty. In front of what had once been Tiburcio Vascos' bedroom, a hedge of plumbago grew wildly.

Amparo came out the front door and shook a rug. She spotted him and waited.

"En todo esta, menos misa. Here you are now," she said.

He hurried up around the truck, up the walkway, over the few steps he had crossed, how many times? "What's going on, Tía?"

She shook her head and went back into their home.

Toño sat heavily at the kitchen table. Pots, pans, clothing, linens, were strewn around canned food, dry goods, stacked on the counter and dining table. "She's got to go," Toño said. "You've got to go, too. There's no more time."

"I'm not going," Amparo said, went to her room, and closed the door behind her.

Toño said, "All morning she's been like this. All morning." He shook his head. "You better pack up your things, right? You two will be staying with us." He coughed, scratched the back of his scalp with his good arm, then said, "You know, until you find something. But me and Chrissie are good to have you with us."

Manuel entered his room, aware of how small it was and

how little he had to pack. He lay on his now naked mattress and inspected his room. Was this the last time he would see this stained ceiling? The slats of wood as his walls? He sighed and stood, gathered a pillowcase to shovel his clothing in. He stopped when he heard Toño walk to Amparo's door.

"Ma!" Toño rapped on her door. "Ma! Come on, we've got to go. Let's get this done. Chrissie's at home with the nietos. They want to see you. Chrissie's got your room done up nice, you'll see."

Manuel heard a skeptical snort.

"Ma!" Toño implored.

He heard Amparo walk to her side of the door. "I am not going anywhere," she said. "This is my home. I know everything here. I know the colors of the sun in the early morning, the songs of the birds at night, the way the flowers grow after the rains. I know everything here. Everyone here."

"No one's here, anymore, Ma. Come on. I know. It's hard," he said through the door, softly.

"If you take me away from here," Amparo said, "you are dragging me away from the land, from the soil that I love. You are yanking me, like a weed, a despised weed, to throw on a pile of other weeds, to wither away and die. You are trying to kill me," she said.

To her own son, she said these words, in a tone Manuel had never heard from her before, angry and pleading and sad and desperate.

"Hardly anyone is left here, Ma," Toño said. "They're all already gone."

"Not the Arechigas."

"They will be, Ma, one day soon, they will be gone, too."

The house was still. Manuel waited to hear what Amparo would say, but he heard nothing.

Toño rapped on his door. Manuel opened it.

"Look, can you talk to her? She's sick of hearing it from me."

Manuel nodded, walked the three steps to Amparo's door. "Tía," he said. "Can I come in?"

She opened the door and returned to her naked mattress. Her eyes were puffy and her face was flushed.

"I don't want to go, son," she said, blinking furiously against her tears.

He sat next to her and held her hand. "None of us want to go, Tía."

"It isn't right," she said.

"No, it isn't," he said.

"I thought God would stop this nonsense." She sighed. "But there is so much nonsense going on in the world, and one old woman's home... You'd think it wasn't so much to ask for?"

"I agree," he said. Like praying for your family to return. It wasn't so much to ask for, was it, after all? "None of it is fair, Tía. But I think how lucky I was that you found me. Maybe that wasn't fair, either, maybe someone else should have been here with you, but it was me. And maybe it's not fair that you have a son who gives you a room, and some people don't have sons or rooms. But there you have it."

She looked at him skeptically. "Are you trying to say I am blessed?"

"In a way," he said, "aren't we both?"

She put her hands in her face so he wouldn't see her cry. "No, mijito, not today. Today I wish I was dead."

"Tía! Don't say that!"

"It's how I feel, it's what I will say. I wish I was dead, to not feel the pain of losing this home. My home. Where I raised my sons."

He clasped her hand, and, as so often she or Hermano Sebastián had, began to pray. "Dear God of the Universe:

Please bless my Tía Amparo. Please show her all of your love and mercy, the way she showed me your love and mercy. Please fill her days with blessings and love. Thank you for sending her son to care for her. Thank you for allowing her son to open his home to me as well. Thank you, dear Father, for keeping this family together, as best as you can. In Jesus's name, Amen."

Amparo nodded. Manuel stood and helped her off the mattress.

It took so little time to pack everything up: her cooking pots and pans, her clothing; the bedding, the kitchen table and chairs. Just as Manuel moved the chairs outside, Toño bumped into the curio cabinet and it fell to the floor, scattering the souvenirs, shattering the tiny clay pots.

She gripped his shoulder. "It's all right. I won't need these to remember my son by when I'll be living right with him!"

Amparo spoke softly to her chickens and gently placed them into cages, then covered them with blankets. There was more space than things in the bed of Antonio's truck, so he strapped down the hens' cages.

They moved her potted plants. Amparo had coaxed from the seeds, hidden in their pits, apricot saplings. Tiny, reedy things, but she hoped at least one would flourish in Antonio's backyard. Everything was quickly loaded up. He watched Amparo walk through her now empty home. Toño slammed his truck's door. Manuel watched Amparo open the animal shed, peer in, then step out again. She walked the front yard, then the back. He watched her put her arms around the apricot tree and press the side of her face to its bark. He saw her lips move.

She beckoned him over. He stood and stepped swiftly next to her.

"I will miss my friend here," she said to him. "I will miss the scents of Palo Verde." She looked up at him. "Oh, my great big little one, I see you, a grown man, and yet in my heart you are that little treasure that Hermano Sebastián brought me. I am blessed," she said. "Two men in my life." She cleared her throat. "'To everything there is a season, and a time to every purpose under the heaven.' Our season in Palo Verde is over. Your season with me is nearing its end. Let me say a prayer for us both." This time she prayed for him and herself, saying, "Thank you Lord, for showing us what you meant when you said, 'For to everyone who has, more will be given, and he will have abundance; but from him who does not have, even what he has will be taken away.'"

Manuel hugged her, rubbing her cold, bare arms to keep her warm.

The three of them piled into the truck and headed to their new home in Whittier. Manuel watched Palo Verde recede in the rear-view mirror. Toño's truck spewed dust behind them, but he could see the outline of the hills, the abandoned homes. The matilijia poppies lining the road waved goodbye and the birds seemed louder than the truck. Amparo gripped his hand.

Later Manuel learned that in the following weeks the police pulled the Arechigas and Romeros away from their homes. After that, the city razed all the remaining houses.

CHAPTER EIGHTEEN

Manuel may have been to Toño's home a dozen times or so, but he'd never noticed how much time they spent watching television on the couch, where he now slept. Or how early the twins got up in the morning and enjoyed sitting on top of him, telling their Uncle Manolo the same jokes over and over again. They were cute kids, sure, and Amparo looked almost gleeful to have them all over her. She, at least, had one of the three bedrooms. Toño and Chrissie did all right, Manuel thought. Him too, he thought, a house, a wife, and kids. A decent job. That's what he'd like, him too, please.

For this, he worked any job he could get and took a bus or the train to Goleta on Saturdays. He met Lizette's father, Mr. Ojeda, a squat man who grunted greetings and wore a straw hat outdoors and in.

He'd earned some money, but he gave most of it to Toño and Amparo each week. He wanted to pay his way, but still have something for Lizette. He needed to find a real job.

He and Amparo had lost their home, their neighborhood—but he could only think on Lizette. Thinking of her moved him in a way he couldn't explain. She was the most beautiful woman he had ever seen, the most beautiful woman to gaze back at him, cool and almost challenging. When she looked at him, Manuel felt as if she could see everything, everything. The parts of himself that terrified him; the parts of him that worshipped her. When thought of her, he conjured her smiling face, her body a stream that gently, teasingly, begged him to follow, so he could know her as well as she knew him.

He laughed at himself. Was he making this all up?

She burned in his head, in his heart, in his groin. All he wanted to do was to touch her, to truly have her, to trace every part of her, to discover the parts no one else had seen. To know all of her.

* * *

On Saturday's bus ride, the morning started cool and damp. They traveled over the roads, jiggling along. There was always a group of young people, old people—today a serviceman who resembled Bobby reading a comic book—and assorted mothers and babies. Lizette was at the end of this bus ride.

He helped an older woman with her heavy bag off the bus. "Dios te bendiga," she called to him.

Bobby's rusting pickup waited outside the bus station. "Hey hermano!" he called out. "Need a ride?"

Manuel headed to the decade-old truck, ducked in, and shook Bobby's hand.

They rumbled up the road, Bobby tapping lightly on the horn as he spotted friends along the way. Manuel could only think about Lizette and got so nervous he hauled his knapsack onto his lap, pretending to look for something, then left it there to cover himself. Would she be as pretty as he remembered?

Did he want to touch her, or just dream of touching her? Did he really want her, or did he just want to dream about her?

Lizette stood on the porch, waving.

Through the dust the truck kicked up, Manuel realized there was something different about this woman he'd been wishing on, dreaming on, thinking of this past week.

She stood in serge denim pants that tapered down her legs and stopped short above her ankles. She had a man's blue work shirt on, except she had tied it right beneath her breasts. A shimmer of flat brown skin showed above the waist of her pants. Was that it?

She looked like an actress, a goddess, a movie star pretending to be a common working girl. She looked glorious and playful and then he realized it was the hair. Most of it was no longer there. He opened and shut his mouth, unable to say a word. He was grateful for the knapsack on his lap, hiding his body's response.

She cast him a playful glance, but there was something challenging behind it. She cocked her head. "What, eres una mosca muerta?"

He cleared his throat. "You look like a goddess," he said, struggling to get out of the car without betraying himself.

She smiled. She reached for his hand and pulled him onto the porch.

How could he have ever doubted? No, it was far better to be right here with her, close enough to see the light hairs on her slim forearms, the ribbon of brown skin above her pants' waistline, the eyes that teased, mocked, and adored him. Even Manuel could tell that.

"Where's everyone?" Manuel asked.

"Where I should be," Bobby said. "Over at the ranch party."

"I told you to go," Lizette said, firmly. "I don't feel like it this year."

Bobby said, "Bring your boyfriend, don't be such a pill. Everybody's going to be asking me where you are, and who this novio of yours is."

"And what of it?" Lizette glared. "It's okay. Those ribs are overrated. Dad makes better beans."

Bobby grunted.

Lizette took Manuel by the hand. "Wash up. I know his truck is dirty, and you've had a long trip."

Dicho y hecho, Manuel used the block of white soap with scarred black lines to scrub his face and hands. He did feel better. He smiled at the reflection in the mirror. His heart had been flipping around in his chest since he saw her.

Yes, she was as beautiful as he remembered. Yes, he wanted to give her everything he had. He wanted her for always. He frowned at himself. He had so little. She'd graduated from her small-town high school, as had her brothers. Everyone worked on the farm. Lizette even. She did the accounting. What could he give her?

Lizette sat at the sofa, a magazine in her hands. When she saw him, she patted the place beside her.

She said, "We can go to the dinner. It's fine. I didn't tell you because I didn't want you to worry about it."

Bobby said, "Look, you promise you'll show up in an hour?"

"Of course," Lizette said with a pointedly exasperated look.

"Don't do anything stupid," Bobby said. "Don't get me in trouble with Dad."

"You do that just fine on your own," she answered.

When Bobby left, Manuel got up and pawed through his knapsack. "I forgot something," he said. There was the wrinkled brown bag with a box wrapped in shiny glossy green paper inside.

Lizette looked at the wrapped box and then back at him earnestly. "Did you get a job, Manuel? You can't spend money that you don't have on me. Not for me. Not for anybody."

"I could afford this," he said, thickly. No. He did not get a steady job. He'd been walking and talking, knocking and talking. He'd been laughed at, shooed away, told to stop pestering them, by white men in expensive hats. He looked at crews where mexicanos and morenos worked, or Mexican and chinos worked. He must have tried to talk to a hundred different men. One of the men in an expensive hat recognized him from the docks. They'd unloaded bananas together.

He had tilted his chin at Manuel. "Check in with me next month. I might have something for you."

He wanted to tell all this to Lizette, but it was as if he told her a dream; there was nothing solid to it, only that it was exciting to him that someone recognized him, someone knew him.

He pushed the wrapped gift back to her.

He watched her face as she removed the wrapping paper and lifted the lid. "Oh," she said, softly with a flush of pleasure across her face. "It's beautiful." She dangled the delicate gold chain at him and said, "You put it on."

Before he did, he traced the line of her jaw. So delicate, so strong. She closed her eyes. He traced the hollow of her neck and brushed the chest bones that protruded so delicately. He unclasped the necklace and clasped it again, where all her hair had once been and was no longer.

He kissed the base of her neck. "I like this haircut," he said. She said nothing.

He lightly touched her shoulders, moving closer.

"This is a beautiful necklace," she said.

Then he pulled her toward him and kissed her. Her mouth was toothpaste and coffee, and sweet, sweet lips. He stroked the side of her face as she clutched his arms. He, tentatively at first, stroked the length of her arm, the taper of her waist, reached for her rear, and she pulled him closer.

He kissed her neck, golden in the sunlight. "You are everything to me," he said as he kissed her neck, gently stroked the length of her body both lean and soft, reached for her breasts.

"Not here," she said, "someone might see."

She tugged him, and he followed, thickly, into her room, her bed made neatly, the shades drawn, the room cool. They sat on the edge of her bed. He picked up her trembling hand and kissed her palm.

"Reina," he said, looking at her huge brown eyes. Was she afraid? She didn't have to be. "Reina, we don't have to do anything."

She nodded. "We don't have to do anything, Manuel, in this empty house, alone to ourselves."

He leaned forward and kissed her. They lay down on the bed and he could feel the length of her body, long and lean and firm, against his. There was no hiding his body's response.

He inhaled her scent: she smelled of soap and cinnamon and something that was all Lizette, all her.

They were halfway undressed and he wanted to stop everything, so he could look at her, the slope of her breasts, the tautness of her nipples, the way her waist curved into her hips.

Then he remembered Nick. An awful man, but he had learned something useful from him. He tugged his wallet out of his pants which now lay on the floor, a tiny slender condom packet he showed to Lizette.

"Is this all right?"

She nodded.

Lizette's body was the world made flesh. When he held her, time and his heart stopped. There was nothing outside of them. He wanted this, he wanted her, forever and always.

Afterward she held him and stroked his back, then whispered in his ear, "Let's wash up and head to the barbecue before any chisme starts."

* * *

Once a month Lizette stayed a few days with a family friend, Mrs. Rivera, who lived in Huntington Park. Lizette shopped, cleaned, made meals, and took Mrs. Rivera out to get her hair cut and dyed. Manuel waited all day until it was time to pick up Lizette from Mrs. Rivera's home. Manuel wasn't clear on the relationship. Was Mrs. Rivera a friend of her deceased mother's? A cousin? A church person?

The truth was Lizette knew so many people he couldn't keep the relationships straight. He liked her brothers fine. They were kind and tolerant. He was respectful to their father, Felipe, when he visited their home in Goleta. But all his days he dreamed of his lithe Lizette, the soft, invisible hair on her arms, the crinkle in her eyes when she laughed. He didn't think he was a funny man, but she laughed warmly at his observations of her family's home and he smiled in return. Her luscious, inviting body. He wanted days with her, just the two of them, just each other together. Days, and nights.

Everything was warmth and light and sunshine and brightness and hope and possibility when he was with Lizette.

He wanted always to be with her.

When they had last seen each other, she had said to him, "Let's do something when I visit. I don't want to spend all my time in church basements and pews. Show me your town, show me Hollywood. You know about Thursday nights?"

Manuel was too busy watching her eager and inquisitive eyes to realize he had to answer.

"Do you?"

"No."

"Well, why would you? You're too handsome to worry about the things we ordinary people care about. Thursdays are the maids' days off!"

Manuel waited for more.

"If all those Hollywood stars have no maids to cook for them, they have to go out to supper then, don't they? Let's go out Thursday night and find some!"

Manuel shook his head and laughed.

"Yes, mi reina," he said, kissing the back of her hand, as he had seen in the movies. How much would it cost? The thought nagged at him. How much could he afford? He would give Lizette all he had, yet he had so little.

Lizette giggled and curled into him. Manuel sighed, inhaling her scent, feeling the effect of her body touching his, feeling himself swell and spread, and Lizette giggled again.

"You must like me or something," she said.

He had no idea where to find Hollywood stars! Who would think of such a thing, except Lizette.

He called Beto.

"Pues, wait 'til you see me when I pick you up Thursday night. I want to meet Lizette, and you'll meet my girl, Sharon," Beto said.

Que lujo to be driven through Hollywood!

Manuel stood at the designated corner at six-thirty. The sun was making its slow, late-July descent; the air was warm and dry. He thought of Lizette, how it would be to sit in the back seat of Beto's car together when he was startled by a car horn. Right on the street next to him was a turquoise Chevy Impala with a white top and dazzling fins. The very car Lizette's brother, Roland, dreamed of owning, and Beto's head was hanging out the window. His hair, which had been an unruly curly black tangle as a kid, was now a thick sheen combed back, his face, pale and proud.

"Is that envy on your face?" Beto said, needling Manuel with a knowing kind of smile. "Let me make it worse. Get in!"

Manuel opened the rear door and scooted in.

Beto said, "Sharon, this is my oldest, slowest friend, Manny. Manny, this is my newest and fastest girl, Sharon." Sharon smacked Beto on the arm and turned to Manuel. Sharon had reddish brown hair swept over and flipped up at the side. Her smile was broad and friendly, and her lips deep red. She held out her hand. "Manny, if you don't believe a word this son of a bitch says, neither will I."

"Agreed. A pleasure," he smiled back as she turned to face the road.

"I didn't realize you liked 'em smart," Manuel said to Beto. Sharon grinned.

Along the drive to Lizette's, Beto talked about his job at the car dealership.

"The best thing is," he said, "is that sometimes clients need extended test drives. Know what I mean?" Beto tapped the steering wheel expressively. "Sometimes they need a car while their own car is getting fixed."

Manuel laughed. "This isn't your car! You had me there, viejo. You really had me. Next you gonna tell me Sharon's a loaner, too."

"I prefer an hourly rate," Sharon said, dryly.

When Manuel brought Lizette to the car, she whooped. "Oh my gosh, if Roland and Bobby could see us!" She slid a hand across the fins and took a moment to admire the car.

Beto had wanted Manuel up front with him, and the girls in the back, but Manuel wanted the warmth of Lizette's body next to him. He wanted the sprawl on the back seat to themselves alone.

"Now if you're a good boy, Manny, I'll let you take it for a spin."

"What's good?"

"A round of drinks?"

"I can do that."

"I'm not sure you can—not where I'm thinking."

"Where's that?"

"Beverly Hills. I hear the girls want to see the stars. Why not? Can't say I've ever seen one up close."

"I saw Joan Bradshaw once," Sharon said, excitedly. "She was more beautiful in real life. I held my breath. She was like a dream."

"Who's that?" Beto said. "You two know who that is?"

"Just a gorgeous star," Sharon insisted.

"What's the good of seeing someone no one else knows?" Beto said.

"I knew her, see?" Sharon turned around in her seat to Lizette. "And her dress? I swear it was cut down to here." Sharon pointed to her belly.

Beto said, "Sharon, you get in the back with Lizette while the men talk."

Manuel said, "No, sir, I am right where I want to be."

"It's gonna be like that then? Fine," Beto smirked.

Manuel shook his head and squeezed Lizette's knee. He rubbed his hand across the fabric of her dress, smooth and silky, like her skin. He pulled her closed and kissed her. The dream was real, vivid, flesh between his hands.

Lizette said, "I like this!" She leaned back and stretched herself against Manuel. He wrapped his arms around her and felt a pang. They would need a car. They would need a home. He needed a job, a real job.

Now the pleasure of Lizette's body next to his was marred.

He pulled her hand to his cheek and tried to feel that wordless joy once again.

"Hey, hey, you two," Beto said, "don't get us pulled over!"

"What are you talking about?" Lizette asked.

"Public indecency!"

The world was different from the back seat of a sleek Chevy Impala. Manuel swore the passengers of this car were the object of scrutiny and envy by the pedestrians they passed. A young kid, who could have been himself years ago, scowled at them.

They made their way across Hollywood Boulevard. The buildings looked bright and promising, everyone crossing the street, Manuel was certain, had a purpose, had a mission. Beto took the car up through the hills, carefully navigating the curves, pulling over to let oncoming traffic through, slowing down, then parked.

The four of them stepped out onto the turnoff. Below them were the lights of the city.

"What's that?" Lizette pointed to a round building that looked like a stack of records.

Beto said, "That's Capitol Records. We'll drive by it on the way down. Look over there—that's Pantages Theater. They hold the Oscars there," he said.

They stood in the chill air marveling at the city lights, trying to find their tiny homes, invisible in the distance. Manuel noticed goose bumps on Lizette's arms and rubbed his hands alongside them to warm her. She leaned back into his chest.

"Nothing like this in Goleta," she said.

"Lemme show you all something else," Beto said. They all got back in the car, descended a bit, and, again, Beto moved carefully cautiously up a long winding drive. "Can't get a scratch on this baby," he said, pulling up to a pagoda-like building with men in red vests looking at their car impatiently.

"Just look at the building—see it? Japanese. This place you eat Japanese food. You take off your shoes and sit on the floor on a cushion, see, just like in Japan."

Lizette said, "Are you pulling my leg?"

Sharon said, "No, honey, we been there. Kinda different."

Beto pulled the car around and they set back down the hill. "Capitol Building it is!"

They slowly made their way down the hill. "Look here—see that place? The Magic Castle. Famous magicians from all over come here."

"Can we go in?" Lizette said.

Beto made a face. "Unfortunately, you gotta be a member."

Manuel said, "How you know so much?"

Beto said, "Cuz I want so much."

They parked near Graumann's, walked around the foot and handprints—Manuel felt a certain pride that his feet were larger than Clark Gable's.

The girls danced around and cooed. They stood at the ticket booth to see how much the tickets were. Then they kept walking. Beto and Manuel followed.

They passed others on the street and came to the doors of a restaurant.

"Ah, come on, let's just look," Sharon said, until a man exited, glanced briefly at the group, and held the door open for them all to enter.

They went in. Beto reached for a menu, already shaking his head, the hostess occupied with another customer. Sharon and Lizette chattered excitedly until Lizette said to Manuel, "Did you see who that was? And all by himself, did you see?"

Manuel shook his head.

"Laurence Harvey! Laurence Harvey! We saw a real movie star!" She kissed him.

Beto caught Manuel's eye and rubbed his fingers together. Too expensive. They walked out again, but it was clear that the girls weren't bothered, they were excited by what had just happened.

Beto led them to the Capitol Building, so different in perspective from their view from the hill. The four of them craned their necks, made noises of awe and approval, then started naming their favorite singers.

"Eydie Gormet," Lizette said definitively.

"I love Betty Johnson," Sharon said.

"Girls, please." Beto held out his hand authoritatively. "Sam Cooke. Sam Cooke. Smooth, suave, cool, debonair. He is the king."

Manuel held the door open as the group entered a diner called Dupar's. Beto winked. This they could afford.

Seated in a booth, Lizette looked nervously at the menu, and then looked at Manuel, as if to say, "You have enough money?"

"Order anything you like," Manuel said.

"All right, then. You have set a challenge!"

Manuel squirmed inwardly but enjoyed this sense of largesse. Beto would cover it if it got too bad.

When Lizette ordered coffee and pancakes it sounded so ridiculous yet so good that everyone else followed.

After supper when the girls made their way to the restroom, Beto scooted around the booth to get closer to Manuel. He said, "You know you're crazy, man, right? Look, you're too easy, too good with her." He made a face, scowling. "Serio, you too nice, they get bored. You play a little rough, or maybe you get a little mean, spices things up. Makes them wonder. That's good. It's like bait. It hooks them, you know?"

"Beto, you have your way of looking at the world, and I have mine." Beto's included glossy girls, flashy cars. He didn't want to talk about it anymore and said, "Now, how about you let me drive that car?"

Beto chuckled, hit him on the back, and said, "Sure—let's hit Sunset. You're gonna like it. By the way, I got something for you. I got a lead for you in a factory. Steady work. Steady pay."

Later Beto and Sharon stood outside the car, arguing. Lizette's head lay on Manuel's shoulder, Sam Cooke sang "You Send Me," and Manuel knew he was alive. Lizette tugged at Manuel's arm, then put his hand on her belly. He stroked her belly until she put her hand on his and pressed it there. Then she looked up at him, meaningfully.

"Really?" he said.

She nodded, solemnly.

A father. He would be a father. His limbs tingled, his chest burned. Joy and shame and terror and ecstasy. "When do we get married, Reina?"

Lizette began to laugh and cry. Manuel gripped her hand. She would be his, morning and night and day and evening.

CHAPTER NINETEEN

1957

Their baby was due months away, in February, yet Manuel was so excited he could hardly breathe when he thought about it. What if it were a son? His son would be an engineer, his son would go to college, goddammit. His son could rise to be anything. How many babies would they have? What if it were a girl? His heart exploded at the thought of raising a girl, a delicate, tiny Lizette. His future would be filled with miniature Lizettes and Manuels. And he would never let them go, they would never disappear. He would never disappear.

* * *

Lizette and Manuel were married in late August, in Lizette's church in Goleta, her father and brothers standing alongside him, her girlfriends standing alongside her, as well as Amparo, who beamed as if she were standing next to Hermano Sebastián. After the wedding ceremony, Manny, as everyone called him now, circled with Lizette, his hand on the curve of

Lizette's hip, welcoming and thanking everyone at their tables in the community room. Streamers were festooned along the walls and hanging throughout.

Lizette's pastor, who had married them, held a prayer in Spanish and English as everyone gathered in the hallway. As the church women helped serve, plates clattered with moles, tamales, fried chicken.

Manuel saw Amparo hug a woman her age and sit next to her. The two were talking animatedly each time Manuel glanced in their direction. Beto came up to him. Manuel hadn't even noticed that Beto was there but would have marked his absence.

"You did it, old man," Beto said. "You went and grew up." Beto smile was half mocking, half proud. "Hey, meet my girl-friend, Nancy."

Manuel glanced at the girl, another glimpse at Beto's aspirations, then hugged his friend. "Thank you for being here."

"How could I not?" Beto said.

At the head table Manuel took care to look around the hall. Beto was the sharpest dressed there, with his suit like midnight blue silk, his date Nancy all ripe and luscious curves in her fitted dress, but Manuel had no sense of envy or lack. Lizette was beside him, in a creamy white dress fitted at the chest and loose underneath, an empire waist, she had explained, hiding the tiny bulge on her belly. The baby that was theirs.

To his left was Amparo, on Lizette's right her father. Her brothers Bobby and Roland were at a table nearby, talking to other pretty girls. Manuel marked them all. Beto and Amparo. Lizette's family. Everyone was there, for one moment, all together. Except, of course, his parents, his Lulu. He shook those thoughts away.

He kissed his sweet, sweet wife. "Mi reina," he said.

"Mi rey," she answered.

* * *

Before they were married, she had gone looking for an apartment for them to rent and was stunned by the Los Angeles prices. They ended up in a small apartment in City Terrace. Here the homes and apartments were practically on top of each other and felt cramped by the weight of their neighbors. The windows on the homes had wrought-iron bars, the yards were fenced in with wire. Their home was on the second floor, where they could hear the heavy steps of the family above them and smell the cooking of the families below them. They had a tiny balcony where Lizette dried clothing. Manuel filled it with potted plants.

Lizette invited her family to inspect, admire, or in Felipe's case, to critique. Manuel's new father-in-law looked at the cracks in the concrete and the slope in the flooring and gave Manuel a look.

"I know, Dad, I know," Manuel said, too happy to feel inadequate for Lizette. "It's just temporary." Her brothers Bobby and Roland collided with each other in the doorways of their tiny apartment, making Lizette laugh full-throated, and told her their stories and misadventures of their farm up in Goleta that each year barely scraped by.

And her brothers were grown-up, long and loping and sangre de leche, as Lizette said, slow to work, slow to rise, but quick for visits that included meals.

"That's fine by me," Lizette said, checking the simmering of the chile verde. Later she dished it out alongside the rice and beans and mounds of corn tortillas.

Roland, the oldest, the tallest, the laziest, was drafted first, but he was rejected, he told them, with a long, slow, smile, removing his glasses and cleaning them with a corner of his shirt. "What can I say? Born under a lucky star, I guess."

"If that were true, you wouldn't have been born Mexican," his brother Bobby prodded at him.

Manuel stopped by the downtown post office weekly now, instead of daily, to check the post office box for letters about Victoria. There was rarely anything, and even then, it would be a false start, a whisper so vague Manuel knew it to be a fortune hunter. He'd crumpled them up and throw them away. Lizette had filled in all that empty space.

Beto had reached out to Manuel with a job as an apprentice machinist. Steady, predictable job. Steady, predictable income. He now drove a 1955 Ford truck, his father-in-law's wedding present to them. On the weekends the two left their hot, dry apartment and drove to the beach, to the mountains, to Goleta to see her family.

Lizette was beautiful. She had a perfectly shaped chest and hips that promised love and childbirth. Her arms were brown and lean, her fingers delicate as they played the piano in her family's home in Goleta as she had played for the church services. Manuel often marveled at how expressive her face was, sharp and mocking with her brother, and sometimes, with him, tender and loving, fierce and outraged.

In 1957 at twenty-two years old, Manuel was excited and overwhelmed. A new life, their baby! His new wife, Lizette. A different job, a different home; everything burst into being at once, everything unfolded as if, as if—Manuel hesitated to even think it—as if it was God's plan. How many babies would they have? How many lives would they bring into the world? What kind of people would they be?

Too much! Too much, life exploded in his chest, in his mind.

If Manuel ever forgot how beautiful his wife was, the furtive looks of the men who passed her on the street reminded him. His eyes narrowed, and he scowled. What was it like for her when he was not walking along her side? What crude and disgusting thing would some ugly man say to her?

She gave him a dismissive look when he brought it up. "I been used to this since I was thirteen. You don't think I know how to take care of myself?" She gave him a pointed look so sharp that both of them started laughing.

But the fact of the matter remained there was a significant part of Manuel that would have preferred she'd stay home. Doing what, God only knew.

"All I want for you is everything," he told her, after scraping the last bit of meaty juice and green chiles up with his perfectly charred flour tortilla.

"Four babies," she said.

He nodded with a smile. "Two of each," he said.

She threw a napkin at him. "I've had enough of boys," she said.

"Lo que diga la reina," he answered. Echoing Amparo, "lo que dios quiere."

Those first few months, it seemed every last thing was sunshine and ice cream.

* * *

Manuel was working the vise on the floor of the machine shop in Vernon when the floor manager called him over. "There's a lady on the phone who wants to talk to you. I told her you were busy, but she says it's important." Lizette? "It was hard to understand her, with that accent." Not Lizette. Who, then?

Manuel picked up the receiver. "Hello?"

It was their neighbor. She'd just taken Lizette to County USC, he should know, and he should get there now.

His body began to tremble. "I gotta go," he said, not waiting for a reply.

His arms were shaking so hard he could barely fit the keys into the car door lock. His foot slipped on the brake, then pushed too hard on the gas.

He didn't remember driving, didn't remember parking, but he found himself at the information desk in a room crowded with people. The woman at the desk told him where to go, and as he strode the hallways, he passed women writhing on gurneys. The fear was now a block of ice on his chest, pressing him, slowing everything down as he pushed forward. Lizette! Lizette!

He found her room and saw two other women sharing the room. He glanced at them only to see they were not his wife. A dull gray curtain shrouded the last bed. He tugged at it, "Liz?" and pulled it aside.

She turned her head to face him. She had been crying, he could tell, but her face was dry. She was paler than he'd ever seen her. He was collapsing inside, but he willed himself to be fierce and alive for his wife. He pushed through the terror, leaned into the bed, pulled her hand between his, and pressed them to his chest.

"I'm here," he said.

She nodded. The two were silent, but the room was filled with noise, the two other women talked to each other, the television was on.

Lizette whispered, "I want to go away."

Manuel leaned closer, smoothed the hair away from her face. "You'll be home, soon."

"Away," Lizette said, "Far away." She began to cry, then choke on her cries, "I lost our baby, your baby—I lost my baby," she said. "I want to die."

Manuel kneeled beside the bed and pressed her hand to his forehead. With her words the block of ice returned to his chest. The terror, the mist, as hard as he tried to make it go away, remained. "Don't leave me, Reina. Please. Please. Live."

When Lizette returned home, Manuel took the week off to care for her. She no longer smiled when she awoke, she no longer turned to him at night in bed. He got her coffee, the paper, a sweet roll. She lay in bed.

Two days of this and he called Amparo. "Ay, pobrecitos niños," she said. Wednesday morning, he drove to Whittier to pick her up. She looked eager and ready. She wore a gray floral dress, and he knew she had made it herself. Years ago, he had helped her cut the pattern and watched as she sewed.

He said hello to Chrissie and the kids. Cristina gave him a tight, tearful hug, and a pot of pozole. "It helps with the healing," Cristina said. Manuel was grateful Toño was out doing his deliveries. He already felt he had failed as a man, as a husband, as a father, to allow his wife to be so frail and withdrawn. Toño, damaged, had managed a healthy, thriving family.

In the car he said, "Thank you, Tía, for coming."

"Son, I am always here for you two. Just not on top of you!"

She had seemed happy enough when he saw her, now, as he drove and glanced at her sideways, he saw that the lines on her face had deepened and he noticed much more gray in the braids that crowned her head than he had noticed before. He was filled with shame and regret; he'd barely thought of Amparo at all.

"How are you, Tía? How is it with your son's family? Do you miss"—he could barely say it because he knew the answer —"Palo Verde?"

"Like one misses a heartbeat." She shook her head and looked out the window. They passed a cemetery. "My grandchildren make me happy," she said. "I thank God for them every day." She patted the back of his hand. "I know this is difficult for both of you. These things happen. She will one day have a baby. Many babies!" She smiled. "But I won't say that to Lizette. This is her first."

He parked on the crooked hillside, took her overnight bag out of the bed of the truck, and walked up the stairs to his apartment's screen door. She examined his entrance. "You need some plants," she said. "You need something alive and green around your home. It will remind you of Palo Verde. It will make you both happy."

Once inside their tiny apartment, Amparo tapped on the door, then walked into their bedroom. Manuel could hear the murmur of two feminine voices. He left them and walked outside.

The rush of moving traffic on the freeways encircled him. He gazed down at the homes, so many, many houses and apartments around them. All those lives inside. He held onto the railing and thought about Lizette.

For a few days Amparo cleaned and cooked and fussed. She did the laundry, changed the bedding. She closed the door against Manuel and talked to Lizette.

When Manuel looked at her questioningly, Amparo said, "I just talk to her about womanly things."

At night he lay next to Lizette, who squeezed his hand and smiled wanly. She let him pull her toward him; he held her and fell asleep listening to the rhythm of her breathing.

* * *

When Manuel returned to work, the floor manager told him to get lost, they'd already filled his job. He picked up his last paycheck and deposited it in his bank. How could Lizette have married him? He had nothing!

Beto had gotten him that job. What would it look like to say, "Yeah, I lost it?" He couldn't do that.

Lizette's dad offered Manuel a job at their farm.

"I'm not going back there," Lizette said. "There's nothing for me there, for our kids."

Eventually, Felipe loaned them rent money. Eventually, Manuel paid it all back, scrabbling earnings together, again from odd and temporary jobs. Construction work. A time spent in a slaughterhouse in Vernon, later an auto shop in City Terrace, near home. Lizette, of all things, baby sat in their tiny apartment! While their mothers went to their jobs.

What had he done to her? He'd given her nothing, grief and poverty and a tiny place to live surrounded by noise and exhaust. He had plucked her flower and crushed it between his hands. Another pregnancy, and this time they both held their breath, another miscarriage.

Manuel was too embarrassed to ask Felipe for more money, and finally overcame his shame by reaching out to Beto again. He couldn't tell him how he'd lost that first job by taking care of Lizette.

When they met for drinks at a bar in Torrance, Beto now drove a sleek Dart that looked like it came right off the lot that morning, crisp and shiny and gleaming and clean.

"Beto, you will be the first Mexican millionaire," Manuel said. Beto was trying to land an aerospace contract to rent them cars; or maybe sell them company cars? Manuel could never keep all the details in his head.

When they went out to drinks, Beto never chose a bar with people that looked like them. Never. If there was cantina music, or a whisper of Spanish, or a brown man in the doorway, Beto kept walking. This place was no different, filled with locals, Japanese and white men sucking at their beers and cock-tails. Manuel ordered a beer.

Manuel paid for the drinks. Softly he started, "Lizette's pregnant again."

Beto said, "That's beautiful, boss. Really." Beto held the neck of his bottle and shook his head. "Who'd a thought that skinny little bastard who couldn't say a word, then couldn't keep his damn mouth shut, woulda turned out so good. Seriously, Manny, you got a beautiful wife and a beautiful life.

"Hey, let's celebrate your manliness. There's this club out here I've heard of called Diamond Ladies." He gave Manuel a knowing look, put his hands in front of his chest, impersonating huge breasts.

Manuel smiled, shook his head, "Nah," he said, finishing his beer. "I prefer the one woman I can touch."

"You want to touch 'em? I'm sure we can arrange that."

"Nah, Beto, that's your thing. Not mine. Lynda's okay with that?"

"It's not Lynda anymore—and why the fuck would I tell her about this?" He waved his hands. "What, are you crazy? Things are good again, don't even hint at something that would spoil it." Beto waved the bartender. "Don't look at me that way."

Manuel shrugged. Beto was his oldest friend, his only friend at times. They didn't have to agree on everything, not even most things.

Beto stood, patted Manuel on the shoulder. "Okay, old man, okay. You remember, if it's a boy you name him after his rich uncle Beto and who knows what I can do for the kid! Okay, I gotta get to this club—I made a promise to myself."

"Beto," Manuel said, feeling the chokehold on the base of his throat but ignoring it. "I need a job, a good steady job. I can't have Lizette babysitting a bunch of strangers' kids while she's pregnant. She's already lost two babies. I don't want her to lose this one. Amparo says she needs bed rest and a good doctor—I don't have the money for that. City Terrace is fine, but it's crowded, you know? Both me and Lizette are used to having some space where you can breathe. Have you got a lead? Anything. Anything at all." Manuel hoped he didn't sound like he was begging. He hated to ask his friend for yet another favor. Why couldn't he do this on his own?

"Jeez, Manny, why dincha tell me sooner? C'mon man, are we friends or not?" Beto promised to send him a lead to Huffy's Bikes in Azusa.

As their third baby, their son, died in the County USC hospital, staff wouldn't let Manuel near her. When she returned home, he hadn't any desire to buy flowers. He couldn't pretend there was any joy, and neither could she.

"I want to sleep in our room tonight," she said.

His chest filled with love and warmth and gladness that they could hold each other, chastely, that they could rescue each other.

"Alone," she said.

That first night was filled with thoughts of inadequacy and failure that rippled over him again and again. Manuel had lost her. How would he live without her? He quietly wept for the babies, for Lizette, and for himself.

Lizette didn't speak to Manuel. He knew it was more that she was *unable* to speak to him, but still it hurt. How could he be so lost without her, when it was clear he needed to find their way? He had no words that soothed or consoled her. She had soothed and cared for and softened him. How could he not do the same for her?

This time there were no family visits. Bobby was in training at Ft. Ord. Roland ducked in and out, sitting in her room while Manuel worked, then headed back home the next day to Goleta.

After Roland left, Manuel came again with coffee and conchas and a kiss on her head. She responded with, "Please go away. Please go to your job."

Azusa. Huffy's bikes. A long drive there to the base of foothills he could barely see because of the dirty air. Took him a couple of days to realize he was the only Mexican there—Colin, the only Black guy there, trained him.

"The boys got a pool on how soon it'll be that you wash out." Colin looked at him sternly. "So don't, got it? I don't need to be carrying that as well around here."

Manuel found he enjoyed the challenge of working with the metal, shaping and punching the sheet, and setting up the next bracket.

During a break Colin introduced him around, introducing each man by his job. "That's Steve, the grinder, over there's Jerry, the fitter." Colin turned to him and said, "One day I'd like to be the patternmaker, but... Who knows? Probably just another pipe dream."

Colin approved of Manuel's work, and they ended up spending their lunch hours together. Colin was fixing up his house in South Los Angeles.

"I wish I had me a house to fix up," Manuel said.

"You got you a wife," Colin said. "She'll be fixing you up." His new friend patted him on the shoulder and the two got back to work.

He returned from his job one evening and the house was quiet, as if it were empty. Terror gripped his chest. Had she abandoned her misery here and him along with it? Had she returned to her family in Goleta?

She lay in their bed, asleep, the coffee and sweet bread untouched.

He sat at the kitchen table. He sat and waited. When it was nine o'clock and she still slept, he pulled out the lunch meat, made himself a sandwich, ate it, then went to sleep in what they had once called the baby's room.

Was it a week like that or a month? When it came to

misery, it was hard for Manuel to keep track, misery became a mist that invaded the days and nights, into the smile of strangers and praise of his supervisor. If Lizette was at the bottom of an unlighted cave, unsure of how to escape, his heart was there with her, without an exit pass, without a treasure map, without a guide.

What was he supposed to do?

He got into the rhythm of his working days. He tried talking to the crew, but they were standoffish. Manuel was grateful Colin had taken him under his wing. Colin taught him skills that weren't directly related to his job, as well. How to work the grinder, just what a patternmaker was, and, in the end, how everything came together in a shiny purple kid's bike.

Sometimes he would return early and her bedroom door was closed. She was already asleep, a book splayed on the bedspread, the light on, her full lips lightly parted.

He wanted to kiss those lips.

Or he could find someone else. He shook his head against the thought. It was Lizette he wanted, Lizette the young girl he married, the golden and smiling, teasing, mocking woman who had once loved him. He wanted her eyes on him, her mouth on him, her love in his direction.

Toño brought Amparo to visit a number of times; each time Amparo cleaned and cooked and fussed. She nodded approvingly of the greenery Manuel slowly, painstakingly attempted to create. She did the laundry, changed the bedding. She closed the door against Manuel and talked to Lizette.

His wife shared nothing with him about those talks.

This afternoon Amparo sat across from him, her hair grayer than he recalled, neatly braided across the top of her head. She reached over the table and gripped his hands. "Let me pray, Manuel."

"Yes, Tía."

"Dear God of the Universe, come and comfort these young people who have known so much pain. Hold their hearts close to you, close to each other. Keep their love for each other alive, so they can find each other in this moment of darkness."

As she spoke, pain burned in his chest, spread to his head. Yes, so much pain! A family, he and Lizette wanted a family, how much was that to ask? Too much, it was too much to ask. Part of him had abandoned his hope for his father, his mother, whom he rarely thought of, but Lulu? Yes, he had prayed with Amparo many nights just like this, and where had that ended? He nearly yanked his hands from Amparo with fury of the memory, but he was no longer a stupid young man. He was a husband. He was a man. Her prayers were born of a love for both of them. To insult her for her love, for her faith, would be contemptible. He calmed himself.

When she finished praying, she moved over to him, to hug him. "May it be as you say, Tía. May God listen to you, in a way he has never listened to me."

CHAPTER TWENTY

As the months passed, Lizette started community college, one class at a time. Manuel continued to work. He dreamed of touching her again. Dreamed of being with her again, dreamed of the warmth and softness returning, dreamed of being a man and wife again. It was if they were both doing a penance for a crime, a sin neither of them had committed.

Lizette began taking classes at East Los Angeles City College to work on her AA. She wanted to be a nurse, a pediatric nurse, if there was such a thing, and if there wasn't such a thing, she'd make it one.

Manuel continued to drive to Azusa, building kids' bikes. Colin had left for some aerospace job in El Segundo. Manuel was sorry to see him go and at the same time impressed. Un moreno like Colin had to be really good to get into that line of work.

He ran ads again for Victoria Galvan. He felt sad and guilty for having abandoned the search for her, but now with Lizette alone in her room without him, he felt he needed to start again.

Bobby showed up, on leave for a few days, slick and clean

and cocky. His time in training had filled out his frame with lean muscle, carving down the fat, burnishing his skin tone. Set against his dark face, his eyes and teeth gleamed, particularly when he smiled, as he did now, like he had found his place in the world and owned it.

That was because of Alice. Alice sat on Bobby's lap and Bobby's arms were always around her, around her waist or her shoulders or her legs in short shorts like he owned them, as the two of them sat on Manuel's couch.

It tugged at him, like baby buggies and baby clothing tugged at Lizette. What the two of them had both lost.

For now, Manuel argued with himself. For now, not for all time.

Bobby leaped up, brushing Alice off his lap, and followed Lizette back into the kitchen.

Alice sat there with plump, freckled, and pale thighs, jiggling as she nervously tapped her leg. "I think your neighborhood is the most amazing place. I've never seen homes scrunched together so tight, you know?" She smiled a shy smile, showing upper teeth that crossed over each other.

"I forget where you two met," Manuel said. The neighbor's radio blaring seeped into their living room.

"Dancing! He was looking so fine in that uniform, and so brown and manly, you know?" She wriggled her shoulders as if laughing at herself. "He came up to me and asked me to dance and I told him I didn't know any zoot suit moves and he laughed telling me that was like a lifetime ago and good thing too cuz neither did he. God made Mexicans so beautiful, you know?"

The way she said that caught Manuel off guard. She moved right next to him, conspiratorially, and now Manuel was overly conscious of the dimple in her thigh, and the cleavage exposed by her halter top. Her chest was rosy pink like her cheeks, either from too much sun or a little nervousness.

"I don't know if Bobby's gonna tell you. You know he seems such an open kinda guy, which is why I think he's so swell, but the truth is..." She looked around nervously, stopped by having heard a door swing, but it was a neighbor's back door. "We're gonna have to get married, if you know what I mean. You're a married man, a man of the world. He wants to make it a civil service, and my old man passed last year, my mother's in Fresno and has already yelled at me for even stepping out with a Mexican, so do you think you two could stand with us at the court this week? You and Lizette are so sweet, and you know, you're so grown-up compared with us."

Manuel looked into those nineteen-year-old eyes, blue, under the thin, stiffly arched, and painted brown eyebrows.

"As long as it's good by Lizette, it's good by me."

"Bobby's probably asking her right now. I wanted to ask you. That's what I love about you two. Bobby says it's always about the other one, it's never about yourselves, you know? How do you do that?"

Bobby stepped into the living room. "Stop giving my cuñado an eyeful!" he said, yanking Alice by the arm, pulling her away from Manuel.

Is that what she was doing? Is that what he was doing? Manuel blinked at himself, trying to scrabble out of this uncomfortable position when Lizette came in holding a tray.

"I'm embarrassed," she said, looking at Alice. "I wish I had something more serious to offer the two of you, but"—Lizette raised her glass of Tang—"to your marriage, and to the young life you two have started together."

They joined her in raising and clinking their glasses, then sipped.

That night Lizette stood at the foot of the sofa where Manuel now slept.

"Come back to me," she said. "Come hold me."

That was what he wanted. Of course he wanted more, but he wanted to hold that warm body close to him, feel the rise and fall of her breathing, listen to the soft purr of her voice. He wanted the nineteen-year-old Lizette back to him, not her body, not the bones, but the brightness of her eyes and her laughter. Now holding her next to him, he could offer himself a little hope that that part of Lizette would return.

"I'd forgotten how good you smell," he said, his arms wrapped around her waist, her back to him. His body was coming immediately to attention, and he was trying to quell it, because he knew, he knew, that was not the reason his wife had invited him back into their bed.

She shook her head.

He squirmed, "Ignore it. Ignore me. I just want to hold you."

She stared up at the ceiling. She sighed. "I don't know if I can explain it to you, Manolo."

"Try me, try." Please, don't ever kick me out of the bedroom. Please, let me stay here, in bed with you, forever. Please, let me be.

"Every time, every time, every damn time I see someone, I can't help but think, they used to be a baby. Some stupid, lucky woman gave birth to them. I can't help it. Every time I see anybody, all I can think is some stranger, some woman, could do, without even thinking, what I've been aching to do, for you. For us."

Manuel listened, inhaled her scent, and stroked her arm. He had almost forgotten how soft her skin was, how smooth, how warm. He had gotten his body under control—if he listened to her words and paid no attention to how sweetly the two of them fit together—

"And then that little girl, that little *girl*, is going to have Bobby's baby. She's going to make us an aunt and uncle before I can make us parents. I just don't understand." She wriggled free from him and turned to face him. "How can I live with this pain, Manuel? Every single day. It just hurts too much."

He picked up her hand and kissed the tips of her fingers. "We haven't even started, I mean, we could go to doctors, see what's wrong with me, see how to fix it—"

She pulled her hand away. "See what's wrong with *me*, you mean." She shook her head. "I had a mother who put three people in this world. I asked Dad if she ever had problems and he shook his head and told me those weren't things they talked about. Maybe she had problems too."

"Maybe," Manuel grasped at the change in her mood. "Maybe we will get through this, and then you can have your three babies."

She turned to lie on her back and gaze up at the ceiling. He watched her breasts move with her breathing. She said, "Maybe that is how things will work out." Then she turned to him mischievously, "I thought you wanted four!"

"You want four. I want what you want."

She lay back down with a heavy sigh. "It's just, part of life like breathing. Do I *want* to breathe? I don't even think about it. But not being able to have a baby, it becomes the only thing I think about. Do you understand?"

He said, "A little." But no. Not really. Lizette's thoughts had a wider range than his own.

"I'm glad, even if it's just a little," she said. "Everything, everything is a sign of God's handiwork, you know?"

"Maybe God's handiwork wasn't ready," he said.

They lay on the bed, quiet together.

Pulling him toward her, she said, "I've missed you."

Manuel held her close to him, inhaling her scent, feeling the tug and pull of her body, both of them falling toward the other.

That night she held him as he had yearned for, for so long.

Friday at City Hall, Manuel noticed that Lizette pursed her lips as she eyed Alice's belly, but she took the pictures.

Alice, in a baby blue dress with a lace-fringed scoop neck, clung to Bobby, grabbing his arm, following wherever he led. Bobby swaggered in his dress uniform, talked to Manuel, Roland, their Dad and Lizette almost as if Alice weren't there, and described his plans for after the Army, where he'd like to live, how he hoped to be a mechanic when he returned, how he hoped he'd be getting a lot of experience doing that where he was stationed.

They hopped in their cars and headed to Olvera Street.

"We don't have anything like this back in Fresno," Alice said.

After putting a second roll of film in her camera, Lizette stopped a stranger to take their picture in front of the band-stand on the plaza. Bobby insisted on taking them to drinks and dinner at one of the fancier restaurants, where Bobby drank seven and sevens and ordered a bottle of Mateus Rosé for the table while Roland and Lizette drank soda pop. Bobby asked the mariachi band to serenade his new wife. Roland fought with Manuel over who paid the check and the loser, Roland, tipped the trio. Felipe, in his omnipresent straw hat, sat and watched them all.

After the songs were sung, the meal eaten, the drinks drunk, and the conversation lulled, Bobby emptied his glass, looked at his watch then at Alice, and said, "We should go." He ran his hand over Alice's thigh, she looked at him expectantly, smiling the way she had done all day. "I need to spend my last few hours of leave with Alice."

Manuel tapped Bobby on the shoulder and said, "Keep your head down, you hear? Come back for your beautiful new wife."

"I got that covered," Bobby said, grinning like the world was his.

Lizette came up to him and hugged him tight. "Come home. Just come home."

They watched Bobby and Alice trail through the street, heading toward Union Station while Roland loped alongside his dad toward the Greyhound bus station.

Manuel and Lizette held hands and walked slowly the other way. Lizette stopped at the fountain, dug into her bag, and stood there, dropping coin after coin into the water.

* * *

So many things had happened after Bobby's civil ceremony that they didn't get around to developing the film until five months after the wedding picture had been taken, three months after Bobby's death had been officially announced, and two months after his funeral at their church in Goleta.

The five of them: Roland, smirking, towering above the group. Lizette, smiling broadly, bright red lipstick against the sheen of her brown skin and dark hair, a green halter top that emphasized the lift of her breasts and made Manuel long for her even more than usual. Alice muffed it, her eyes closed, a goofy grin revealing the two tangled front teeth. Bobby's hand proprietarily around her waist, provocatively close to her breast. And Manuel, a small, strained smile.

Manuel was terrified they'd lose the baby when they got the word that Bobby had been killed in action. Lizette insisted on getting out of bed to attend his memorial service in Goleta. Manuel didn't want to put their baby at risk.

"I'm not going to lose this baby at eight months. It's coming with me, so I can show my brother my love one last time."

The church in Goleta was filled, but Alice, pregnant with Bobby's baby, was not there.

Lizette's pregnancy held. They never saw Alice again.

CHAPTER TWENTY-ONE

D ahlia was born March 23, 1965, whole, breathing, live, squalling, and Manuel didn't know what to do with himself. The baby had all the right number of toes, fingers, limbs, eyes. The baby nursed and slept and wailed, and Lizette was young and old, wise and foolish, beautiful and tired. She was everything, Manuel was everything, the baby was every-thing. The baby was their world. Lizette exhaled and looked up at him with glistening eyes and said, "Now we are a family."

He had a daughter! What did that mean, who would she be, what would she be?

Manuel stared at that unformed face and wondered, what would she even look like?

They had a cradle in the bedroom. The curtains Lizette had sewn three years ago now served their purpose. But it wasn't so much a newborn's room as a playroom, filled with toys that an infant didn't need, waiting for a toddler to clamber over.

Manuel was already worried about the next baby. What if the next baby were a boy?

"Calmate," Lizette told him, smoothing the hair on his forehead. "Could we please just not rush ourselves?"

Lizette was self-conscious of the angry jagged scar, where they had ripped Dahlia out of her. He kissed it, to reassure her. Of course he still loved her and wanted her. But even so, he wondered why they had to disfigure her this way?

The biggest fight they had was over teaching Dahlia Spanish. Manuel tried to explain what the notary had told him, long ago, about not teaching his kids Spanish so they would always be seen as Americans.

"Stop it, Manuel. Stop it right now. Bobby died for this country, you can't get more American than that *and* he spoke Spanish. My dad came from Campeche, and he's a US citizen. He's an American. My mother's family came from Texas, and they were there, Americans for decades, the border crossed them! My children are speaking Spanish."

And that was that.

Manuel, now skilled on the lathe, the grinder, and the punch press started hunting for jobs nearer to home. When Bethlehem Steel hired him as a tool and die machinist for union wages, he took the entire family out, Amparo, Toño, Chrissie and their kids, to La Fonda to listen to the mariachi players while they dined. All evening Dahlia sat on his or Lizette's lap or Amparo's lap. Manuel felt proud, truly proud of himself. Bethlehem Steel, years ago when he left the docks, had been his dream!

This time there were more Mexicans and a handful of Blacks. He wished Colin were there with him.

As Dahlia grew, Lizette hadn't gotten pregnant again. It was strange. Not even a failed pregnancy. They hadn't done anything differently. It seemed to Manuel, once Lizette stopped nursing Dahlia, they were with each other as much or almost as much as before all the heartbreak of the babies. But it was strange, each month would come and go.

Lizette only rolled her eyes. "If God thinks it's not the right time, it's not the right time," she'd say to Manuel. "But I hope he doesn't wait too much longer. I want Dahlia to be close to her little brother. Or sister."

And they lay together and held each other and loved each other and another month without a pregnancy would roll by.

Then another. And another and it was now four years, nearly five. Dahlia had perfectly even and white baby teeth and smiled everywhere. She was so smart! Did every parent think their child was the smartest most beautiful one in the world? Probably! But in Dahlia's case it was true.

"Que chula ese niña, ese muñequita," Amparo said, each time she visited, spending the night sharing Dahlia's bedroom.

She had a musical, high-pitched voice and loved to sing all the songs she learned from Amparo or at preschool while Lizette took morning classes. Lizette cut Dahlia's hair into trim bangs and pulled ponytails on the side of her face, and Dahlia was their muñequita, big smiles, bold hugs. Fearless. Manuel kept her close, never wanted her out of his sight, but even so once when he stepped into the bathroom, she, at age three, walked out the apartment door, down the stairs, and kept walking. Manuel and Lizette were terrified, looking through the car port, knocking on the neighbors' doors when a woman from down the street brought Dahlia back, neat as a pin in the pale blue short set Lizette had sewn, looking up at the three adults with her large brown eyes as if she had just gotten a taste of adventure.

He kept her close. He held her hand tight as they hailed the paletero who walked their neighborhood while Dahlia made her choice. Lizette teased him to relax. He worried about her. If he could, he'd hold her, carry her everywhere, never let her out of his sight.

"You got to give her room to explore!" Lizette said, exasperated.

When Lizette attended summer evening classes, Manuel could hover around Dahlia as much as he liked. He'd mess around with her in the kitchen and serve her a hot dog in a flour tortilla squirted with mustard, or seared bologna on a corn tortilla smeared with mustard—that worked for both of them. Or a frozen pot pie heated in the oven. Or for something special they'd head to Carl's for foil-wrapped chilidogs.

Dahlia was like her mother. People in the neighborhood smiled at her, talked to her. Manuel held her hand, kept her near him, and Dahlia answered, made conversation, as if it were perfectly natural for a four-year-old to find her place in the world, everywhere she went.

Where did she get that from? Manuel wondered. Not him, he knew, only Lizette. Lizette who went through the world with her halo of beauty, cutting through his wrongs and rough edges. She was his. She had chosen him.

During one visit Amparo showed Dahlia how to roll out flour tortillas. Dahlia's pudgy fingers pushed the rolling pin obstinately. She said to him, "Are you happy, son? These are the days. For where your treasure is, there will your heart be also. Family is your treasure."

He was. And yet. He couldn't reconcile his faded memory of Lulu to search for her in Dahlia's face. Again, his ads had cost him money and harvested cranks and psychics and grifters. He thought about his visit to Jean Shiro's home, with her daughter in a cap and gown, and smiled at the thought of Dahlia, one day, dressed up in the same way.

There were some things he could not bring himself to share with Lizette. This love he felt for Dahlia, had his parents felt this, too? What had kept his parents from fighting for him and Lulu? If someone ripped Dahlia away from him, what would keep him from fighting for her?

In the darkness of night, the thrum of the freeway traffic, the light breathing of his wife, these were the thoughts that oppressed him.

What a crime, he thought about what had been done to his young self. What a crime.

Over dinner Lizette told Manuel and Dahlia all about the battle of Puebla. "Did you know," she told Dahlia, who gazed with adoration up at her mother, "it was about slavery? France was rich and powerful and wanted to help the Confederates in the States. Mexico and all the Indian soldiers didn't want slavery so they fought. And guess what? Mexico won!"

Dahlia clapped her chubby hands at her mother's face. Manuel shook his head and smiled at the silliness, at the strangeness of it all. Lizette loved her college classes. Each time she smiled in delight at something the teacher had said or shared an idea, Manuel had the tiniest pinprick of—of what? Something like misery, inadequacy, jealousy, sadness, and fear all in one.

Lizette, now growing into a beautiful woman, even more than the gorgeous young girl he married, loved her daughter, loved her husband, and her college classes. In that order.

"Did you hear about the high school students?" she said to him.

Manuel shook his head. He learned so much from his wife.

"Thousands and thousands of them walking out. It's like we're finally waking up," Lizette said. "It's like we're getting to know who we actually are. Chicanos."

"Such an ugly word," he said.

"I like it," she said.

One night as they lay in bed, he said, "I'm glad to have a wife smarter than me."

She shook her head. "Not smarter, more educated."

"Just don't leave me for some pendejo profe," he said.

She sat up, mock outraged. "Don't tell me who to leave you for," she said. "I'll make that decision on my own, thank you very much!"

He laughed and pulled her toward him. "You know, when you get your degree, you don't have to work. We're doing pretty good."

"Manuel, raising kids and running a house *is* work. I want to be a nurse. Even part time."

He held her tighter and inhaled her scent. "Lo que la reina diga."

During the news programs that they watched after dinner, he held her hand. Scenes from anti-war protests rolled on.

"Nobody can say Bobby died for nothing." He looked over at her. "Nobody can say his death was pointless."

She looked at him. "What if it was? Maybe if we just admitted these lives were wasted, we wouldn't go to war."

"That's crazy," he said.

"The world is crazy," she said. Then, "All those boys." The two of them thought of Bobby.

* * *

When Lizette got her nursing degree, they threw a party in their home. Her dad showed up. Toño brought Amparo and his family. Dahlia was the center of everyone's attention. Beto brought a redhead in a slinky shimmery dress, whose name Manuel promptly forgot. His friend nudged him, pointing at Dahlia, "You stopping at one? I thought you wanted more?"

On weekends they drove out of City Terrace and through dazzling neighborhoods and dreamed about owning their own home, a real home, with a yard and a sidewalk and a place their kids could roller skate or learn how to ride a bike. Manuel knew exactly which Huffy bike he'd be buying for Dahlia.

Lizette and Manuel gathered their paperwork, their taxes, Manuel's pay stubs, and went to apply for a home loan.

The first time they were denied, Manuel shrugged it off, until they had enough savings to make an average man sit up straight. They learned that cities like Bell, Lynwood, Maywood, and all the Los Angeles neighborhoods that were trim, clean, and sparkling like Mrs. Shiro's wouldn't sell to Mexicans.

Lizette said, "Bobby's Mexican. Bobby was drafted to fight this goddamned American war. Would he, too, be too Mexican to buy a goddamned house in this goddamned white world?"

Manuel hated it when Lizette cursed. The fifth time they were denied, Manuel called Beto in, angry and frustrated.

"Hells bells, Manny, you shoulda called me first. You tell them Lizette's French. You tell them Galvan is Spanish, from Galicia. Anything but Mexican!" Beto gave them a phone number, his connection, and, within a week, the loan was approved.

They found a single-story Spanish style with thick walls, an unused fireplace, and a brittle stucco roof in need of some repair in the hills of Mt. Washington. It was in their price range, being sold by an older couple downsizing to join a daughter in Texas. The streets were narrow and terrible for bikes or skates. But the house had an unfinished patio that looked over hills that lighted up at night.

City Terrace had been on the hills, but in a way that was cramped and on top of each other. Here, looking out over the patio, Manuel could see other homes in the distance, hints of other lives. When he inhaled, the air, the scent, brought him back to Chavez Ravine. He looked at Lizette.

"This is the one," she said.

When they signed the paperwork, the covenants stipulated that they must be white.

That night in bed, Manuel said, "Today we are white. Do

you think white people make love differently?"

Lizette said, "Let's find out."

* * *

When they moved in, Manuel insisted on carrying Lizette over the threshold. Dahlia danced alongside them. He forbade Lizette from helping move or unpack.

"I mean it!" he said while she laughed at him.

Their home filled with sunshine.

The three of them often sat on the back patio that Manuel had begun to reshape and mold into his vision. He wanted the patio to be an oasis, where he could sit and sip a beer, watch the houses across the hills light up. He was working on building a rock garden into the walls that framed the patio. Toño came over to help while Chrissie hung out with Lizette. Beers and dinner and help with the garden. The irrigation was the tricky bit; he already knew which succulents he wanted. Something about it all, the colors, the birds, the sounds, evoked Palo Verde.

Lizette worked part time at a doctor's office in Bell. Nobody wanted to hire her full time, everyone knew she'd be getting pregnant again and raising her family. She started working on her master's degree, class by class. "Let's see what I can squeeze in before we have our next baby," she said, kissing Manuel on the neck, and pulling him to bed.

Afterward, he lay in bed while Lizette got up, rummaged around, checked on their daughter and started humming in the kitchen. He lay and felt the warmth of their bed, the scent of his wife.

Had it been this way for his parents? Had they loved each other like this?

He felt a gash of regret slice through his body. He would never know.

CHAPTER TWENTY-TWO

1969

Manuel had followed the progress of the Apollo flights at home on the TV set, at work through his transistor radio. Look at those engineers, he thought to himself. What must it feel like to be a man who made those flights happen?

He infected Dahlia with his enthusiasm, and although her fingers were too thick, her movements too clumsy to do this on her own, she helped him as he recreated the Apollo modules in his workshop. She held her breath each time he pressed the glued pieces together and exhaled when he let go.

On the day of the moon landing the three of them watched the black and white screen and cheered. What a moment. What a time to be alive. The world, the future, had changed. He briefly wondered, was Lulu watching too?

Late July, as he returned home from work, he could see from the street there were no lights on in the house. This was unusual. Manuel could usually spot movement from the drive, his wife or Dahlia darting around, sometimes waiting on the front porch. As he stepped into his home, it was as if he'd entered that "Evil Ways" song Santana was singing everywhere, where the woman was wicked, there were no lights on in the house, and no food being cooked. He laughed at his own dramatization. Then, he paused.

Where was Dahlia?

Where was Lizette?

True, the two of them could be on the back patio, perched on the cliff's edge, watching the hills light up as families returned home and began cooking supper, but it was a soggy, sodden evening, and there wasn't even a porch light on.

"Liz?" he called out, walking into the house, setting down his tools, his lunch pail. He headed deeper inside, flicking on lights as he went, a little worried, an unhappy sense of foreboding, anxiety, brooding. "Dahlia?" Lizette was always calming him, telling him he was getting worked up over nothing. He spotted their bedroom light under the closed door and walked in.

There was a note on his pillow, clearly and simply written, yet Manuel read it over and over. "I have taken Dahlia to my family's in Goleta. I need time to think. I will call you in a few days."

Why? Why would she be in Goleta with Dahlia? What had happened?

Their bed was made. The kitchen was clean and spotless. Dahlia's room was tidied, the blocks and toys and stiff books for small children all neatly arranged, as if an actual, breathing, reckless child no longer lived there.

He lifted the phone to dial her father in Goleta, then put it back down.

He walked into their bedroom and looked at her closet and drawers.

Most, if not all, of her clothing was there. He nodded to himself, feeling mildly calmed and appeased, the fist in his guts unclenching.

Manuel showered and shaved as if Lizette would know what he looked like on the other side of the phone. He dressed in clean fresh jeans and a white T-shirt. He picked up the phone and dialed Goleta.

It rang and rang and rang.

He threw the pile of work clothes in the washing machine. In Dahlia's room he tightened the screws on her bed frame. He patted the tiny wooden rocking horse in the corner, realized there was a rough edge, then went to the garage where he found fine sanding paper. He sanded down the rough area and checked for chipped wood which might give his small daughter a splinter. There were none. He looked around the room, picked up one of the stuffed animals, a furry blue creature with oversized eyes, and propped it on the bed.

He dialed Goleta. It rang and rang and rang.

He went out to the back patio, wet and slick under the day's drizzle. He returned to the kitchen and called again. This time a voice answered. "Yeah?"

It was her father.

"Hey, Dad, it's Manny. Is Lizette there?"

"Hey, Manny. I gotta tell you, I don't like being in this position—never come between a man and his wife is the way I've tried to get through my life, you know? But here we are, and I feel just terrible about the whole thing."

"Is she there?"

"Well, I'm trying to get to that."

"Just tell me if she's there or not, and let me talk to her, please?"

He felt himself getting riled up. He couldn't let that happen. He couldn't take it out on the old man, he couldn't take it out on Lizette; she wasn't gone, she wasn't leaving him, she didn't say she'd be leaving him. She wouldn't take their daughter away from him. Would she?

He read her note again. "I need time to think. I will call you in a few days." Nothing that she would be back either. Her dad was talking to him.

"I'm sorry, what'd you say?" Manuel asked. There was a buzzing in his ears that was growing louder.

"I said, son, I'm awful sorry. They're not here yet. Roland went down to pick them up. They're not back yet."

"Could you tell her, could you ask her, to give me a call when she gets home to you? I just want to make sure she, my girls, are safe."

"Will do," he said before hanging up.

Manuel's arms shook with their impotence.

He looked around the home, struck by its quiet emptiness. He pulled out a couple of boxer shorts, another pair of pants, and a clean shirt and placed them on his bed. He sat impatiently in his living room, watching first CBS then NBC then KMEX. It was all about the war and he turned it off, brushing thoughts of Bobby away.

He wanted to leave this empty home and expend the energy that kept his feet tapping or his knee jiggling, but then he might miss her call.

Something kept him back from following her. Some sense that his trailing her would only make whatever had driven her out of their home worse.

Would he ever see her again? Hear her voice again?

Calmate, calmate, he told himself. Of course he would.

But would she call?

He forced himself to not dial her father's home again. She would call him when and if she wanted to.

The phone rang at nine-thirty that night.

"Lizette?" he answered.

"It's me." Lizette's voice was empty.

"Hey, are you okay? I've been worried, I been out of my

mind." He didn't mean for it to sound accusing, but there it was. He tried to move quickly past it by saying, "How's our girl?"

"She's fine." Again that flat voice. "Her uncle, you know, bought us supper and ice cream and now she's in the house with Dad's dogs."

Manuel had wanted to hear her voice, and with it the assumption that all was well between the two of them, for the three of them. The silence grew, his tongue thick in his throat, the tone of her voice was distant, frozen, removed.

"This is an expensive way to not talk," she said, at last.

Manuel cleared his throat. "Are you leaving me?"

"Manny, if I could, right now, I would leave everyone." She paused. Was she weeping? He wasn't sure. He was about to ask when she said in a strangled voice, "But I'm not going to do that to our daughter. Do you understand? I need time away. I need time away."

His fingertips were cold, his chest was cold, he couldn't feel his legs. "What happened?"

"I don't want to talk about it."

"How long?" he forced himself to ask.

She said, "I don't know. I just don't want to feel the way I feel."

During the week that passed, he called each night and Lizette quickly passed the phone to Dahlia. The five-year-old sounded bright and bubbly and didn't seem to miss him at all. "Did you know," she said in her bright and happy voice, "cows have to have babies to give milk? Did you know, cheese comes from milk?"

"Everything's going to be okay, baby," he said to her.

"Everything *is* okay, Daddy," she said, which both concerned and comforted him.

Saturday morning he called. Surely Lizette would realize it

was time to come home. Surely she would understand he needed her; their daughter needed her, right here. She would understand that, wouldn't she?

Life went on. Life went on after every miserable loss he had ever had, didn't it? Parents he no longer remembered, the whisper, the barest thread of a memory of a sister. After everyone he had lost, each and every time, life stubbornly went on.

But not his wife, not Dahlia. Please God, do not take them from me.

When he slept in their bed at night at the edge of sleep, a cold mist swirled around him; his tongue thick in his throat, powerless, powerless.

The next morning he hated that the phone rang for so goddamned long in Goleta. Probably feeding the fucking pigs or mucking the sheds or whatever goddamned thing her father and brother did.

He should be ashamed. His wife couldn't bear to face him and had fled to be back home with her father. Fine, he was ashamed, and also royally angry.

"Hello?" he nearly yelled in response to his father-in-law picking up the phone.

"You wanna speak to Lizette, I imagine. Sorry, son, but she's left."

A brittle blossom of joy in his chest. "Coming home?" Where else would she go? Why else would she leave?

"Nah, she said she wanted to go to Monterey. Always wanted to go to Monterey, never had the chance."

"How the hell is she getting there?"

"She's going with her brother, Roland, of course, what are you thinking? What are you implying? I wouldn't have accepted any dirty nonsense—"

Manuel hung up on el viejo.

He spent the morning pulling out the weeds between the

succulents in the front yard. He scowled at the destruction he had wreaked. He walked through the home. He put away his laundry. He made their bed. He wanted Lizette back in their bed.

He stepped into Dahlia's room and sat on the floor. There was a shelf with all the Apollo modules he had made with her. He'd already organized the toys and now he wanted to see her things scattered, he wanted to see her singing to herself. He couldn't bear any of it.

But he couldn't leave.

He was asleep in front of a droning TV set when the phone rang.

"We're in Carmel," she said, her voice slightly lighter and more expressive than the last time they spoke.

"Your brother too?"

"Yeah. I told him to go home, but he doesn't want to leave me alone and that's really ticking me off."

Manuel smiled inwardly. Not even her brother was safe.

"But I'm serious. I want to be alone one goddamned day of my life."

"But Dahlia's there."

"Of course she's with me. That's not what I meant."

What did she mean? Away from him? From men? He said, "You got enough money?"

"Yes."

"What's the room like?"

"Fine. A big comfortable bed in its own room. A pull-out sofa in the front. They've got a kitchen. A big family with four kids could stay here just fine." She started to cry.

"Reina, you're breaking my heart."

She cleared her throat. "Roland's out now, picking up steaks. We're gonna walk to the beach in the morning. And then I'm kicking him out of here."

"Where are you, mi reina, what's the name?"

"Carmel's Cottages by the Sea."

"What if you kick him out, and I'll be there..." He wanted to say Sunday, desperately, he wanted to say Sunday, he wanted her in his arms, in his heart forever, but he stopped. "Monday?"

"I just said I want one day to myself. Please, Manuel, please."

"When can I come?"

Pause. He silently pled, he silently begged.

"Tuesday. I'll see you Tuesday."

CHAPTER TWENTY-THREE

He called in sick. "Really bad," he told his boss. "Might be the whole week." Fire him, he didn't care. All that mattered was Lizette and Dahlia. On the drive up the coast Tuesday morning, the ocean sparkled and shimmered, but Manuel was blind to it. He took the inland route, part of it new and glossy and unfamiliar to him. He kept his eyes on the dividing lines, the cars in the distance ahead and behind, the cars that shimmied too close to his left or his right.

He paid attention to the green-trimmed signs that announced the distance to San Francisco. Nearly four hundred miles! Monterey would be south of that, and Carmel a bit closer.

Two hundred miles out, he filled his car, bought an RC Cola, and took a handful of quarters to the pay phone.

The room rang and rang until the receptionist interrupted. Manuel left a message. "Tell her I'm on my way."

He passed fields and fields of crops, guessing at the heads of lettuce or cabbage, recognizing the squat fields of strawberries. Acres and acres of orange groves. There were people squatting in the fields, their heads covered in straw or cloth hats. He thought he saw children there.

He looked again and cursed. Yes, there were children working in the fields.

Past Bakersfield he turned toward the coast, glancing at the sandwiches he had packed, leaving them there because he had no appetite at all.

By the time he hit King City, he had eighty miles to go.

The sun warmed the aging interior of his car, smears of insects streaked his windshield. He had rolled the windows down but found himself steeped in sweat.

He crested a hill and saw the coast.

The streak of sky and shimmering sea penetrated his obsession and self-absorption. For a moment he felt calmed by the vast beauty.

He found the cottages after filling up at a gas station and being told the way. It was a right turn off the Pacific Coast Highway, heading south and straight for the ocean, humble homes scattered on the right and left, a number of beach motels with their signs offering rooms and color TV.

He pulled up into the lot of the Carmel Cottages, paused, then parked. He skipped the guest sign in and followed a pathway thick with pink hydrangeas and deep magenta bougainvillea. As he inhaled the salt air, he felt his nerves gather in anxiety at the pit of his groin.

Is this how they ended? In a sweet shamble of a motel, with a sky blue enough to pierce him, and a breeze gentle enough to cool him?

He rapped on her door, C, a bungalow. No answer. He rapped again. "Lizette?" he said. "It's me." A fist clenched where his nerves and anxiety perched. Had she left him, here? He scrambled over a hedge and peered through the window.

Strewn on the pine floor, he saw a familiar scattering of Dahlia's toys.

His terror allayed, he knocked again, then headed down the pathway to the beach, taking off his shoes, the ones he had polished the night before to make an impression on her.

He could spot his wife a hundred yards away at any angle. There she was, propped up by one slender brown arm, the other raised, holding her straw hat down on her head, against the breeze which was stronger by the sea. With a pang he recognized the yellow frilly bikini she had bought, abandoning her attempts at hiding the gash on her belly; the ruffles emphasized her breasts and the jut of rear. He followed her gaze and spotted their daughter.

Dahlia squatted on the wet sand. She filled her pail with the lapping wave that flowed up to her and emptied the water back onto the sand.

He didn't recognize the bathing suit on his daughter, he didn't know if she'd ever had one before. He felt immediate regret for not going more often to the beach, for not going at all to the beach, and he paused before he approached his wife because the two of them appeared so idyllic and perfect and all to themselves that he didn't want to interrupt this scene with anger or bitterness or shame.

He wanted them, right there on the beach, forever in this moment. The waves, the sky, an afterthought, a backdrop, brought alive by the presence of his family. His family. For this moment, none of them, not one of them, would ever grow old, or sick, or die.

Right here, please.

He held his breath and watched. He exhaled and waited. He inhaled again and approached his family. He didn't want to startle Lizette, so he made his way sideways, out of his way, and now strode to her where if she tilted her head, ever so slightly, she would see him.

She did, the expression of her eyes masked by unfamiliar sunglasses, a lazy wave of her arm, a smile, thank God, a smile! Out of her radio came a tinny soundtrack, a paperback splayed against the sand. Dahlia sprang up and ran over to him, covering the legs of his pants with clods of sandy mud. He dropped his finely, meticulously polished shoes on the sand and scooped her up.

"Do you like the ocean, my girl? How've you been? How's your mommy?" he asked while kissing her fat cheek and plump arm.

Dahlia pointed at a sea gull and was telling him about the birds here, and he concentrated on his daughter, the scent of salt air just like at Goleta, and he tried not to turn too quickly to his wife, too needily, too demandingly. Just him, as he was.

When he turned, she was still looking at him, waiting.

"Let's fly to Mommy." He swung her up and sailed her screeching over to Lizette. He stepped on the warm sand and saw two new beach towels and one small white towel that he assumed came from the cottage. As Dahlia shrieked, "I'm flying!" an old ache in his body awoke. Briefly, he felt an old mist cover his face, a sense of suffocation—he pushed it aside to concentrate on his wife, his love, his Lizette, who waited, an odd expression on her face.

Before he could stop himself, before he could put his arms around her, or his lips on her skin, he angrily demanded, "Who's that towel for?"

Her mouth went hard, she stared at the ocean, and in a low menacing voice she said, "My lover."

He shook his head, "Is this what you wanted to tell me?"

"You, Manuel, you, you fool, you are my lover. The only one. My only one." She said it angrily and bitterly and the knowledge left him unconsoled. Her tone confused him and made him miserable.

He sat down heavily on the sand. Polished shoes wouldn't have changed this, sleekly ironed trousers wouldn't have changed this. All he had was who he was. He kissed Dahlia and let her go, her arms outstretched to the mother who wouldn't look at either one of them.

"That towel is for you. You said you would be here today."

Dahlia wandered away, away from their silent anger and toward the foam that lapped at the wet sand. Manuel kept his eyes on his daughter. Was she too close to the waterline?

"I'm so upset," Lizette said, in a low voice. "I come to be alone, and you follow me, and what am I hoping for? I'm hoping for you, your arms. I'm hoping for you, some under-standing. I'm hoping for you, but I'm angry, and ashamed, and angry that I'm ashamed and ashamed that I'm angry." She glared at him. What was she talking about?

He looked away from Dahlia and at Lizette. "What happened? What happened?"

"I don't want to talk about it right now. I can't talk about it right now." She looked at Dahlia. "When I can, I will. I prom-ise. I just couldn't face you. Even though I wanted you here, now, I can't face you." She looked away.

She just said she wanted him here. He wanted to pick up her hands, to kiss her face, to hold her, but he knew better. Her entire body screamed not now.

"What is it?"

She shook her head, biting her lip. Against the words? Against tears?

He knew she would tell him when she was ready. He didn't want her to sense his impatience, his frustration on her behalf. His rage. He would make this right, whatever it was. He walked to the edge of the water and scooped Dahlia up.

Strong and willful, like her mother. She laughed when he twirled her upside down. She giggled when he held her above the water and dipped her toes into the crashing waves. Dahlia was many shades of brown, deep brown hair, golden brown eyes, skin soft and downy and bronze, nearly copper. He placed her back on the ground, and she bounced off ahead of the waves.

"Let's take a walk," he said to his daughter. And they did. Dahlia scampered ahead, rushing in and out of the foam. Gulls hovered and dove. Dahlia chased the roosting ones away. They walked and walked, then turned around, and Dahlia began to hug him at the thigh, and he scooped her up and held her and carried her back in the direction of her mother.

Dahlia, in his arms, wide-eyed against the wind, the sun, the gulls, the clouds, the spray, the breeze, held on. His daughter's small puffs of breath against his neck melted his anger into sorrow.

Lizette watched them as they returned and held a towel out for Dahlia, who went running into her arms.

He recognized that scene. He had lived that scene before. But this was now, this was his child, and his wife, and there was something not right. He gathered up the beach towels. Dahlia, wrapped in her beach towel, sang an unfamiliar song.

Back at the motel, Manuel settled Dahlia into a chair as Lizette draped towels on the patio furniture. She came into the room and examined him. "Let's just pretend for a while. Can we? Pretend things are fine."

He nodded, "Of course, of course! What are we pretending?"

"Kiss me," she said. He did. Her lips were the ones he had known for ten years now, soft and pliant and loving as she kissed him back. Then she pulled away.

Lizette fried the steaks in a skillet filled with onions and peppers. The flour tortillas she bought were light and airy. They drank RC colas and ate in the kitchen nook.

Lizette told Dahlia she would make a special bed for her; Dahlia thrilled to the sofa being pulled out and made into a bed. Lizette and Manuel played gin in the nook, Manuel with an eye more on Dahlia than his own cards. Once Dahlia fell asleep, her lips parted and her eyelids were thick and sealed.

"I'm going to lie down now," she said. Manuel understood it was not an invitation. He sat where he was, watching Dahlia. He could hear the waves crashing in the distance. He listened to his wife move around, then settle in. He waited, then waited some more, then gave himself permission to join her.

Lizette was curled, enveloped by bedding, facing the wall.

"Are you sick? Can I get you something?"

"I don't know how to say it," her voice was thick.

He sat on the bed and stroked her hip. "Take your time. I am here."

"Is Dahlia asleep?"

He got up again to look. From the bedroom light he could see her, sprawled out and half-uncovered. He covered her with the bedding. "Yes."

She turned to him. "Remember County USC? Remember how it was when Dahlia was born? You were at work, and our neighbor drove me over, all that pain, it all happened so fast, too fast, she was early, and I lay on the gurney waiting. I didn't tell you. We were both so happy to have our daughter, at last, alive and breathing, that I pushed so much of that away."

"What? What did you push away?" He had no idea what she said, what she meant. "What can I do? What can I say?"

She shook her head. "When it was over, we had Dahlia. I didn't think about it." She was quiet for a moment. "Did you ever wonder why we only have Dahlia?"

He shrugged. "Things just happen."

She shook her head. "All those miscarriages, and after Dahlia, no more?"

"Your body sorted itself out."

She snorted. "My body." She shook her head. "*My* body." She moved her hand over her face. She sat up against the headboard. She pulled a tissue out of its box and wiped at her nose.

"When I was studying for my test a few weeks ago I thought maybe I misunderstood what I was reading. So, I"—she cleared her throat—"I went to the goddamned doctor for a follow up, Manolo." She paused. "He told me some things, he told me some things about my body. He looked at my—I had to go back a second time. He didn't have my files the first time around. He got my files from County USC."

He pulled her close to him and shook his head. "What? I don't understand." It was hard to understand what she said, what this meant.

She pulled away from him as if she didn't want him touching her. "We were so happy, so relieved when Dahlia was born." She briefly covered her face with her hands. "They asked me how many times I'd been pregnant, and I told them, five, counting Dahlia and the miscarriages, all the while the pain is building, and I know there's something wrong. I told her, counting all those miscarriages, and something was wrong. They said, she said, they said they were gonna help me." She stopped and picked up a glass of water on her nightstand. "How could I have been so fucking stupid? Do I think just because you have a white coat and a nice face that you're going to help me? How could I have not known?"

She shuddered. "It was a nightmare. So many of us in the corridor, some women wailing with their pain, others crying, and then these doctors or orderlies or students, I don't even know anymore, it was a horde of them that descended on each of us. Someone gripped my left breast, someone else gripped my right breast, and another man spread my legs and looked in me." She made a face and turned away from him. "Like a rape," she whispered.

"I wish I were the kind of woman who could break things and hurt people, really hurt people, like the way they've hurt me." She didn't move away when he held her hand tight.

"When I had Dahlia, there was pain, so much pain. They said they would make the pain go away. I must have been out of my mind, out of my head, I had no idea—" She paused. She wiped at her eyes and took a deep breath.

She said, "They told me the baby would die if I didn't. I signed it, I signed it. *I* did this to us. Me. And that fucking doctor. They knew. They knew I didn't understand a fucking thing."

"What, Reina, what did you do? You didn't do this thing."

"Last week the doctor said it was there in my record, there for me to see, right there was my signature. I'd given them permission to give me a tubal ligation." She stopped. "That means my tubes tied. That means I can't have another baby."

"And now"—she pulled her hand away—"you know."

She looked at him with an expression he had never seen before, sorrow and fear. "Can you forgive me? I had no idea what I signed away. I signed our babies away."

"I don't understand." What she said wasn't making any sense.

She turned to him, mascara smearing beneath her eyes. "They tied my tubes. There was so much pain—there was so much pain, I thought I was signing for the pain medicine. I swear to you that's what the doctor said. I swear." She choked. "Because I thought our baby would die, because I couldn't bear the pain, we will never have another baby."

He sat heavily. He felt as if bricks had landed on his chest, sunk into his center. "What did they tell you? Who told you?"

"The nurses said to sign it. The doctor said to sign it. I didn't know that was the price. I want to die."

He gripped her wrist. "Don't say that."

"I want to die! I am so stupid. How could I have signed that? How did I not realize? Was I out of my mind with pain?"

He thought back to that day and all he could remember was the joy of Dahlia, the relief that both of them were alive and whole and well. They did not know Lizette was not whole.

She said, "It's all my fault."

"No, no, no. You didn't do this." Then added, "We'll find a lawyer."

"Who can give us back our missing babies?" she asked.

They were silent. She turned away from him. Manuel held her slender wrist in his hand.

"Just lay down with me," she said.

His body trembled all over, was it sorrow? Was it rage? How could he join and comfort her, when all he wanted to do was hunt down and murder the doctor who had wrenched the gift of life from his wife's body.

"Please," she said.

He waited for the roar of emotion to ebb, to fade the tiniest bit, then he joined her, fully dressed, in the bed.

She was crying, softly. "Do you forgive me?" she said.

"Mi reina, you did nothing to forgive." He cradled her, softly crooning into her ear. "I will make it up to you. I swear. I will make them pay. Every day. I will make it up to you."

"Shh, shh, shh," she said. "I can't lose you too."

And the two of them lay together, silently, separately eviscerated.

* * *

In the morning when he thought his heart would crack and her body would break and Dahlia would awake, they lay in their bedroom, behind the closed door. Manuel pulled the blankets and sheets off, to admire the beauty of her body, her nakedness, her womanliness. In the lighting her gaze at him seemed challenging and unapologetic.

How could she love a man who couldn't protect her?

How could she love a man who could not right this wrong?

He looked away from her and traced his finger on her jaw, to her breastbone, so fine and delicate, skated the curve of her breast, and stroked her belly.

Lizette told Manuel that when she found out, she thought her life was over.

He kissed her belly and lay his head on her. "If you ask it, I will kill the butcher that did this to you."

She stroked his scalp with her fingertips. He could feel the tingle spread from his head and radiate to the ends of his toes.

Her response was one of measured calm. "Never would I inflict that on you. Too many murdering men in this world." She stroked his head.

Bobby and the war. He wanted all of her, always, to himself, but part of him realized that was a violence in itself. There would always be a part of Lizette that was hers, and hers alone. Her grief for Bobby. Even her grief for her own body. He could only mourn alongside her.

"This is never going to happen to her," she said, both of them knowing she meant Dahlia. "I am angry, Manolo, about being stupid and ignorant and in pain. This will never happen to my daughter. This will never happen to any women I work with. I've been thinking about this. There's a women's clinic near us. I don't know what they pay, but I want to work there. I think I do. I'll go talk to them when we get back, about everything."

She said, "Things are going to be different when we get back home."

She was coming back home with him. That's all he heard and all he cared to hear.

They slept late into the morning, and when they awoke, they found Dahlia watching morning cartoons, the volume on low. He pulled Lizette's warm body closer to his. He never wanted to move. He wanted this forever and always, his daughter happy and safe, his wife, warm and wondrous next to him, while the sea outside crashed around them. Thank you, dear God, he thought, again and again.

After breakfast they walked to the waterline, Dahlia dancing in front of them, the pale moon visible overhead. This was the only child they would ever have. All the lives that might have been. These small breaths, these small steps, these tiny weights, these tiny lives, all this Lizette mourned. She had wanted children. He had only wanted what she desired. And now they were both barren. That butcher was a murderer. Life would have to go on, in its own broken way; it would be better for both of them if they held onto each other as life crashed around them.

CHAPTER TWENTY-FOUR

1970S

Manuel and Lizette grieved together, grieved alone. At a birthday gathering at Toño's and Cristina's, Lizette, with Manuel, took Amparo aside and told her. Amparo clutched their hands, wept, and prayed for them.

Manuel silently cursed the doctor who had mutilated Lizette.

Lizette began to interview for jobs. At the Mt. Washington clinic, so near their home, the hiring clinician looked at her and said, "I guess we won't have to worry about maternity leave."

"Can you believe that?" Lizette said, still offended, recounting her day to Manuel. "I walked right out of there."

Again, Manuel wished he could kill that doctor.

Lizette found a job in Cypress Park, a bit further. "Plenty of hardworking comadres go there," she told Manuel. Lizette came home with stories of mothers and children and young women; Manuel came home and planted a cactus or moved rocks or sealed a wall on their patio.

Union strong, Manuel made good money. He spent some of it searching for his sister. The memory of his parents was utterly and absolutely gone, a gentle murmur of an ocean breeze, a joyful flight in the sunshine was all he had. And the distant memories of his sister, fading, fading. Still, he paid money for searches, for ads, for misplaced addresses and wrong phone numbers. He paid a private investigator to dig into city archives.

Lulu, or Victoria, his parents who abandoned him, thoughts of finding them, were all too foolish. Like Amparo's curios, he would put them all on a shelf but out of sight. He would stop blaming himself for having misplaced them all.

He had stopped going to church long ago. Lizette stopped after she realized she'd been sterilized. It didn't matter—he tried to not let it matter—during Lizette's strange silences, her mouth hardened in a way he could never have anticipated—the coolness of the sheets on the bed between them made him long for her warmth.

Yet the church stories remained. "When I was a child, I spoke as a child, I understood as a child, I thought as a child: but when I became a man, I put away childish things." Was the longing for his sister, his parents, such a childish thing? Or was it as Amparo had said, Porque donde esté tu tesoro, allí estará también tu corazón. His treasure was his family, the one of his past. And this family, the one in front of him.

Dahlia, a bundle of energetic expressions and questions he never would have thought of as a child, wide smiles, and move-ment! *Of course* she was brilliant, she was Lizette's daughter. All the brains from his wife. All the joy.

He tried not to brood on their terrible trip to Carmel—never would he return there, never! Its beauty had pierced him like knives. Had it indeed been *their* trip? She had gone, he had followed, she had returned home, however reluctantly. The following week he took both his girls to Disneyland as if to dispel forever thoughts and memories of that horrible week.

Lizette began to teach Dahlia how to sew. Lizette, who had often made her own clothing and Dahlia's, pored over patterns with Dahlia, took her to fabric stores in downtown LA, had Dahlia help her make the curtains for her bedroom with a strange gauzy fabric that looked ethereal. Like an angel's wings.

He realized, slowly, painfully, that there would be no sons. What would a son of his have been like? What things would they have done together? In any case, he enjoyed his daughter tagging alongside him on the patio, watching him replace a damaged paver, carefully grouting between the stones. Because tool and dye was his job, he explained to her all the reasons for drill bits, just as he would if he had had a son. He gave her an old electric hand drill to play with and watched as she delightedly drilled into scraps of wood. He wanted to share with her his planes and chisels, but feared the damage they might do—not yet, he told himself. When she was older, twelve or thirteen.

On the weekends they went to Griffith Park or Whittier to visit Amparo and Toño and Cristina, family, where Lizette fussed over the four growing kids and Amparo smiled and cooed over Dahlia, who called her Gran Mom. Or to the beach, or to Goleta to visit Lizette's family where Dahlia's Uncle Roland and Grand Pop would show her the fields, introduce her to a few of the workers, take her to the beach to splash in the waves, and spoil her with ice cream and dime store toys.

"We are all each other's families," Amparo told them. The braided hair she wore as a crown was now completely gray. Manuel watched as Amparo, Lizette, and Cristina made this true with visits, with dinners, with celebrations. Dahlia in the midst of Toño's two boys and two girls some weekends, the girl cousins spending others with Dahlia at their home.

On some weekends they'd stay at home, Lizette studying for an exam—she was working on her master's of science in nursing—that woman was always doing something! She'd made him invite Colin and his family over, two boys, strong and energetic, and his wife, Julie, who moved like silk. While the two of them sat alone sipping beers, Colin told him how he worried for his boys, and Manuel felt for him. You couldn't hold onto a son like you could a daughter. He wanted Dahlia close by, always.

Other weekends, Dahlia, bored of TV or playing in her room, would trail him to the patio where he dug or moved stones, or the garage, its door open to the drive, where he puttered on a project.

Amparo and Lizette, in a rare moment of stillness, sat with him on the back patio that Manuel had begun to reshape and mold into his vision. He had built a rock garden into the walls that framed the patio. The irrigation was the tricky bit; he already knew which succulents he wanted. Something about it all, the colors, the birds, the sounds brought back Palo Verde.

Amparo said, "I see a little bit of our first home together here, Manolito." He leaned over and kissed her on the cheek.

* * *

He checked the fluids in his green Mercury, the one Beto had got him such a great deal on. He explained this all to Dahlia, now twelve and tall and wearing a yellow midriff that irritated him to see, with jean shorts, but Lizette had told him not to say a word, ever. Now he demonstrated: how to open the hood of the car; how to latch it securely so it didn't come crashing down on the back of your head, how to take the cap off a radiator, safely; how to add water, without scalding steam sputtering out. He demonstrated, then had her dip the oil wick in, check the level. He held the funnel while she poured.

She wore two long braids down the sides of her head,

looking a little like Lizette, but not quite. He tried to push the thought away, but it formulated before he could stop himself. Is this what Lulu had looked like at that age? Is there a trace of his sister in his daughter?

"What?" Dahlia saw him looking at her.

"Nothing," he grumbled, clearing his throat, then sighing.

Dahlia wiped her hands on her coveralls. "Uncle Rolis said we should go visit them real soon."

"Did he, now," Manuel said, still recovering.

"Yeah, Uncle Rolis says we can watch the ocean at night. It glows."

Manuel was irritated by this nonsense. They didn't have to lie to Dahlia to get her to visit.

Dahlia traced the hood of the Mercury with her finger. "Can I help you wash the car?"

Manuel nodded. He took a swift glance at the engine to ensure that everything was in its place, twisted the radiator cap again, made sure Dahlia was arms' length from the hood, and slammed it down.

As he started a bucket of sudsy water and gathered wash rags, Dahlia recounted her last visit to Goleta. "Grand Pop doesn't say a lot," she said, "but Uncle Rolis is so funny. How can he make so many funny faces?"

As she began to laugh and twist her own sweet face into weird, distended shapes, Manuel blurted, "You have an aunt, too."

"You mean Tía Cristina."

"No. You have another aunt."

Dahlia looked at him skeptically.

"I do?"

"Yes."

He splashed sudsy water on the trunk.

"What do you mean?" Dahlia stood up straighter and scrutinized him. "What's her name? Where does she live? When can I meet her?"

Now he'd really stepped in it. Why had he even mentioned it, why had it come out of him, like a pedo, and he'd now fouled the air with it. Sometimes he couldn't believe his own stupidity. He stopped washing. "Her name is Lulu. She's my sister."

"You have a sister?" The frown was deep across her face.

Manuel nodded.

"Can I meet her?"

Manuel nodded again. "Absolutely." As soon as I find her, he thought. "She'd love that."

He scrubbed the trunk some more, and this time Dahlia joined him. She was on to her favorite subject: buying a dog. Manuel listened and nodded along, grateful that it was she, and not he, who had changed the subject.

* * *

They went to the movies. Lizette loved the movies. Manuel loved watching the faces of his family. The first movie they took Dahlia to was *Mary Poppins*, and Manuel loved watching her eat a hot dog as she bounced on the cushion of her seat. The screen was so large, towering over them, just like when he was a child.

Sometimes it felt as if their lives were punctuated by movies. *The Ten Commandments* took the place of religious education. There was a Marx Brothers film festival; Lizette and Dahlia laughed all over themselves.

So did Manuel. He was so full of pride. It was true, he was proud. He was proud of his home. He was proud to have a wife so beautiful and a daughter so smart.

He tended to grumble through the musicals. They were challenging, and people breaking out in song in the middle of a crisis was unseemly and confusing to him. It didn't make sense. People didn't do that.

On a November Saturday afternoon, they piled in the Mercury he enjoyed so much, and he pulled out of their steep drive and drove to the Nuart in Bell. Lizette wore a flowering halter dress and Dahlia wore a smock dress Lizette had sewn for her.

Manuel bought the popcorn, the sodas, the hotdogs, Milk Duds for Dahlia, and ice cream bon bons for Lizette while the girls found seats.

It was a plush theater with crushed velvet seats and long drapes that covered the screen. The seats were a bit worn, he noticed as he rubbed his hands over the fabric.

"What's this about again?" he asked.

"You'll see," she said.

When he realized *Fiddler on the Roof* was a musical, he groaned inwardly. But, by God, he was with the two people he cared most about in the world. He would make the best of it, instead of regretting the afternoon, thinking that he could have spent the time working on the patio, fixing the cracks in the cement, finding the perfect planter for the rock and succulent garden he tended. Searching the nurseries for the right cactus.

While he was mulling all this, Tevye's story swept him up.

It was hard not to be swept up with this jokester, with this man with such confidence. As he watched, he wondered, and then believed, that he was Tevye. Sure, he didn't have four daughters and an aging wife, his wife would always be more beautiful than any woman, but he was Tevye. He was the Poppa, trying to support his family, trying to make this the best of all worlds. He had succeeded, hadn't he? His own little plot of land, his own job, back and forth, first as a machinist, then tool and dye. He could be proud with what he'd done. Their own home. He filled with pride when he thought of his home, and the patio he had built. The home he and Lizette had created, that Dahlia completed.

Oh God, he laughed at the rich man song. "When you're rich, they think you really know!" Oh God, didn't that explain Beto? Everyone went to him as if his money were the answer to all questions.

As he watched that boy sing about miracles, he squeezed his wife's hand. That was how he had felt when he had found Lizette. It was a miracle that she loved him, this unformed boy who had so little to offer.

Anatevka—that was Palo Verde! That was Chavez Ravine! The way people got along or didn't, the muddy roads. Okay, there were goats instead of a mule. But a small community of outsiders. Look, the rabbi, would be Hermano Sebastián!

This was his life on the screen. A bunch of Russian Jews. Who would believe it? The music wasn't annoying or irritating, it was strangely wonderful, stirring, emotional. This was his life —it had better have a happy ending.

He wasn't ready for the wedding scene. He wasn't. Why would those Russians come in and destroy everything? Why?

He looked over at Lizette and Dahlia, and they were staring up at the screen. He squeezed his wife's hand, and she ignored him, fully immersed in the movie.

And he, Manuel, would never disown his daughter. Never. Never. What was Tevye thinking? Of course, her getting married in the first place would be natural, but a jolt. Who would Dahlia have to marry for him to never want to see her again? What about Colin? What if Dahlia married one of his sons?

He couldn't imagine not talking to his daughter again, but maybe marrying Colin's son was going a bit too far.

Maybe he was closer to Tevye than he thought.

The daughter was leaving them. There was another song

that shredded the heart. It ended. The daughter said, "Only God knows when we will see each other again."

Lulu, his heart whispered.

Manuel found himself bawling from that point on until the demolition of Anatevka/Chavez Ravine. As the lights went up, he turned away from his family; he didn't want them to see him so weak. He didn't want them to know that this was his story.

CHAPTER TWENTY-FIVE

1975

Beto sent an invitation for them to spend a weekend to celebrate the new year with him in La Quinta and to meet his second wife. Manuel was feeling pretty good, he'd moved to an aerospace company, which turned out to be the same as Colin's, same toolroom, and they were both making good money. Feeling good and proud until the moment they drove over a gravel-lined road and pulled up to this desert home, a stark, low, rectangular building—all glass, concrete, and aluminum. Whisked inside, they had their own bedroom suite with a small refrigerator stocked with fruit and beer and wine. The pool was flanked by the dramatic shadow of the mountain and palm trees outstretched to the stars.

Beto smoked a thick cigar in the Jacuzzi. Beto's wife, Aubrey, tiny, in her twenties, with stiff blond hair and string bikini, sat poolside while Lizette, in her simple black one-piece, did laps in the shimmering turquoise pool. Dahlia was staying with her cousins in Whittier.

Beto could have rubbed it in, could have mocked him, could have rolled his eyes and meant, "See what I mean? I told you so:

sap," but he never did. He offered drinks and cigars, and warm laughs to Lizette's stories of Dahlia. Aubrey minced in and out, directing the brown server, who kept bringing the drinks, the brown cook, who made their meals, the brown housekeeper, who set and cleared the outdoor dining area.

* * *

Late at night, their legs in the luminous pool water, warm air on their arms, Beto asked them, "Why'd you two stop at one? I thought you were gonna over-populate the whole damn county."

Manuel saw Lizette wince. "Not sure," he said. Then, "You know, it's getting late for us."

In their bed made with sleek silk sheets, the thick blackout curtains drawn against the night outside, Lizette said, "Wouldn't you feel strange surrounded by so many people?" She was having trouble getting comfortable in the unfamiliar bed. "Makes me think he needs their help wiping his ass," she said distastefully.

They were silent the entire drive home; he was in a miserable mood. Everything he had been proud of, his home, his family, his job, revealed as modest, simple dreams. He had a wife, he had a daughter, and he had a home, and all that now felt strangely inadequate. He hadn't found his parents, he had abandoned his search for his sister, or he took it up sporadically until it pained him too much to even consider continuing. He now felt as if he were responsible for misplacing his family. As if he were responsible for Amparo's home in Chavez Ravine being razed, its pieces strewn in a landfill, all for Dodger seating in the bleachers. As if Lizette's sterilization were his fault. If he could get his hands on that doctor—

Logically he knew none of this was true. But he felt guilty

that he had never followed the notary's advice to go search for his parents in Mexico. That he gathered money for a home instead. That he avoided traveling there, even Tijuana or Rosarito Beach, where anybody with a day or two to spare traveled, talking about the clam cocktails and the flour tortillas—and that he hated all things Mexican—all things dark and cursed.

He saw himself for who he truly was: powerless.

"What is wrong with you?" Lizette complained the next morning, slipping on her nurse's uniform, a shirt decorated with teddy bears and lollipops over her blue scrub pants. "I married someone alive! And you act as if you're dead—trust me, you will be soon enough!"

It had been years now, since they'd found out Lizette had been sterilized. No mas bebes por vida. And yet the thought of that arrogant doctor still haunted him, angered him, ruined the two of them at times, just at the moment they lay in bed embracing each other. The thought of Lizette writhing in pain while someone mocked her, scarred her, eviscerated her. That doctor haunted him, haunted their lives.

Manuel had plenty of accrued vacation time, he didn't like being loose and unplanned, so he rarely took the time. He began to take a day here and there. He started with Dahlia's birth certificate.

It was the doctor at County USC who had told her to sign the paper and the pain would go away, Lizette was sure of that. On Dahlia's birth certificate was the name of the man who had delivered their baby.

Dr. Williams.

Manuel drove to County USC and found that Dr. Williams was still there. There were framed portraits of the doctors in the waiting room. "The white world," as Lizette called it. The murderer's portrait displayed a pale man with black-framed glasses and blond-gray hair in a military cut. In the photograph, he smiled; to Manuel the smile looked artificial, but everything about the man struck Manuel as contemptible.

He examined the waiting room: Los Angeles condensed and now seated and crowded into plastic chairs, some with cigarettes, others with baby strollers, and women with hair in curlers. There were white people, Mexicans like him and Lizette, Black people, and people he couldn't identify. Chinese. Japanese. There were people in hippieish clothing, women in short skirts, men in scruffy business suits, women in faded house dresses.

Had Dr. Williams ripped the babies out of some of these people as well?

They weren't all here for babies, of course. This was County USC, they were here for anything.

He waited in line at the reception until his turn, when he asked the woman with the gnarled hands when Dr. Williams would be in, he wanted to deliver a gift. She looked at him, back to a chart on her desk, then back at him.

"Dr. Williams comes in tomorrow at noon. But things change, you know, depending on the baby."

Manuel nodded in what he hoped was a reassuring and understanding gesture. He glanced at his watch: it was ten-thirty.

The next day at eleven he drove his car slowly around the vast lot that spread out around the hospital until he found what he was looking for: the staff parking lot. This one had an attendant in a small, covered building.

He wondered if doctors considered themselves as part of the staff or if there was another separate, more special lot for them. He idled his car, the engine a little rough, reminding him that he should change the oil this week. He listened to the news on the radio. People were upset. People were always upset, and now he would be, too.

He watched a man in a loose-fitting gray suit and a maroon briefcase move swiftly out of the staff parking lot and toward the hospital. Seemed a sure bet this man was a doctor, although he couldn't say he could remember his face from the portraits—all his energy had been spent hating on Dr. Williams.

Manuel circled the public lot again, and this time fit into a slot adjacent to the staff lot. He listened to the news. He listened to music, hearing neither the melody nor the words, intent upon finding Dr. Williams.

What would he say when he met him? What would he do?

Eleven-thirty, then twelve. Then twelve-thirty. Cars arrived and entered. Men left the lot and headed to the hospital. Dr. Williams was not one of those men.

At twelve-forty-five the attendant left his stall and headed toward the hospital. Manuel figured he was headed to the toilet.

Soon after, a deep-blue Lincoln with a darker-blue vinyl rooftop pulled up to the attendant booth. The driver stepped out, a man with black-rimmed glasses, silver blond hair in a military cut, who pushed up the barrier-arm and drove through.

Dr. Williams.

Manuel was swiftly out of his car, following Dr. Williams and the sound of the Lincoln's engine into the parking structure. He hurried as the doctor leisurely made his way back to the attendant booth to lower the barrier-arm. In five paces, Manuel came face-to-face with the doctor, blocking his way forward.

"Excuse me," the doctor said.

Manuel scowled at him; the man's face was older than that contained in the hanging portrait.

He had found him, now what had he wanted to say?

Williams blinked at him, uncomprehending, his lashes nearly invisible against the pink ridges of his lids. "Let me by," he said.

Manuel glanced around. There were people one hundred yards away at the hospital entrance. There was a car pulling into the public lot. The attendant booth was visible from here, but the attendant had still not returned.

As the doctor moved to get by, Manuel thought of Lizette home in bed in a dark room; of the way her face had crumpled as she blamed herself; of the months and then years they waited for that second child that was never to come; of the rage that flooded his chest and torso when she told him the reason. Of the years since.

In rushed the desolation he associated with his missing parents and absent sister; abandonment by the counselor who told him what Mexicans couldn't do. Lizette, Lizette who had rescued him from bleakness, from despair and misery. She had saved him from his miserable self, and he hadn't protected her.

He stared at the doctor's blank eyes, pale lashes. The edge of the man's mouth turned downward; Manuel saw the contempt, scorn, and derision that allowed a man like that to do what he had done to Lizette's body, to their lives, blithely, without regrets, compunctions, or even a second thought to the lives he shattered.

"Hey Doc," he said. "You sterilized my wife. I wanted to give you something."

With the hands of a manual laborer who had been working since sixteen, Manuel swung his rage-filled fist into the doctor's jaw and heard bones crunch under the impact. As his body crumpled forward, Manuel threw the force of his left fist into his gut, and the body collapsed.

Manuel glanced around. There was still no one. He pulled

the heavy body deeper into the parking lot, panting with rage and anger as he lay him on his side.

He could kill him. Just as he had killed their possibilities, he could kill this man with blood dribbling out the side of his mouth.

He could kill him now, easily, simply, and slip away.

Using his steel-reinforced work boots, he kicked the unconscious doctor with all his force in the kidneys.

May he piss blood for the next year, Manuel thought, walking swiftly to his car. And may he consider his sins, every time he does.

He registered the trembling of his hands as he reversed the Mercury and pulled slowly out of the lot. He spied the attendant sedately returning to his station; two cars entered as Manuel exited. He drove carefully home.

That night as Lizette read in bed, he checked in on Dahlia, asleep, kissed the top of her head, her dark hair matted, dull, a little dirty. That was when he realized his hands were aching. He went to their kitchen, filled a bowl with ice, added water, and stood at the sink, soaking his hands in the icy water, wishing for Amparo's concoction that had soothed him his first day on the docks.

One day, on the day when Lizette needed it most, he would tell her what he had done.

CHAPTER TWENTY-SIX

As Lizette aged, Manuel was grateful that she remained beautiful in that mature, elegant way some women were lucky enough to possess. As Dahlia grew, Manuel couldn't help but admire his daughter. There was nothing tentative or diminutive or shy about her. She was loud and forthright in a way that surprised him. As if his fear and timidity were turned inside out by her. Dahlia was a wild girl with a big smile, and she couldn't stop moving, couldn't stop arguing, couldn't stop finding something wrong with the world, but what Manuel didn't understand was couldn't she see that her world was *magic*. Her world was a Mt. Washington home with the two people who had conceived her, family who adored her, a room to herself. Stability. She knew who she was and where she came from. She knew the secret of her existence, like Lizette. Like Lizette, she knew who she was and where she came from. Nothing at all like him.

Lizette also explained to Dahlia why she had no siblings, thankfully when Manuel was not in the house, because he might have punched his way through a number of doors—filled with shame, embarrassment, and anger that there was nothing he could do to change this.

In her senior year, in 1980, Dahlia had already been accepted on a full scholarship to UCLA, USC, and two tiny colleges in the Midwest whose names were strange and unfamiliar. Manuel blamed Lizette. What had he wanted? Lizette. A good job to raise his family. He did not want Dahlia leaving to some strange state she'd have to fly to. Was that what Lizette wanted? When would they even see her?

Lizette was always talking to the women she met, Spanish speakers, English speakers. What kind of job did they have? How were they paid? Did they need a doctor's note for their time off? She recounted all their answers to Dahlia. Lizette made sure that what had happened to her never happened to Dahlia. That Dahlia's body was hers and hers alone to control.

Dahlia. Yes, Manuel wanted the world for his brilliant daughter. Yes, he wanted whatever her dreams were, but he hoped her dreams were to stay close by, to get married, have a lot of kids. To never leave them.

Dahlia came into their kitchen with a ripped envelope and a smile that took up half her face. She wore stone-washed jeans that were pleated in the front, like men's from an old movie, and a T-shirt that made her look curvy like her mom. He wished Dahlia wouldn't wear tight shirts like that outside of the house or anywhere for that matter, but he had lost that argument with Lizette when their daughter was in tenth grade.

"It's her body," Lizette said. "She is never going to be ashamed of her body."

Here Dahlia was, crushing him with her arms. "Columbia, Dad." She practically bounced up and down. "Columbia. The only thing it's gonna cost us is the travel."

He hugged her back and squeezed, nearly choking. "Beautiful girl, felicidades."

That's what she had been doing the past years, studying for the PSAT and SAT. Filling out the college applications, the scholarship applications, the financial aid forms. Lizette. She got this all from Lizette.

"Remind me, where is Columbia?" Manuel asked.

"New York City, Dad," Dahlia said, a hint of exasperation in her voice.

Pride and love and loss and abandonment. He dropped the glass of water he was drinking from. It shattered on the tiles, and he cursed silently and swept it up, grateful for the distraction, afraid to look at his daughter as Dahlia ran to tell her mother.

That night in bed together he admitted to Liz, "I'm not sure she should be going."

Lizette sat up in the bed and glared at him. "Why is that?"

"It's far, it's cold, it's—" He faltered under her gaze. "It's New York City, it's dangerous," he said. What if she doesn't come back? What if she dies on the plane? What if she falls in love and decides to live there forever? What if, what if, what if?

Lizette scolded him. "Viejita! Old woman! Old man! This is her life, this is her adventure. I wish, I wish," she added, "I wish I could be going."

It was as if he didn't know her at all. Why would his Lizette want to be going?

* * *

He couldn't help himself, he tried to not think of it, but he did. "It" being Lulu. Of course it was Lulu, and his parents, but his parents? Could they even still be alive? Who knew where they were? Lulu, she had to be alive. She had to be. What would she even look like? Manuel wished he could see her face. Wished he could hold her hand. Hoped he would see her, please God, before he died.

He decided to go to the Mexican Consulate. He was proud of himself, he had come up with this idea on his own. He didn't tell Lizette, he didn't tell Dahlia. The consulate could help, they'd have to, right? Maybe something good would come of this, and he could share the news with them like a miraculous surprise. A gift.

The Mexican Consulate stood in a brand-new boxlike building on the corner of Park View on Sixth Street on the edge of MacArthur Park. He and Lizette had brought Dahlia to the park a few times. It seemed to him more worn down, filled with more bums than he recalled. He wasn't supposed to call them that, according to Dahlia, but he'd forgotten the right word. He flashed briefly to the men Amparo had housed and fed. Poor bastards, he thought.

He drove past the building to find street parking. He was disappointed by the blank, uninteresting architecture of the boxlike building. In his mind he had an image of an imposing Spanish/Mediterranean building with a courtyard, guarded by fences of black wrought-iron, a place striking and compelling. Nothing like this generic office building. A huge Mexican flag wafted on its flagpole.

There was a line about twenty people deep, waiting to enter the offices. He got in line. He double-checked to be sure he had his ID with him, his birth certificate, the picture of his parents. The line moved slowly, and he was glad he'd gotten here to stand in the cool morning air. He spent his wait examining the people, the structure, glancing over at the noises coming from the park. He was surprised to read "Los Estados Unidos de México" over the entrance door. Another United States.

An hour later he was inside the building. Mexican

nationals followed the green strip on the floor, while non-Mexican nationals followed the red strip painted on the floor. There was no one in front of him, so Manuel followed his designated pathway down a narrow hallway to an open door on the left. He was now in a never-ending line, like those at the amusement parks, where he'd waited alongside his daughter. There were a handful of people, perhaps Americans like him, in front of him. There were two people behind glass, like at his bank. One, a tall man with glasses spoke softly to the two people in front of him. At the other window was a woman with elaborately died and teased hair, a kind of copper brown, intently reading a book while eating something. She had a plaque reading "cerrado" in front of her. She was oblivious to the souls waiting for her.

When Manuel was at the head of the line, the man leaned over to the woman. Manuel watched intently. She had gold bracelets that jangled each time she turned the page of her book or brought a morsel of food to her mouth. Whatever she was eating smelled delicious and was making him hungry. The last client ahead of him left the window. As Manuel stepped forward the man turned his plaque to "cerrado" and again leaned over to the woman.

She took a heavy sigh, wiped her hands with a moist towelette, made a big show of marking the page where she was reading and slowly and deliberately turned the plaque to read "abierto" and looked straight ahead, definitely not in Manuel's direction.

He noticed now she was older than he previously thought and that she was adorned in gold jewelry. The golden bracelets on her wrists were strands of gold coins. On her chest hanging on a heavy gold chain was a huge golden coin with an eagle on it. "50 pesos" read the embossing. Mexican coins.

She sniffed.

"Good morning," he said, addressing her through the slot in the glass window. He saw now what she had been eating. There were little Styrofoam containers of chopped onion, quartered limes, sliced radishes. And a huge bowl of soup. It looked like pozole. She sniffed.

"Don't they give you a lunch break?"

"Of course they do! This is just a snack," she answered, annoyed. "What is it you want from me?" she asked, raising and spreading her arms in an exaggerated gesture.

Before he could respond, she picked up her book, closed it, set it aside. Pushed her cup of coffee and thermos aside and leaned toward the pane of glass between them. Manuel became nervous and self-conscious, but the man in the next slot had disappeared, and there was no one waiting behind him.

"Day after day people like you come here, interrupt my tranquility and fill my days with questions. Questions, questions, questions!"

"I'm looking for some help," he began and waited for her response as she waited for him to continue. He went on. "I'd like to get the copies of my parents' birth certificates. Here are their names." He pushed his birth certificate into the steel tray, like a bank teller's, that separated them.

The woman's eyes turned to slits, and she slowly moved her head from side to side. She said, "You have to go to their hometowns to get those."

Here he thought his plan had been so brilliant. He stopped, faltered, regrouped. He began again, "I have been told that in the '30s, '40s, and even '50s Mexican families were taken from their homes here and taken to Mexico. I was wondering..."

"Ah," she said, "You need window 53 B."

"What?"

"53 B. Here." She wrote something on a slip of yellow paper. "Take this, tell them your story." Her English was

immaculate with some kind of florid ring to it. Commanding.
She turned her sign again and reached for her book.

"What are you reading?" he asked because he was
intrigued by her utterly disdainful presence.

"*Rain of Gold*, young man. *Rain of Gold*. It should be
required reading for all of you pochos."

Stung, Manuel clutched the scrap of yellow paper and
walked out of the room, in search of window 53 B.

There was no line on the fifth floor at the office window
marked 53 B. Behind the glass wall, another woman, crisp and
fresh and immaculate, listened to him as he told her what he
was hoping for, and he held out his supporting documents.

She examined it, pushed it back to him, and blinked her
eyes.

He told his tale again. What could they do?

She kept her perfectly arched eyebrows raised as he told
her his story. Of missing parents, a missing sister. He spread out
his birth certificate, and she impassively inspected it.

"Do you know how many people this happened to?" she
said.

He shook his head.

"I heard one million."

Manuel waited. She continued. "One million pobre creat-
uras condenados. Think of it. What was it like for the kids to be
dumped in a land you'd never come from? My cousin lived in a
village and the kids that were dropped there didn't speak a
word of Spanish." She shuddered at the thought. "They did not
do very well, I'll tell you that."

"My parents? Can you maybe help me find them?"

She shrugged. "I can put in a requisition." She shrugged
again. "I cannot promise much. We are a big country."

They would keep his request, add his name and the name
of who he was searching for in their files. She verified his

mailing address and phone number multiple times. If they knew anything, they would share it with him.

He walked back to his car. He had been so proud of this idea. He hadn't let hope grow within him, but it had, despite his own caution. Grown and gushed like the fountain in the park. Getting into his car, without anything known or to show for his day here, was painfully anticlimactic.

CHAPTER TWENTY-SEVEN

"Manny," Toño's voice was on the phone. "Ma's gone. I wanted you to know."

Amparo, aged eighty-two, had died.

"How?" Was all Manuel could choke out.

"She just didn't wake up."

Tía Amparo. He had foolishly thought she would always be there, her love would always surround him and his family like a force field. Tía hovered around his life with so much love that he could take it for granted, squander it, even. The woman who had saved the terrified little boy.

He blinked back tears. "Thank you, Toño. She saved my life." He hung up to tell Lizette.

* * *

The funeral was not at all what he expected. He, Lizette, and Dahlia sat in the front row alongside Toño, Chrissie, and their kids. The pastor, a benign man, spoke platitudes in front of the open casket. The hymns and prayers were in English.

Manuel had half-expected the congregation from Iglesia Pentecostal de Dios to be there, for Hermano Sebastián to speak, for the church to be filled with the flowers and birds of Chavez Ravine. And afterward a huge potluck with freshly made flour tortillas, steaming casseroles, and pots of beans.

Instead, Toño invited the family to Mimi's, a local restaurant, for an early dinner.

Perhaps, wherever Amparo was, she was surrounded by the families and flowers of Chavez Ravine. That was Manuel's prayer for her.

A few months afterward when Dahlia moved away to college, he found himself not wanting to leave the neighborhood, his home, their bedroom. The cold mist had returned, and now he trudged through the swamp daily. When he lay in bed there was an ache like a quarry full of stones on his chest that oppressed him. When he opened his eyes, he saw the world in deep and miserable grays.

The neighborhood had changed throughout the years. More Central Americans, a few Vietnamese, a handful of Blacks. White faces creeping in. In 1986 Reagan gave people amnesty, and now, it seemed, Mexicans were everywhere. Mexicans different from him. They spoke Spanish better than him, listened to unfamiliar music. He felt different from them. He worried that they all made the real Mexican Americans, like him and his family, look bad.

Before he visited the consulate once a year or so he'd place his ad in the papers. *Orange County Register, Long Beach Pilot, Los Angeles Times, The Penny Saver, La Opinión.* He'd abandoned the post office box long ago and sifted through the letters that arrived. He got onto a lot of junk mail lists.

Lizette said he should hire an investigator, so they did. When he went through their ten thousand dollars in savings, they had nothing to show for it. Nothing at all.

His annual advertisements were his way of daydreaming a different life story, a different ending. He refused to spend another dollar on a useless investigation.

* * *

"You need to go to the doctor," Lizette told him, slipping out of her scrubs and into velour sweats.

"You need to see the doctor," Dahlia told him on her calls home.

"You need to pull your head out of your ass," his supervisor told him, after he'd fucked up another progressive die.

What he didn't want to tell Lizette or Dahlia was that he was pretty sure he was dying. That was what made sense to him, all the juice for living had leaked out and soaked into the ground. He was dying, and he would only be in their way, lying like a warped log, ruining Dahlia's years in college—what shit that would be to have to live with. Dragging Lizette down, still a beautiful woman, she could find someone, she would find someone to care for her even better than he had. Damn well better not be that bastard Beto!

He didn't want them to know, he didn't want them to make a fuss over him. He just wanted to slip out as quietly, as silently as possible. He wanted to stay in bed, invisible, and fade away.

* * *

"Wake up, Manolo. Wake up!" Lizette shook him, roughly. "Are you all right?"

Manuel blinked around, for a moment not recognizing the room where he lay, the room where they lived for twenty years. He blinked at his wife, filmy from the sleep in his eyes.

"Are you all right?" she repeated and leaned down. "You

were crying, Manuel. It broke my heart to hear you. You were crying. What were you dreaming?"

He shook his head—whatever the nightmare, it had slipped out of his head. Torn between embarrassment, grief, and gratitude, he looked at his wife with admiration.

"I don't know what I was dreaming." She looked at him with concern. "Kiss me," he said.

Her kiss led to another, then another, and soon they got up to things they seemed to not have had time for recently.

"I thought you didn't love me anymore," she said.

He was shocked. "Why would you think that?"

She shook her head. "You just don't seem to look at me that way much anymore." He wanted to protest, to say she was wrong. Lizette was, and remained, beautiful. With the birth of Dahlia her nipples had darkened and spread in a way that was almost unbearably erotic. Her body throughout the years had thickened, only making her curves more pronounced. He pulled her close and stroked her thighs, her hip, and gently, the cleft between her legs that embodied the mystery of her being. He wanted to say that he always looked at her in that way, but she was right. That was part of the juice that had leaked into the ground.

"Ah, Reina. It's just that..."

She looked at him pointedly.

"I'm just tired."

"You don't look at your wife, you're not excited for your daughter, you're jealous of Beto."

"Now that's not fair, everyone's jealous of Beto."

"You're right. Even me, a little bit."

They lay in bed together and Manuel could feel her breast on his chest. Little heart explosions were going off. What a strange existence, to have your wife wake you up from a bad dream you can't remember, then love her, only to be told by her that you're a screw up.

He said, "Sometimes I feel..." He searched for the word, then said, "Empty."

Lizette said, "What do you mean?"

"I didn't do things right. I should have done things differently. I..." He faltered. "I should have found my family."

He felt her bristle beside him. "You created a family," she said, evenly, in a way that he knew—she was controlling her temper. "You built a home for your family."

She sat up, her naked breasts exposed, distracting him, as she said, "I don't mention my mother to you, because she was gone long before we met. Yet I miss her, wish she was with me, every single day. Why would we talk about the impossible? And Bobby, God, what would Bobby be today?" She smiled. "Can you see him? I can, him and Alice in our lives, and their family. I can see it. Sometimes I think about it. But our lives are right here, Manolo, right here in front of us, here in our bed, Dahlia in her studies. Right now."

He pulled away and sighed. "I don't know what you want from me."

He stopped talking to Lizette about this. He didn't want her to know that there was a part of him forever lost, trudging through a swamp, the stones around his neck, or the weights in his clothing when he stepped into work. He remembered feeling all this a long time ago. People, even Lizette, seemed farther and farther away.

He needed to let go of hope. To give up, if not looking for them, to give up hope of finding them. He wasn't going to talk to a therapist, he wasn't going to complain anymore. He was going to suck it up, be a man.

When the weights got too heavy, or the mist at work too thick, he'd just blink and focus. At home he spent more and more time on the concrete patio, rearranging the stone wall, setting in and transplanting the succulents.

* * *

He watched the hillside light up as the sun went down, the warm and welcoming interior lighting gradually blinking on, showing domestic scenes. Kids' voices outside, kids playing, kids screaming, kids crying. Sounds reminding him of when his daughter was young, reminding him of when he walked in the darkness as an angry young man.

Right now, in the present, a pang of regret about Amparo made him sit back down.

Last year the open casket in the Pentecostal Church had displayed Amparo with a gray skin tone and the feeble smile on her face had looked like a smirk. He had never seen Amparo smirk in actual life. Just a full-throated laugh and smile that would make you think she was young and rich and beautiful and happy.

Manuel scolded himself. How would he know if she were happy? He had gone to her with all his problems, with all his outrages, longings, aches. She teased him, pulling his hair at the crown of his head, but she didn't mock him. She listened.

And now, seated at his rustic kitchen table of his own home, inspecting the gnarled veins on the backs of his hands, he drowned in a wave of shame.

Had he ever asked her whether she wanted a partner? Had she wanted other children of her own?

How had his wife wept when she realized she would never be pregnant again; what of Amparo?

From the day he joined her, it was always about his loss, his pain. He had never once wondered about the longings and dreams of the woman who had taken him in and saved him from the world.

He was disgusted with himself.

He stood abruptly and decided to take a walk. Maybe shake the ghost of Amparo out of his head.

* * *

Dahlia did return from Columbia, from New York City, from that world strange and foreign and exotic to Manuel, if not to Lizette who made sure to make an annual pilgrimage to New York City.

During those four years Manuel couldn't countenance it. Couldn't see himself getting on a plane. He made it once, for the graduation. It was the best he could do.

Dahlia did return! Back to her old bedroom, which she stripped of its posters and repainted and began hanging angry posters filled with worker slogans. He appreciated the sentiment, but why were her causes so angry?

Dahlia was his daughter, but like women in general, a deep mystery. He'd see women on the street, or in the movies, or on television, with thick flowing hair, wavy, puffing out around their faces. Lizette's hair was long and straight, something easy to manage for her job. Dahlia? When he first saw her hair, he didn't know what to say. It was cut short and spiked upward. If you didn't look too closely, she could pass for a guy. Why'd she do that?

Was she trying to tell her parents something? He'd asked Lizette, who just shrugged, "Y que?" she'd responded.

They returned to a household rhythm, whereas once there had been two parents and a child, now there were three adults.

* * *

He would come home from work and listen to Lizette and Dahlia talk. Dahlia in graduate school at UCLA, driving there three days a week. Dahlia always intent upon pointing out some injustice in the world, whether about tenants or landlords or field hands or the women who were at the clinic where Lizette worked. Lizette's long slender fingers poured the three of them coffee in the morning before Manuel left for work. And when he returned? Both of them, back at the kitchen table, Dahlia with a book and a notepad propped in front of her while Lizette fussed over her with a small snack.

He loved watching the two of them drink coffee and argue or gossip or laugh to the point of tears. One day as he kicked off his work boots and washed his hands in the kitchen sink, brushing up against the warm curves of Lizette, a thought came to him: Both the women in his life would have master's degrees. Oh, lord, his heart soared. He was proud to the bursting. It was enough. It was all he wanted. This was enough, wasn't it?

There was Lizette, now fifty-five, looking twenty-five, so fierce in her concentration at the stove. He tugged her toward him and kissed his wife with all the love and pride in his heart. Her lips were soft, welcoming, spicy, she must have sampled the sauce she was simmering.

She said, "Hold on, Romeo, our daughter's here."

Dahlia, head in a book, snorted.

He kissed his wife again.

"What's that for?"

He said, "For all the times I've forgotten."

This time she kissed him back.

* * *

After dinner Lizette sat in the living room watching news on KMEX, while Manuel washed up and Dahlia continued to study. Lizette had often told him she had a thing for one of the broadcasters. "If you don't watch yourself, I'll leave you for that guy!" Jorge Ramos's intent face shone from the screen.

"Dad," it was Dahlia interrupting the scrubbing of the saucepan.

"What?" He was strangely nervous, she looked so serious. What could she be serious about? Did she want to move out? Did she find someone to love her? All love was fine by him, he just didn't need to know all the details—

"I know this is sensitive, so, could you sit down with me?"

"You want your mother here, too?"

Dahlia shook her head. "No, just you."

He dried his hands, took a deep breath, and sat down.

"Please don't get upset," she started, "but—"

Well, of course that upset him from the get-go. Those few words and now he felt his skin as a casement for his anger— such a stupid phrase, why would his brilliant daughter of all people start with that—he had lost track of what she was saying, and she was waiting for his response.

"What?"

She started again, "Dad, I know it's hard to talk about this. I know we don't really talk about it, but I just can't, you know, try to help our community without starting with my own family. I think about Grand Mom, you know, and what she did for you, but I think about why she had to step in. Why? You know. And Mom told me about the notary you went to, and what he said—"

Now he was angry. Pride and anger combined, and he flushed with shame. Why had they both betrayed him in this way? Highlighted his stupidity? He stood to get away, get away, flee, run, take another goddamned red car to San Pedro...

"No, please sit down, Dad, please listen to me."

The beaded earrings she had made dangled from her ears,

the short spiky hairstyle of hers now looked short and angry; but she wasn't angry, he was. And embarrassed. How much he wanted to protect her from all the hurt and pain and everything. All of life, all of it, he wanted to shield her from.

But she was an adult now, and he had been one for a very long time.

"What do you want to ask me?" he said, terrified of what might come next.

"I'm not asking you anything. I want to tell you something. Can I?"

He nodded.

"Dad, hundreds of thousands of us were sent to Mexico. Hundreds of thousands of us, Mexicans, US citizens, men, women, and children who lived here, worked here, loved here. This is what our country did to us."

Manuel shook his head, this did not make sense. He felt like Nick, who claimed, since he'd never heard of it, it couldn't possibly be so.

As if knowing what was going on in his head, she said, "There's a lot of bad things this country has done, and we don't always know about it. I want to make the world a better place, I do. Like you and Mom have. But I gotta start here. There's a professor who studies this at UCLA. Maybe you could talk to him, you know? Maybe there's something he could help us with."

"Us?" He raised an eyebrow. This was his burden.

"Us," his daughter insisted. She got up, gave him a hug, and left him at the table.

* * *

Manuel avoided discussing it further with Dahlia. She kept offering to take him, and he kept telling her he was busy. He would do this on his own, and if he found out something, so much the better. The prouder he would be, of her, of himself, when he had something to share. He called, made an appointment with the professor, and one Wednesday he took a half day and drove the interminable drive to Westwood, the West Side. After a couple of wrong turns and misdirections, he found himself at the parking structure where he'd been directed to, and he set off for Professor Enrique Esparza.

On the phone the man had sounded noncommittal, but Dahlia had been on his mind, pushing him along.

But look at this campus!

Manuel scanned across the expanse of green between gorgeous brick buildings. He went up to one and rubbed his hand against the brick and grouting. Beautifully done.

He looked at his watch. He had plenty of time. How big was this place?

Look at the students. They all looked like they knew they belonged here. They walked like it was their place, and it was, right? Not like a doddering old man, like him, gaping at the masonry, the shrubbery, the sculptures.

He walked through the sculpture garden. He admired the big and bold structures, the gleaming surfaces, the boxlike structure that gushed water in the center of a shallow pool. He came across one that was smooth yet disjointed and made him uncomfortable. "War Remembrance" the title read.

This is where his daughter went. By God, he hoped she walked like she knew she belonged here.

He looked at a campus map and started walking. There was a building he wanted to see.

The engineering building wasn't what he expected, but still, he held his breath as he watched young men and sometimes women go in and out. There were Mexicans there, he could tell. There *were* Mexican engineers as Amparo had said. Hell, maybe even Guatemalans or Salvis.

How stupid to believe the lies he had been told in high school. No Mexican engineers! How ignorant he had been.

He navigated his way back to where he was heading. The spaciousness of the campus made him feel small and yet buoyant. He entered a poorly lit building, navigated his way to the stairwell, and rapped on the door bearing the plaque Professor Esparza, Endowed Chair.

"Come on in." And so he did.

"I'm Manuel Galvan, Professor."

"Call me Enrique."

Enrique Esparza sat in a stiff armchair. He had a tailored white shirt on. A jacket hung neatly on a hanger behind. Enrique's face was plump, with lines on his forehead, wisps of hair brushed across the top of his head. On one wrist was a heavy wristwatch, on the other hand a simple gold band.

"Come in, have a seat."

Manuel sat down, little echoes going off within him. A wall was lined with bookshelves, with photographs of Esparza surrounded by students in cap and gown. All the students looked Mexican.

Manuel cleared his throat. "Thank you for taking the time out of your busy day to meet with me." He didn't know if this man had a busy day. He didn't look busy at all. He looked like he was lounging in an easy chair surrounded by books. His colleagues probably never got injured by machinery. Tension and unease began to build in his chest.

"How can I help here?" The professor nodded encouragingly. He looked like a patient man.

What had his daughter said? He cleared his throat again. This shouldn't be this hard, he'd talked to the management, he'd spoken at union meetings. But this was about him, that was the difference, this was about him and his life. Could this man unravel the mystery? Surely, it was too much to ask. That was what choked him. Hope.

"Long story short," Manuel began, willing himself not to get choked up, willing himself to put all the emotion aside, as if this was not his story, but something that had happened to a stranger. A stranger he was sympathetic to but removed from and distant. A stranger. A ghost of a ghost. "When I was a child, I lost both my parents. I have the sense that one day they were there, and one day they were not. A former neighbor told me they were swept up in the mass deportations. I have a sister, too. I've been looking for her, off and on, for years and years. I was hoping—" Damn, there was that word again. He changed course. "I was wondering if there was anything you knew that could help me find them."

Esparza nodded, encouragingly. Manuel pulled out the large envelope he had been carrying. He withdrew his birth certificate and the photograph Jean Shiro had given him decades ago and placed them in front of the professor.

Esparza examined both documents carefully and nodded. "That's interesting," he said.

Manuel's heart stumbled. "What is?"

"It's interesting to me, it doesn't impact your question to me. Your parents are listed as Indian, and you're listed as white. They could have listed everyone, including you, as Mexican. I mean, it's interesting to me, as a scholar. These kinds of things impacted the 1940 census, nobody wanted a bunch of Mexicans claiming Indian tribal rights."

Manuel's heart slowed. This was of no concern to him.

"And these are your parents," the professor said, "so many years ago."

Manuel nodded. He had no more to say.

Finally, in place of the silence between them, Esparza said,

"Not a common story, but not uncommon either. And it's not just shame that keeps us from sharing these stories, it's as if, if we don't bring it up, maybe it won't happen again. If we just toil quietly, in our little part of the world, maybe we won't bring attention onto ourselves, maybe they'll just ignore us and leave us in peace." Enrique raised his eyebrows at Manuel. "Right? I interviewed so many families, Manuel. Not to diminish your tragedy, not in any way."

They sat again in more silence. Manuel was nervous now, the man had not answered his question, and more and more Manuel felt the weight of his work shoes and the calluses on his hands, contrasting against the softness of the man across from him.

At last, with impatience prompted by the professor's indifference, Manuel asked, "Do you know of anything, anyone, who can help me find them?"

The professor leaned back on his chair. "You ask the most important question—is there any organization that can help you relocate them, contact them, find them. You are right to bring me the birth certificate, but as you yourself can see, there is no city or village of origin listed for either of your parents." The phone on his desk rang. The professor let it ring.

"What can I do?" Manuel asked.

"I am so sorry you are in this position. I do know others like you. Some have been able to find their families, but to be perfectly honest, they knew what towns to look for them in. Others are still quite wounded by the destruction of their families."

The professor paused and looked across the desk at him. "I could put you in touch with them. You could share your stories. That could help in not feeling so alone, in not feeling like you were targeted by all this."

Manuel scratched at his forehead. Strangers. Talk to

strangers about the worst thing in his life. But what if he returned empty-handed without anything to offer Dahlia? She and Lizette would shake their heads at his lack of follow-through. He couldn't have taken the afternoon off for nothing. But it was far from what he had hoped for.

What had he hoped for? A treasure map, a magnifying glass, and a trail to follow. He was ashamed of himself to speak it, too ashamed of this deep hope, this misbegotten dream. He was ridiculous.

"Yes, thank you," he said. "I would appreciate anything you can offer."

The professor slid a notepad across the desk and handed him a pen. "Just write your name and address here," he said. "When I get their permission, I'll mail you their information."

Manuel noted the professor's hands were smooth, his nails neatly trimmed, nearly gleaming. He wrote his name and address, taking time to ensure its legibility. The backs of his hands were age-spotted, the veins thick. His fingernails were clean but rough and chipped in places; his fingers thick and calloused. What was the point, he wondered, of books and papers and soft hands and education, if you couldn't actually help someone?

He thanked the professor for his help and time and made his way out the door, through the corridor, down the dank stairway, and outside into sunlight that, by contrast, was dazzling.

The disappointment wasn't going to break his heart, was it? No, not this time.

This campus was so beautiful though, he thought. He inhaled the greenery, paused again at the architecture, threaded his way through a sculpture garden. He might not belong here, but, dammit, his daughter did.

Wasn't that tremendous?

All the little threads and missteps and tragedies of his life—

but he had Lizette, and he and Lizette had Dahlia, and, by God, *she* belonged *here*. Her mere existence was a gift to him. She was the gift.

He didn't have Lulu, he didn't have his parents, only God knew if any of them were alive. He didn't have Amparo. But he had his wife, and he had his daughter, and the day was beautiful, and the young people made him smile.

He decided he would have to add a sculpture or two to his rock garden.

CHAPTER TWENTY-EIGHT

1992

D ahlia said, "Dad, if this passes, it's gonna be a permanent underclass."

It was a cold October evening. Manuel nodded at her across the dinner table. "Save our State" billboards and posters were everywhere, along with radio and TV commercials. Twenty-five years old with a master's in community organizing, and now Dahlia was focused on staging student walkouts. She was so worked up over Prop 187. When he first heard about it, he thought it was sick joke. Not let kids go to school because their parents didn't have the right papers?

He said, "Tell your friends not to wave a Mexican flag, all right?"

She said, "Everybody else gets to wave their flag, Dad, why not us?"

"We're not Mexicans, we're Americans. We're not illegal. Maybe it's good, this law, so people can tell the difference. Some of us have been here for generations!"

Dahlia got that funny smile on her adult face. It was so much like her funny smile from childhood that he let it drop.

He'd be there, he told her.

That's how he and Lizette ended up Sunday morning in a throng, heading to City Hall.

At first the protest was a surreal walk through downtown, the streets closed to traffic, families walking on the streets, vendors pushing carts of paletas, elote, cotton candy, even balloons as if this was a stroll in the park. Dahlia held her poster up, her hair too short and spiky, wearing a tight T-shirt with the Mexican flag on it. The poster read, "NO ON 187" on one side and "No RE-PETE" on the other.

He gripped Lizette's hand so tight she laughed at him, but he held on. He spotted his union, SEIU 660, on a banner. He looked for Colin and was surprised by how many Blacks and Asians were in the crowd, too.

As they walked, they chanted, "La Raza/Unidad/jamás será vencida." It was a nice thought. He wondered if it was based on any real event. All he could think of were the vanquished, starting with his family of origin, followed by Palo Verde, now a parking lot or worse for Dodge Stadium, continuing with the lost children he and Lizette would never know. But here they were, winding their way slowly, slowly to the steps of City Hall. Here he was, yelling and chanting with everyone else.

They made it to the far edge of City Hall and saw a mariachi band. A trumpeter played the "Star Spangled Banner" with mariachi sway.

"That's my America," Dahlia said, a tiny tear trickling down. When a month later the state of California voted for Proposition 187, Dahlia and Lizette hovered between rage and depression while Manuel wondered why everyone was so fucking afraid of Mexicans.

* * *

Saturday morning Manuel worked on repairing the fountain he had recently installed. Lizette enjoyed watching the ravens, pigeons, and other birds gather, and now the water had drained. He couldn't find the source of the leak in the basin, so he figured this was a plumbing problem and began to dig up the base. That's when the phone began ringing and ringing.

Manuel stalked into the house, grabbed a dish towel, and picked up the phone ringing on his kitchen wall. It had a long, loopy coil that stretched for miles, even so it wouldn't take him to the length of his patio where he was working on the fountain. He cursed himself for forgetting again to buy a cordless phone at Circuit City. How many times had Lizette asked him to do just that?

"Hello?" he said in a tone of voice designed to discourage the caller from any further contact.

"Is this Manuel Galvan?" the caller, a woman, asked.

"Yes," he said, impatiently. The dish cloth was now covered in mud. Better that than the phone.

The caller switched to halting Spanish, "Te portaste bien, hermanito?" There was something distinctly familiar about the voice, about the words, but the memory was distant, so far away...

"It's Lulu," said the voice on the phone.

Manuel slid to the floor, dropped the dish cloth, cradled the phone with shaking hands, blinked furiously, cleared his throat against the congestion of emotions, tried to speak while the voice on the phone said, "It's Lulu, little brother. I've been looking for you. And here you are."

He found his voice, "Lulu, how is this possible? Am I dead?"

"You sure as hell better not be!" she said. "I looked for you so long."

"Me too, I swear!"

"I'm sure you did, I'm sure." Now it was her voice that was clogged with emotion. "It wasn't easy, I'll explain it when we meet. Can we meet? Just the two of us the first time. Then I want to meet your family. Do you have a family?"

"Of course."

"And afterwards you can meet mine. But not the first time."

The voice she now had was new to him; the words she spoke she had never said to him, not in a grown-up authoritative manner, but the cadence, the rhythm, the music was the same.

He had stopped blinking against the tears and simply let them fall as the two of them spoke.

It turned out she lived in Downey, a suburb not too far from his home in Mt. Washington.

"Can I see you today?" he asked. He didn't want to risk another day, another hour. Who knew what terrible thing might happen, a car accident, a heart attack, an earthquake? Years back a plane fell out of the sky and wreckage crashed onto homes in Cerritos. Not one more day.

He heard her laughter, a throaty, worldly woman kind of laugh, and he briefly panicked, wondering who his sister had become, realizing he had no idea, swiftly filled with an anxiety that they would have nothing in common, nothing to say, worse, that they might not even like each other. Could that be possible?

"Ay, Manolito," she said. "I've missed you every day of my life."

They agreed to meet halfway, at the Carrows across the street from the Citadel, the Assyrian/Egyptian/exotic shopping center that Manuel still considered the Firestone center.

"I need to warn you," Lulu said, "I'm kinda big. I'll be easy to find." She giggled. Then, "I'm warning you cuz I don't want you making any faces when you see me." Her voice became serious. "That would be too painful."

"Never!" Manuel said, but he instantly worried that he might.

"If I'm late, don't leave!" he said and asked, "What's your phone number and address?" As Manuel wrote it all down his heart was thrummed. For the first time in fifty-five years, he was speaking to his sister. He read the number and address back to her, fearing the smallest mistake in this.

"How did you find me?" He said, "I tried to find you, so hard, so long." Not long enough, his head argued, not hard enough.

"I'll tell you when I see you. I'll tell you whatever you need to know."

They murmured goodbyes. Manuel hung up gently, looked at the information he had written down, and copied it down again, his hands trembling.

Lizette was out, doing errands. In his excitement, he had forgotten she had the car.

He waited fifteen impatient minutes and had just realized he could easily call a taxi when Lizette pulled up in their aging Maxima and began to unload the groceries. She wore a deep-blue crushed velour sweat suit.

Manuel rushed down the sloped driveway and said, "I need the car, right now."

"Give me a minute, take out the groceries, old man, and you can have it."

"No, really, now."

Lizette gave him a look that could have sliced off his arm.

"It's Lulu," he said, barely breathing. "I'm going to see Lulu."

Lizette gaped, then pulled him by the elbow and steered him into the car. She drove, and Manuel was grateful because his hands still shook. During the drive down the 5 freeway, the industrialized stretch of land that belied any vegetation or greenery or beauty of Los Angeles, Manuel could see nothing, he could only hover and guard this overwhelming sense of anticipation that threatened to explode, like a buried grenade, like a depth charge, like a time bomb in his torso.

"Take that turnoff," he told Lizette.

"I know where we're going," she replied, mildly. Manuel was filled with impatience and irritation at her moderate speed, and his wife's calm tranquility, but he bit his tongue. He prayed, prayed as he hadn't since he was a small child, one long repetitive chant of a prayer: *deargodletnothinghappentoeitherofusuntilweseeeachotheragaindeargodletnothinghappentoeitherofusuntilwemeeteachotheragaindeargod...*

Lizette parked and he leaped out, then leaned back into the car. "Do you mind?" he said. "Do you mind just sitting here for a little while? She wants us to meet alone."

"You mentioned it a few times on the way here." She squeezed his hand.

Manuel slammed the car door shut behind him, his mind empty of his wife and the life she represented. *Lulu, Lulu, Lulu* rang through his head, the little girl he looked up to, the little girl who crooned to him, the little girl who dragged him along, carried him, hugged him always so tight, then bravely said goodbye. Then without her, the silence, the mist, not feeling even alive.

Could she really be there?

Would she really be there? Could this be some kind of terrible hoax?

He pulled open the glass door and was hit by an icy blast of manufactured, chill air. He scanned the restaurant. She would be a mature woman, an old woman, older than himself. They had taken longer than he had anticipated, surely Lulu would have waited for him—after waiting over fifty years...

"Manolito," came a soft voice. He turned his head.

The voice came from a very large woman, seated in a padded corner of the waiting area, that in his intensity he had somehow overlooked. Lulu now stood to greet him.

He rushed to her and they hugged in silence.

This was his sister. This was Lulu. This was a little boy running to her at night and crying. This was a little girl pointing out the caterpillar on the wall. This was warm buttered tortillas. This was a mother singing them a song he could only half remember now. This was a father, rough and smiling, carrying Manuel on his shoulders, sun and shadows both dazzling Manuel's tiny eyes, his sister, Lulu, jumping alongside, telling a story about what she had seen that day.

This was his sister, telling him to be a good boy. Telling him to be brave because she was going to be.

Lulu in his arms was all those things, all those colliding thoughts. He inhaled and smelled flowers and onions and jasmine and cilantro. He could feel the layers of her clothing under his touch, it was a warm day, he realized, and all of her, from neck to ankles, was completely enveloped under fabric.

At last they broke apart. She said, "You are a man now, Manolito. You were just a tiny boy when I saw you last. Are you a good man?"

"When you meet my wife, ask her." He smiled. He stepped back. "Let me look at you," he said.

Her thick hair was dyed a deep black-red, her adult features enlarged by weight and age, a full expressive face with few wrinkles—but her eyes were those that he remembered: mischievous, sparkling, and filled with adoration for him.

"It's you," he said. "It's really you. Thank God!"

She cleared her throat. "God had nothing to do with it," she declared. "Or if He had, we wouldn't have been separated in the first place."

He hovered, overwhelmed, tongue-tied.

"Let's sit down. Let's get a table so we can talk," she said.

At their oversized table, large enough for Lulu to sit comfortably, the waitress handed them two slick laminated menus, each the size of a large map. Lulu handed the sheet of plastic back and said, "Just an iced tea," and Manuel ordered the same.

She reached over and covered his hand with both of hers. He noticed her hands were so soft and pale against his, as was her face. She tried to say something, but apparently all the tears the two had spilled while on the phone had not yet found their end, their very last tear. She made a face, smiled at him, then tugged at her napkin, wiped her face, and blew her nose.

"You have no idea how happy I am today," she said.

"Pues, I think I do."

She shook her head. "You kept it, then? Spanish? You lucky thing. I don't have it at all, hardly a word, just what I said to you, earlier, on the phone. I practiced." She smiled at him, mischievously, teasingly. He saw her again, briefly, as she once had been. How could more than fifty years vanish?

The waitress set down tall plastic tumblers filled with ice and tea. Lulu—she would always be Lulu to him, Victoria would never replace his name for her—ripped open three pink packets and emptied them into her tea, swirling the mixture with the elongated spoon. She sipped, smiled, then held out her hand to him across the table.

"Why are you so far away?" She blinked at him with tenderness.

He scooted closer to her on the vinyl bench.

"We have so much to catch up on," she said.

"Lifetimes," he said. "Yours, mine," he stumbled, choked out, "Our families."

She smiled and said, "But can I just sit here with you right now? Just the two of us? Only you know what this means to us."

They sat in a humble silence, the cascade of diners and dishes around them, the whoosh of opening and closing doors, the jangle of the cash register and the rumble of conversation of strangers. Lulu pressed his hand.

More silence.

"I can die happy, almost," she said, smiling at him, their silence apparently ended.

"I had given you up," Manuel said with a pang. "My wife told me I was getting old and bitter and angry."

Lulu shrugged. "We get old. And we have a right to our bitterness and anger. Anger is fuel, Manolito, fuel for any changes in this world."

There was a steely anger in her voice that reminded him of his wife, his daughter, and Tía Amparo. Hell, is that what a Mexican woman was? Better than defeat.

"Your wife thinks you're old and angry? Once they took me from you, I became old and angry. I was eight! I didn't have the words, but I had the emotions. I knew they were not going to keep you away from me, goddammit, and look! Here we are."

All this swearing! She sounded like Lizette!

"You knew all this then, Lulu? And you were eight? I thought you were so grown, such a little woman, such a little mother. That was how you've been in my memories, in my heart, all these years."

Lulu picked up her napkin and wiped at her eyes. Her mascara had long been washed away.

He said, "Where did they take you when you left me?"

She shook her head. He could tell she didn't trust her voice. He waited. She took a sip of her drink, patted her face with the napkin, and said, "Manolito, I honestly don't want to poison my first visit with you by my memories of that place." He caught a glance of a shudder that went through her body. "Not now," she said. "Maybe not ever."

He nodded in silence. Whatever she wanted, whatever she wished. He told her of his wife, of his daughter.

"You're really here," she interrupted him, patting his wrist, then squeezing his hand.

"You found me," he smiled. "You made this happen."

Then it was her turn to talk, and his turn to listen attentively to each word, to try to trace her family, four children, two divorces, working two jobs, then an administrative assistant, finally a paralegal, and looking, searching, looking for him threaded throughout her entire life.

He worried that he couldn't keep track of all the names, the cities where she'd lived, the schools she'd gone to; he panicked at the thought of forgetting a single detail. He patted his pockets and realized he didn't have a pen or pencil; then he made a face and relaxed.

"What are you smiling about?" she said. "There's a strange look on your face. Did I say something funny?"

"I just sat here worried that I couldn't remember every single detail you're telling me right now. I won't remember everything! I panicked; I wanted to grab a pencil and take notes, or a recorder to make sure I keep everything. Then I smiled because I realized."

"What?"

"If I get confused about your daughters' names, I can ask you."

"Damn right."

"That this isn't the only time I've ever going to see you."

"No, no it isn't, little brother. You will never be free of me again." They both laughed.

"The worst thing was to think I'd die without finding you," she said. Lulu reached across the table and clutched both his hands. Manuel trembled inside. He worried he'd bawl like a four-year-old, like the small boy he had been when he had last seen Lulu, but he didn't. He cleared his throat, and he blinked his tears away and said, "You are so beautiful."

She laughed and shook her head and shoulders.

"You are, Lulu, you are beautiful to me." Yes, she was, this woman with thick arms and legs had the same eyes he remembered, deep brown with a hint of hazel, and they looked at him with all the love he had kept in his heart.

Then he moved alongside her and buried his head in her neck to hide the tears he could no longer contain. He could smell the shampoo in her hair, the soap she used, the scent of her skin. Fifty-five years. Fifty-five years. Bridged.

He felt her consoling hand pat the back of his head, and the rhythm seemed so familiar. A physical memory. What else did his poor soul carry? Not so bad if she were here with him, now, today, something to be grateful for, alongside Lizette and Dahlia. Here she was. Here they were, together.

He didn't mean to weep, but he remembered the small boy in a cold car alongside Lulu. He remembered her when she told him to be behave and be brave. "I can't believe it's really you," he choked out.

She patted the back of his head.

It took a couple of attempts to recover himself; he went through all the napkins on the table then excused himself for the men's room.

"Don't go anywhere," he told her.

She shook her head and said, firmly, "Never again."

In the restroom he rinsed his face and dried it with coarse paper towels. He looked at himself. What did she see? The little boy within him was buried far and deep. He was a man and had been one for decades. What did Lulu see?

Back at the table, Lulu smiled as he walked toward her. Their iced teas were filled to the top.

He said, "I tried looking for you, I really did. I spent years, I always thought of you."

"I never stopped thinking of you. The moment they took me from you, I thought what can I do? But what could I do, a girl of eight? I moved around in families"—she appeared to shudder—"then I was adopted. I looked white. They put their name on me. I was Vicky Hammond. We lived in Wisconsin." She placed her elbow on the table, a fist to her face, and leaned on her hand. "You never have to visit Wisconsin," she said.

Manuel laughed at himself. "Here I was so excited, proud almost, when I discovered your name was not simply Lulu, but Victoria Galvan."

"So I was when I was with you. Then I was married and became Vicky Caley, then divorced and remarried, and now, widowed, Vicky Branch."

"I'm sorry you're widowed."

She tilted her head. "It's been some time, now. He was a good man, and he brought us to California, thank God! You see, how could you have ever found me?" She shook her head.

"But you found me."

She sighed. "It should have been a hell of a lot sooner. Vigil. I thought our last names were Vigil. That's what was on my birth certificate. But whoever recorded it mixed up the last names! Used our mom's on me. For years I phoned strange men named Manuel, or Immanuel, or Victor Vigil. Yes, I remembered your middle name, too. Victor was our uncle."

Manuel listened.

"It was when I got good at being a paralegal that I figured out the steps. I went into court adoption papers. Child Services. That took time, that took money, I had the money, I had the time. Nothing."

"Then how?"

She pulled a slip of paper out of her handbag. There was his advertisement in the Penny Saver. "When I saw this, I couldn't stop shaking. There was your address, right there. There was your name."

He covered his mouth with his hand. His ad.

"Then I looked you up in the phone book. Then I called you. And here we are."

He didn't want to start crying again, so he just kept his hands on his mouth. Finally, when he could trust himself, he asked, "What happened to our parents?"

"They were expelled from this country," she said. "You must have heard something about that?"

"A little," he said.

"This county keeps trying to get rid of us," she said. "This whole Proposition 187 bullshit? It passed! This country hates us." She shook her head. "I don't understand why. I'm not done looking, Manolito. I'm going to find our parents if it takes every penny in my bank account, every cell in my body. I've been working on this for decades. I've been to big cities in Mexico and small pueblos. They made this my life's work. I will find our parents."

How did she dream so big? It was too much to hope. The mere thought compressed his chest, but of course he pressed through that. "What can I do? How can I help? What do you need from me, you fearless avenging angel?"

She looked at him, at first suspiciously, then a smile cracked her love for him wide open.

"I've got a lead. Come with me when I find them."

"Of course! Help you! Give you money. One favor."

"Anything."

"My wife's waiting outside in the car. Can I bring her in now?"

CHAPTER TWENTY-NINE

On a June evening before their flight to Hermosillo, everyone came to their home in Mt. Washington. Lulu brought her four children, ranging from nineteen to twenty-six. Jean, the baby, was a neat, trim, girl, very light-skinned with hazel eyes and dark brown hair. She was nineteen and thinking about going into teaching. Gloria, very brisk and businesslike, very brown and beautiful. Lulu's first born, named Manuel after her brother—Manuel's heart skipped a beat when Lulu told him—was a sandy, tall, white-passing boy, who worked as a salesclerk in the men's section of Robinsons'. Phillip was younger, darker, taller, with a scowl that seemed familiar to Manuel. A scowl worn by a young man trying to sort out his place in the world. Manuel had worn that scowl, it seemed to him, for decades.

Dahlia and Lizette were there of course. Roland brought his family from Ventura: Roland's wife Marie, their twins Gabriel and Marina. Toño and Cristina came with their children and now grandchildren.

Lizette made enough chicken and rice for more than twice

that number of people. Victoria brought a huge cake she bought on the way, and Dahlia made a salad that only she and the teenage girls would eat.

Lizette served the food in the Mexican bowls she had brought with her from Goleta, a relic of her mother's that she brought out only on special occasions. Large, beige bowls decorated with hand-brushed strokes of red and green glaze. Bowls that glowed with celebrations.

Manuel stood on the patio, the patio he had built, paver by paver and stone by stone; he seasoned the rib eye steaks, sliced extra thin, with salt and pepper and waited for Lizette to tell him when to grill the meat. There was so much noise and commotion in his own home, he barely recognized it.

Lulu's lead had brought sad news: their mother had died decades earlier, of TB, shortly after returning to Mexico. But Lulu had found their father in a small town in the state of Sonora. A group of them were flying out in the morning.

He watched Lizette, hugging and fussing over everyone as they entered, directing her new nephew where to set the cake that they had brought.

All those missing years!

He pushed that away.

Lizette came over to him. "You need to talk to people, Manny, you can't just stand there like an old bigornia."

He shook his head. "What am I supposed to say? Can't I just watch? You do the talking. That's what you're good at."

"Try getting to know them, okay? This is what you wanted, viejito. This is what we both wanted."

"I wish my Tía—I wish Amparo were here to see all this," he said.

Lizette hugged him.

Lulu drank wine while Roland sipped his beer and the two of them talked about the Central Valley and their shared hatred for Pete Wilson. Later he watched her at the head of the table, talking with her children, with Lizette, arguing lightly, like now, with Roland, about the Central Valley. Was all this real? Was she real? Would the plane take off tomorrow? Would it land?

Lizette had the kids help Dahlia clear the table and bring out the cake Victoria brought from Lucky's.

"Congratulations," the script read, "to all of us." Lizette looked pointedly at Manuel, who stood.

He said, "I kinda get the feeling this is an occasion for toasts. And you may not know this, those of you new to me, me new to you all, but I really don't talk a lot, which is why I married Lizette. She talks and thinks for both of us. Even if she says she doesn't. How smart was that? Marry a woman who can do thinking, and get it all right the first time.

"But's that not what I want to say, right now."

He looked around the long table they had set up on the patio. Even the kids, his new nieces and nephews looked up at him expectantly. Roland had that slow smile on his face, his smirk had permanently disappeared at Bobby's funeral. Around the table they held up glasses of wine, bottles of beer, cans of Diet Coke. Lizette looked at him inquisitively.

"I have to tell you all, I had given up a dream." He started to choke up, pushed it aside.

"I was angry and desperate, for everything that had caused this separation, from my parents, from my sister. Angry about this pain, in my life and who knows in how many lives of others?

"We cannot be the only ones..." For it had to be true, they could not be the only ones. He thought back decades to the notary who had been the first one to tell him what had happened, the only one unashamed and unafraid to tell him the truth.

"How many others, I worry, how many others?" He continued, "I had always wanted to find my sister. And I have to apologize to you, Lulu, in front of all our families, I have to apologize for having stopped my search."

Lulu shook her head, wiped at her eyes, and softly said, "No, you don't."

"But she found me! Isn't that just like a woman. You give up, and she's got to prove you wrong." There was a small titter of laughter from around the table.

"Miracle number two, if you weren't keeping score, is tomorrow. Tomorrow some of us here, you know who you are, set off to Hermosillo to meet my father. Our father. The grandfather. Miracle number three, Lulu's getting me on a plane in order to do just that." Laughter.

He was getting choked up again, again he pushed it aside and raised his beer. "This is for you, my beloved Lulu, my miracle maker."

Bottle and cans and glassware clinked.

Roland and Manuel washed up. Roland rinsed the plates and sorted the silverware into the dishwasher. "You doin' okay, man? Kinda strange, huh?"

Manuel had had a tingling throughout his body all day. He'd been dizzy getting out of bed. Right now was no different, the prickle of energy ran from his chest to the tips of his fingers. Was he having a heart attack? Was he really going to die the night before he met his father? Was he a hypochondriac?

"Nah," he shook his head. "I am not doing okay."

After the house cleared, Lizette went around with a broom, sweeping out the crumbs and crusts the meal left behind.

He closed the dishwasher he had installed seven years ago. He didn't like the way it caught. He opened it again, felt along the edge, and found a screw that had been working its way out.

He twisted it back in with his thumbnail and closed the door again. It shut flush and firm.

He called out to Lizette, "I better not die in my sleep tonight. Cuz if I did, I'd have to come back as a ghost and kill someone."

Lizette pulled out the suitcases they had bought years ago at Gemco and set them on their bed and began packing.

After they packed, and Manuel triple-checked their tickets for their flight in the morning and mentally tabulated what time that absolutely had to leave by to get to their gate an hour before departure at nine in the morning, he could not sleep.

* * *

On the plane, Dahlia sat by the window, Lizette in the middle, and Manuel on the aisle. His sister sat directly in front of him with her two oldest children. Manuel found himself unable to eat any of the food set out in front of him; found himself impatient with the glare of the sun across the body of the plane; in need of many glasses of water and then in need of numerous trips to the compact restroom.

He paced back and forth on the plane until a flight attendant implored him to take a seat. Lizette rolled her eyes at him as he did.

They went through customs in Hermosillo, showing their passports, and walking into the country.

Manuel paced the airport lounge, which appeared smaller than the one where they had waited in California. The light was different, too. Dimmer? An attendant waited in the restroom that he used, and, not knowing what to do, he emptied the US coins he carried onto the tray beside the attendant.

"Dad!" Dahlia said, with some annoyance, as he passed her in his pacing. "We'll get there, we will. Calm down."

"Don't you tell your dad to calm down," Lizette snapped. "This is a hard day."

He picked up his wife's dry hand and kissed the back of it. "Mi reina." Then he ruffled the spiky, stiff hair of his daughter, and she ducked away from him.

"It is a hard day," he said.

Their group climbed onto a smaller plane, sitting two by two. He sat at the window, and Victoria on the aisle. The backs of her hands were pale and hinted at hidden frailty. He held her hand and felt pangs on her behalf.

* * *

The plane sets off, rises, and it seems like an eternity and then only moments later it begins its descent. They are heading to a bare air strip surrounded by greenery—more lush greenery than he has ever seen in his hometown, or home state for that matter. A tiny traffic control tower emerges larger and larger. As the plane lands, scraping its wheels and skidding and bouncing against the runway, Manuel grips his sister's hand.

It seems to Manuel that they wait an interminable amount of time for the seatbelt symbol to be dismissed. His mind is a blank, he hears the blood rushing in his ears, he can't hear what Lulu is saying as the staircase attaches to the plane, then the doors unlock, and at last the people now gathered in the aisle begin to slowly make their way out of the plane.

Stepping onto the stairwell, Manuel's eyes follow the trail of passengers. They lead to a building entrance where a group of people are clustered, waiting. Two children hold a banner painted in vibrant fluorescent colors: "Bienvenidos, a todos mis hijos." In the center of the crowd of waiting people is an elderly man with salt and pepper hair seated in a wheelchair, eyes sweeping across the descending passengers.

"There he is." Lulu points to the man in the wheelchair. "There's our dad."

Manuel and Lulu hold onto the railings as they carefully make their way down. Once their feet are on the ground, they make their way around the other passengers and begin to run.

ACKNOWLEDGMENTS

As a third grader in love with the printed word, I thought books sprang fully born from their magical creators. I wanted to possess that magic. As a young adult, I tapped at my keyboard, alone, and hungry for the voices of others, convinced that writing was a solitary pursuit.

As a mature writer, I fully appreciate the reality that nothing is ever done alone. So many people have kept my writing dreams, and this particular novel, afloat over the years. I would like to take a moment to list so very many of them, with love and appreciation.

Naomi Hirahara, amazing writer and supreme connector: thank you for those Hill Library meetups.

What a vibrant community I have come to know and belong to, thanks to the organization Women Who Submit.

My writers' group: Bonnie Kaplan, Kat Wright, Lisa Cheby, Lauren Eggert-Crowe, Xochitl Julisa Bermejo—your insight and thoughtful feedback have kept me focused.

My long-distance cheer team: Erika Wurth and Natalia Sylvester—sharing our struggles and your encouraging words have extended my writer life.

My beloved very first readers: Elisa Callow, Lucia Vigil, Rachael Warecki—in appreciation of your indulgence and insight.

To my next draft readers: Tisha Marie Reichle-Aguilera,

Kim Fay, Kate Maruyama—thank you for so much time and attention.

I am grateful for the supportive Macondo Community. And for all the buoyant voices of the Grotto!

Marcela Fuentes, who has been a wonderful, positive presence.

Cody Sisco, who with insight and compassion strengthened these words on the page. Special shout out to Lisa Kastner of Running Wild Publishing and RIZE Press for embracing Manuel's story.

Lastly, my family's constant belief and support of me, my sister Stefané, my adult children Simone and Leo, my husband Barry. And lastly, my mother. Who absolutely *is* my biggest fan.

RIZE publishes great stories and great writing across genres written by People of Color and other underrepresented groups. Our team consists of:

Lisa Diane Kastner, Founder and Executive Editor
Cody Sisco, Acquisitions Editor, RIZE
Benjamin White, Acquisition Editor, Running Wild
Peter A. Wright, Acquisition Editor, Running Wild
Resa Alboher, Editor
Angela Andrews, Editor
Sandra Bush, Editor
Ashley Crantas, Editor
Rebecca Dimyan, Editor
Abigail Efird, Editor
Aimee Hardy, Editor
Henry L. Herz, Editor
Cecilia Kennedy, Editor
Barbara Lockwood, Editor
Scott Schultz, Editor

Evangeline Estropia, Product Manager
Kimberly Ligutan, Product Manager
Lara Macaione, Marketing Director
Joelle Mitchell, Licensing and Strategy Lead
Pulp Art Studios, Cover Design
Standout Books, Interior Design
Polgarus Studios, Interior Design

Learn more about us and our stories at www.runningwildpress.com

Loved these stories and want more? Follow us at

runningwildpublishing.com, www.facebook.com/running-wildpress,
on Twitter @lisadkastner @RunWildBooks @RIZERWP